WILLIAM SHAKESPEARE

*

THE THIRD PART OF KING HENRY THE SIXTH

EDITED BY
NORMAN SANDERS

PENGUIN BOOKS

PENGUIN BOOKS

Published by the Penguin Group
27 Wrights Lane, London w8 5tz, England
Viking Penguin Inc., 40 West 23rd Street, New York, New York 10010, USA
Penguin Books Australia Ltd, Ringwood, Victoria, Australia
Penguin Books Canada Ltd, 2801 John Street, Markham, Ontario, Canada l3r 1b4
Penguin Books (NZ) Ltd, 182–190 Wairau Road, Auckland 10, New Zealand

Penguin Books Ltd, Registered Offices: Harmondsworth, Middlesex, England

This edition first published in Penguin Books 1981
3 5 7 9 10 8 6 4 2

Made and printed in Great Britain by
Richard Clay Ltd, Bungay, Suffolk
Set in Monotype Ehrhardt

CONTENTS

INTRODUCTION 7

FURTHER READING 39

THE THIRD PART OF
KING HENRY THE SIXTH 43

COMMENTARY 165

AN ACCOUNT OF THE TEXT 283

GENEALOGICAL TABLES 299

INTRODUCTION

In the most haunting choric scene of *Henry VI, Part Three*, the King himself, having been chased as a hindrance from the battlefield at Towton by his Amazonian queen, sits on a molehill and reflects on the nature of war:

> *Now sways it this way, like a mighty sea*
> *Forced by the tide to combat with the wind;*
> *Now sways it that way, like the self-same sea*
> *Forced to retire by fury of the wind.*
> *Sometime the flood prevails, and then the wind;*
> *Now one the better, then another best;*
> *Both tugging to be victors, breast to breast,*
> *Yet neither conqueror nor conquerèd;*
> *So is the equal poise of this fell war.*   II.5.5-13

The ebb-and-flow motion described here has struck many readers of the play not only as an accurate evocation of the Wars of the Roses, but also as an apt description of the structure of the play itself. There is unusual critical agreement about the episodic character of the action: the way the scenes deal repetitiously either with political manipulations and family discussions leading to military action or with events of the battles which result. But the attempts to find some principle of ordering in the plot are frustrated by the uniformity of emphasis, the tonal monotony imposed by the dominant rhetorical modes of vituperation and lamentation, the varieties of personal violence echoing each other mechanically, and the very evenness of dull

7

horror which seems to preclude any emotional climax to compensate for the obvious lack of a structural one.

Shakespeare seems deliberately to have arranged the materials he found in the English chronicles to produce just this non-climactic design. The historical events covered by the play stretch from the aftermath of the first Battle of Saint Albans in 1455 to the year 1475, when a poverty-stricken King Reignier pawned his kingdoms of Naples, Sicily, and the county of Provence to King Lewis XI in order to pay the ransom demanded by Edward IV for Queen Margaret. Although the chronology of Edward Hall's and Raphael Holinshed's accounts is generally followed in the play, there is a good deal of telescoping of time and fusing of events. For example, the opening scene takes place dramatically immediately after the Battle of Saint Albans, with which *Henry VI, Part Two* ended; but the determination of the Yorkists to seize the throne and Henry's bequeathing his title to the Duke of York are based upon arrangements made after the Battle of Northampton in 1460. Similarly, the conflicts of Mortimer's Cross, Ferrybridge, and Towton are run together in the second act to end in the temporary Yorkist triumph, with Edward on the throne and Warwick departing for France to secure his title with a marriage between the new English King and Lady Bona, the French King's sister. A historical five-year gap is ignored in the following acts so that Edward's wooing of Lady Grey may lead directly to Warwick's and Clarence's defection to the Lancastrian side and ultimately to the release of Henry from the Tower. The capture and escape of Edward himself from Middleham Castle, his successes at York, Coventry and Barnet, and the recapture and murder of Henry are all spliced breathlessly together to bring the play to its conclusion in a Yorkist triumph.

Faced with this unsyncopated construction, some critics have claimed that Shakespeare had simply lost interest in his theme after exploring it for two plays. Others have seen an arrangement of the action based upon a shifting concentration on political affairs and their military results. Still others have attempted to perceive a design in the balancing of the leading figures on the two sides, or in the emerging self-centred villainy of Richard of Gloucester.

However, the very variety of these structural theories may suggest that it is wrong to seek for the sort of clearly articulated shaping of the action that is found in *Parts One* and *Two*. The subject of the play is obviously the erosion of all values that people have traditionally shored up against the encroachment of chaos in public life; and Shakespeare seems to have refused to impose upon his materials the kind of ordering suitable for the stark confrontations between virtues and vices found in the earlier plays. Instead he decided to follow the remorseless pressures to act that events force upon men; and, by means of the selection of scenes he made from the chronicles, to convey the cyclical nature of all history that is rooted in Henry's image of wind and tide. The method for this dramatic exploration of the flux of time is the employment of a number of dramatic, poetic, and structural devices which, working together in the theatre, offer a vivid experience of how human beings are both the agents and the patients of their most selfish compulsions.

*

The institution at the centre of the play is kingship, which is Shakespeare's stage metaphor for man's aspiration to a governed, ordered existence. It is noticeable that the play opens in the Parliament House of England, the place designed for rational deliberation about social issues. But here it is the scene of rebellion, as armed men fresh from battle burst in and lament their inability to seize their king in the conflict just ended. This is a 'bloody parliament'; rights are to be decided in a council where blows rather than words prevail, where the celebration of victory means bloodthirsty gloating, where the heads of slaughtered enemies are cast down as proof of martial prowess in a spirit of gloating mockery. In the account of the parliament by Edward Hall on which the scene is based, the emphasis is on York's measured speech setting out the validity of his claim to the crown; but in the play the whole treatment of succession is differently focused. Certainly there are references to Henry's and York's ancestors, and a brief recital of the old business of Richard II, Bolingbroke, and Mortimer; yet the stress is on the connexion between possession and power rather than on the truth of dynastic claim.

King Henry's own attempt at justification by birth comes down to his being the grandson of Henry IV, who 'by conquest got the crown' (I.1.132), and the son of Henry V, who 'made the Dauphin and the French to stoop | And seized upon their towns and provinces' (lines 108–9). His personal claim will be re-established if necessary by a war which 'shall ... unpeople this my realm' (line 126). In a similar manner, York's claim is one that his sword 'shall plead ... in the field' (line 103) and that is backed by his sons' incitements to violent assertion: 'Armed as we are, let's stay within this house. ... tear the crown from the usurper's head' (lines 38, 114). More importantly, it is supported by the less emotional power of Warwick, who views the crown simply as a gift to be distributed at his will:

> *Neither the King nor he that loves him best,*
> *The proudest he that holds up Lancaster,*

Dares stir a wing if Warwick shake his bells.
I'll plant Plantagenet, root him up who dares. . . .
Or I will fill the house with armèd men,
And over the chair of state, where now he sits,
Write up his title with usurping blood.

I.1.45-8, 167-9

Henry's own supporting nobles take a scarcely less personal, if differently motivated, view of their allegiance: Clifford, Northumberland, and Westmorland will fight to be revenged on York, the killer of their fathers, rather than York, the illegal claimant. As Clifford puts it: 'King Henry, be thy title right or wrong, | Lord Clifford vows to fight in thy defence' (lines 159-60).

Despite the opening scene's emphasis on brute force as the establisher of rightful possession of the crown, both historically and by dramatic reference the rival claims are based on family relationships, the details of proper succession, the blood linking parent and child. Henry's political response to the combined pressures of Warwick's soldiers and his own consciousness of weak title is to disinherit his only son and adopt York as his heir. On a personal level, this action is as unnatural as Margaret perceives:

Ah, wretched man! Would I had died a maid,
And never seen thee, never borne thee son,
Seeing thou hast proved so unnatural a father!
Hath he deserved to lose his birthright thus?
Hadst thou but loved him half so well as I,
Or felt that pain which I did for him once,
Or nourished him as I did with my blood,
Thou wouldst have left thy dearest heart-blood there,
Rather than have made that savage Duke thine heir
And disinherited thine only son.

I.1.216-25

And the dispossessed Prince Edward himself adds to his mother's words the sheer legal impossibility of Henry's decision: 'Father, you cannot disinherit me; | If you be king, why should not I succeed?' (lines 226–7). On the political level, Henry's compromise has far wider implications; for it makes the crown cease to be the symbol of effective power in England, passed from one holder to the next by the principle of primogeniture, untouched in its essence by the individual character of its particular wearer. Henry's oath renders the crown his personal possession, to be owned by the permission of some of his subjects, under restrictions which neither his own supporters nor the Yorkists are long disposed to maintain.

This link, established thus early in the play, between unnatural violation of the family structure and the nature of civil war becomes an explored metaphor for one aspect of the national chaos. The connexion between the conflict and a personal revenge code is made by Henry's appeal for support –

Earl of Northumberland, he slew thy father,
And thine, Lord Clifford; and you both have vowed revenge
On him, his sons, his favourites, and his friends –

I.1.54–6

and also in Warwick's equally specific reminder of his power:

You forget
That we are those which chased you from the field
And slew your fathers. . . . I.1.89–91

York's decision, at the urging of his sons, to rebel against his newly-adopted 'father' and Margaret's military action to repossess her son's right set in train the series of horrors which result when the political life of the nation amounts to little more than rendering wrong for wrong.

Immediately it is in familial terms that we witness the outcome of these violations. Clifford, driven to support Henry-right-or-wrong by his adherence to a manic code of all-transcending filial duty, acts out the reductive behaviour his fury demands. Throughout the scene of Rutland's murder, his narrowed mind reveals itself in a revenge litany that is his reply to all appeals for mercy:

> *As for the brat of this accursèd duke,*
> *Whose father slew my father, he shall die. . . .*
>   *my father's blood*
> *Hath stopped the passage where thy words should enter. . . .*
> *Thy father slew my father; therefore die.*
>
>   I.3.4–5, 21–2, 47

Rutland's imaginatively phrased pleas stand in sharp contrast to this obsessive response; and Clifford can employ verbal elaboration only to indicate the direction which such insatiable destructiveness as his inevitably takes:

> *Had I thy brethren here, their lives and thine*
> *Were not revenge sufficient for me;*
> *No, if I digged up thy forefathers' graves*
> *And hung their rotten coffins up in chains,*
> *It could not slake mine ire nor ease my heart.*
> *The sight of any of the house of York*
> *Is as a fury to torment my soul;*
> *And till I root out their accursèd line*
> *And leave not one alive, I live in hell.*   I.3.25–33

Clifford maintains his stance of avenger in the scene of York's capture; but there Margaret's refinements of cruelty are added to it. She has marched to Wakefield to re-establish her son's right to the throne; but the form her triumph takes is a mocking of parental love:

> *where is your darling Rutland?*
> *Look, York, I stained this napkin with the blood*
> *That valiant Clifford, with his rapier's point,*
> *Made issue from the bosom of the boy;*
> *And if thine eyes can water for his death,*
> *I give thee this to dry thy cheeks withal.* I.4.78–83

It is this rather than his humiliating accession to a molehill or the wearing of a paper crown that breaks the Duke who reached at the moon and saw his only felicity in the English diadem. Shakespeare's handling of York's response to this torment has puzzled many critics, chiefly because of the muted allusions it contains to the passion of Christ. But it is by such means that the audience's attention is led away from the culpability of the sufferer and focused on the monstrous perversion that develops when a universally recognized value – family affection – can provide the impetus for the infliction of pain that is rooted in that emotion itself. York's speech distils the nature of this agony rather than conveys the particular suffering of one Richard Plantagenet:

That face of his the hungry cannibals
Would not have touched, would not have stained with blood;
But you are more inhuman, more inexorable,
O, ten times more, than tigers of Hyrcania.
See, ruthless Queen, a hapless father's tears;
This cloth thou dipped'st in blood of my sweet boy,
And I with tears do wash the blood away.
Keep thou the napkin, and go boast of this;
And if thou tellest the heavy story right,
Upon my soul, the hearers will shed tears;
Yea, even my foes will shed fast-falling tears,
And say 'Alas, it was a piteous deed!' I.4.152–63

This is Shakespeare's counterweight to those filial emotions that turn Clifford into a pent-up lion that looks 'o'er the wretch | That trembles under his devouring paws' (I.3.12–13), and to the maternal ones which transform Margaret into a 'tiger's heart wrapped in a woman's hide' (I.4.137). The audience's response is voiced on stage by the formerly vengeful Northumberland:

> *Had he been slaughter-man to all my kin,*
> *I should not for my life but weep with him,*
> *To see how inly sorrow gripes his soul.* I.4.169–71

However, Northumberland's humanity is not what prevails in the play; rather it is the adapted animal reflexes that Clifford articulates in one of his calmer moments as a lesson to Henry:

> *Unreasonable creatures feed their young;*
> *And though man's face be fearful to their eyes,*
> *Yet, in protection of their tender ones,*
> *Who hath not seen them, even with those wings*
> *Which sometime they have used with fearful flight,*
> *Make war with him that climbed unto their nest,*
> *Offering their own lives in their young's defence?*
> *For shame, my liege, make them your precedent!*
>
> II.2.26–33

Almost every character in the play is associated with the image of basic family loyalties issuing into violent national division. Early in the opening scene, the Battle of Saint Albans is conveyed by the Yorkist victors in terms of brothers and fathers slain:

> *Lord Stafford's father, Duke of Buckingham,*
> *Is either slain or wounded dangerous. . . .*
> *And, brother, here's the Earl of Wiltshire's blood. . . .*
>
> I.1.10–11, 14

The head of the Duke of Somerset, thrown to the floor by Richard, the arch-family-violator himself, is immediately identified as a relic of 'the line of John of Gaunt' (line 19). Warwick's flagging spirits at Towton are revived by a vivid account of his brother's death and dying words:

> *Thy brother's blood the thirsty earth hath drunk,*
> *Broached with the steely point of Clifford's lance;*
> *And in the very pangs of death he cried,*
> *Like to a dismal clangour heard from far,*
> *'Warwick, revenge! Brother, revenge my death!'*
>
> II.3.15-19

Even so insignificant a character as the Earl of Oxford is drawn into the same pattern, as he proclaims at the French court his equation of political alignment with family feud:

> *Call him my king by whose injurious doom*
> *My elder brother, the Lord Aubrey Vere,*
> *Was done to death? And more than so, my father,*
> *Even in the downfall of his mellowed years,*
> *When nature brought him to the door of death?*
> *No, Warwick, no; while life upholds this arm,*
> *This arm upholds the house of Lancaster.* III.3.101-7

It is by such means as these that Shakespeare personalizes civil strife, as the principals involved justify their commitment by reference to a revenge code of geometrical simplicity. He also, by following the war's effects down the social scale, demonstrates emblematically the ultimate products of this large-scale actualizing of personal emotion. Henry, seated on York's stage molehill, looks on as the battle washes to his feet '*a Father that hath killed his son*' and '*a Son that hath killed his father*'. The Son bends over his parent-victim to utter the insanity of life-values leading to acts of death: 'I, who at his hands received my life, | Have by my hands of life bereavèd him' (II.5.67–8); and the Father echoes him: 'O boy, thy father gave thee life too soon, | And hath bereft thee of thy life too late!' (lines 92–3). At this moment, Young Clifford and Old Clifford, York and Rutland, Margaret and Prince Edward are fused into two stage figures holding their murder weapons and nursing their grief. The napkin soaked in Rutland's blood is generalized in Henry's words as the two roses of the warring houses and the fluctuating emotions of guilt and grief on the face of the unknowing filicide:

> *The red rose and the white are on his face,*
> *The fatal colours of our striving houses;*
> *The one his purple blood right well resembles;*
> *The other his pale cheeks, methinks, presenteth.*
>
> II.5.97–100

With the stichomythia that follows, the three mourners in this triptych of suffering balance poetically the national, the familial, and the personal:

SON

> *How will my mother for a father's death*
> *Take on with me and ne'er be satisfied!*

FATHER

> *How will my wife for slaughter of my son*
> *Shed seas of tears and ne'er be satisfied!*

KING

> *How will the country for these woeful chances*
> *Misthink the King and not be satisfied!*   II.5.103–8

*

At first sight, the unity of the Yorkist family seems to provide a strong contrast with the destructive kinship of the Lancastrian party. Whereas in the opening scene Henry

17

strips his son of his birthright to ensure his own possession of the crown, York ceases to press his personal claims to guarantee his children's ultimate accession to the throne. Even the scene of York's decision to seize the crown by rebellion is infused with his sons' eagerness for their father's advancement and the ready family support of uncles and brother. It is York's position as *pater familias* that is stressed in his death scene, so that the audience's memory of his political culpability is erased by his paternal suffering. His three sons are closely supportive of each other. If Clarence defects, it is only to be reconciled with Edward at a crucial military moment, on the grounds that consanguinity outweighs an oath sworn to his father-in-law Warwick. Even Richard, for all his mental reservations and plans for the future, refuses to desert his brother, rescues him from captivity, and encourages both his taking of York and his proclamation as king. The final scene too is, on the surface at least, one of brotherly concord and family triumph.

Yet this united Yorkist movement towards success that the play's narrative line follows is shot through with elements of family division. In the opening scene, York's paternal affection is doled out in proportion to his children's capacity for slaughter. Edward displays the blood of the Duke of Buckingham on his sword and earns his father's approval thereby; but 'Richard hath best deserved of all' York's sons because he can produce the head of the Duke of Somerset, his father's old rival. The apparent warmth of the scene of York's decision to rebel is generated by oath-breaking and Richard's specious arguments to justify it. Shakespeare's treatment of the vision of the triple suns at Mortimer's Cross also seems deliberately ambiguous. Edward interprets the phenomenon as a symbol of brotherly unity and vows to adopt it as his

badge: 'Upon my target three fair-shining suns' (II.1.40).
Richard, on the other hand, is aware of another possibility
in the illusion: 'See, see! They join, embrace, and *seem* to
kiss, | *As if* they vowed some league inviolable' (lines 29–
30). The truth is they are really 'one lamp, one light, one
sun' (line 31), of which he denies his brother possession
by means of a bawdy quibble: 'Nay, bear three daughters;
by your leave I speak it, | You love the breeder better than
the male' (lines 41–2).

To York's death the response of his sons is predictable.
Richard's lines on revenge convey the same inner corrosion
and the same honing of affection to a killing edge as do
Clifford's:

> *I cannot weep, for all my body's moisture*
> *Scarce serves to quench my furnace-burning heart;*
> *Nor can my tongue unload my heart's great burden;*
> *For self-same wind that I should speak withal*
> *Is kindling coals that fires all my breast,*
> *And burns me up with flames that tears would quench.*
> *To weep is to make less the depth of grief;*
> *Tears then for babes, blows and revenge for me!*
>
> II.1.79–86

And at Clifford's death also he echoes his victim's own
desire to have his enemy alive to kill again:

> *I know by that he's dead; and, by my soul,*
> *If this right hand would buy two hours' life,*
> *That I in all despite might rail at him,*
> *This hand should chop it off, and with the issuing blood*
> *Stifle the villain. . . .*   II.6.79–83

It is once Edward is crowned that overt division in the
family makes its appearance. Lady Grey seeks out the new
king to plead for the restoration of her slain husband's

lands, and Edward's lust is aroused by her presence. In the seduction scene that follows, it is noticeable that much of the exchange – *double entendre* though it be – is based upon those pressures which can be exercised on the parent through the rights of the child:

> *How many children hast thou, widow? Tell me.*
>
> *'Twere pity they should lose their father's lands.*
>
> *Now tell me, madam, do you love your children?*
>
> *And would you not do much to do them good?*
>
> *Therein thou wrongest thy children mightily.*
>
> *Thou art a widow and thou hast some children;*
> *And, by God's mother, I, being but a bachelor,*
> *Have other some; why, 'tis a happy thing*
> *To be the father unto many sons.*
> *Answer no more, for thou shalt be my queen.*
>
> III.2.26, 31, 36, 38, 74, 102–6

Thus in the vocabulary of kinship does Edward arrive at the decision that is to alienate his father-substitute, Warwick; and Richard's first soliloquy quickly follows to detail for the audience the fullest development of familial perversion:

> *Ay, Edward will use women honourably.*
> *Would he were wasted, marrow, bones, and all,*
> *That from his loins no hopeful branch may spring,*
> *To cross me from the golden time I look for!*
> *And yet, between my soul's desire and me –*
> *The lustful Edward's title burièd –*
> *Is Clarence, Henry, and his son young Edward,*
> *And all the unlooked-for issue of their bodies,*
> *To take their rooms, ere I can place myself.*
>
> III.2.124–32

From this point onwards the splits in the Yorkist side are manifold. Edward's selfish marriage to Lady Grey provokes the desertion of Warwick and the loss of the French alliance, because Lewis XI takes Edward's action as an insult to *his* family pride. Clarence soon joins Warwick in France because Edward has placed the ties of his new wife's brothers above the claims of his own, thus burying brotherhood in his new bride.

It is true that Richard remains ostensibly loyal to Edward and rescues him from Middleham Castle; and that Clarence changes sides again at Coventry because he will not be

> *so harsh, so blunt, unnatural,*
> *To bend the fatal instruments of war*
> *Against his brother. ...*   V.1.86–8

The three also act in Yorkist concert when they stab the young Prince Edward and sadistically bait his mother, Margaret, in a scene which balances the earlier slaughter of Rutland and York. But the apparent fraternal accord of the final scenes is darkly overshadowed by Richard's lines in the Tower: 'I have no brother, I am like no brother ... I am myself alone' (V.6.80–83). And it is the same note that is carried by him into the conventional triumph with which the play ends, as he kisses Edward's heir, Judas-like, and vows in an aside to blast the family harvest. Well might the first Yorkist king himself allow a doubt to creep into his optimistic curtain-line: 'For here, I hope, begins our lasting joy' (V.7.46).

*

The object at the centre of this family-fuelled civil strife is the English crown; but the issue of kingship emerges quite differently from its treatment in *Parts One* and *Two*. Like every other human value in the play, majesty is debased, stripped of any suggestion of its sacramental dignity or ritual splendour. Here it is merely a prize to be fought over by warring animals. The formal discussion of rightful claim in the first scene is reduced to a minimum. Its concern with due succession serves only to remind the audience of what has been lost in the present reality of brute power, which is appropriately conveyed by Warwick's lines with their combination of personal assertion and verbal violence:

> *Do right unto this princely Duke of York,*
> *Or I will fill the house with armèd men.*
>
> I.1.166–7

Henry's humiliating compromise to ensure that 'York and Lancaster are reconciled' leads only to solemnly sworn oaths which are immediately shown to be quite unbinding.

For York and his family the crown is quite blatantly a possession which permits ultimate personal gratification. Either in conscious imitation or from subconscious admiration, Shakespeare makes the Yorkists fall into the rhythms of Marlovian intoxication:

> *How sweet a thing it is to wear a crown;*
> *Within whose circuit is Elysium*
> *And all that poets feign of bliss and joy.*
>
> I.2.29–31

York's own vow in response to his sons' persuasions to 'be king or die' is worked out with grotesque logic. Instead of the throne he mounted in the Parliament House, while surrounded by friends, he stands at Wakefield on a molehill, faced only by enemies. The crown he finally achieves is a paper mockery, whose greatest value in the face of his torment is to provide him with a gesture of renunciation to accompany his last curse:

There, take the crown, and with the crown my curse;
And in thy need such comfort come to thee
As now I reap at thy too cruel hand!   I.4.164–6

For his sons, kingship is devalued in other ways.
Edward, like Richard, would 'break a thousand oaths to
reign one year' (I.2.17); and after his father's death he is
very aware that the title is now his and not his brothers'.
As he reminds Richard rather unnecessarily, 'His name
that valiant Duke hath left with thee; | His dukedom and
his chair with me is left' (II.1.89–90). However, once he
actually possesses the crown, he loses all aggression and
curiously falls into a submissive lassitude that is typical of
Henry himself. After Mortimer's Cross he submits the
fortunes of his monarchy to Warwick's control; and he
asserts after Towton that the Earl's power is co-equal with
his own: 'Warwick, as ourself, | Shall do and undo as him
pleaseth best' (II.6.104–5). The crown for him is not a
responsibility; it is a licence to give free rein to his particular faults. 'I am Edward ... and must have my will',
he tells his brothers (IV.1.15–16); and his will is the indul-
gence of his strong lasciviousness. We hear late in the play
that he has once before abused Warwick's hospitality by
offering sexual wrong to his niece; and we see for ourselves
his blunt physical pursuit of Lady Grey. By the play's end
his plans for his reign are characteristically to

                          spend the time
With stately triumphs, mirthful comic shows,
Such as befits the pleasure of the court.   V.7.42–4

Despite all his relish for kingship's privileges, Edward's
various possessions of the crown during the last part of
the play are tinged with the same sense of being at the
mercy of Fortune that Henry so strongly projects. At his

capture in Warwickshire, Edward is strikingly passive and resigned –

> *What fates impose, that men must needs abide;*
> *It boots not to resist both wind and tide –*
>
> IV.3.59–60

and he has a similar reaction to his rescue from Middleham Castle:

> *Yet thus far Fortune maketh us amends,*
> *And says that once more I shall interchange*
> *My wanèd state for Henry's regal crown.*
>
> IV.7.2–4

Even the decision that leads to his final accession is taken only under the threat of desertion by Montgomery and his forces.

The cycle of possession and non-possession of the crown that both Edward and Henry experience is reflected in the behaviour of other characters. Lewis, King of France, distributes his support with all the fickleness of Fortune herself. With initial sympathy for his countrywoman Margaret, he promises her that 'France can yield relief' to re-install Henry on the English throne (III.3.20). Then, with an advantageous marriage for his sister in the offing, he embraces the notion that seizure approved by the populace alone proves legitimate title:

> *But if your title to the crown be weak,*
> *As may appear by Edward's good success,*
> *Then 'tis but reason that I be released*
> *From giving aid which late I promisèd.*
>
> III.3.145–8

However, he can again reverse his decision in the face of Edward's slight to his sister and decree him a 'supposèd king', affording Margaret and Warwick military and naval aid to uncrown him.

It is in the character of Warwick that the reduction of the crown to a bauble is most marked. This kingmaker prizes his power to bestow the crown where he pleases more highly than kingship itself. By means of a biblical echo, Shakespeare reminds us of the godlike presumption inherent in Warwick's role as 'Proud setter-up and puller-down of kings' (III.3.157). From his first appearance to his death, he is a character created in terms of this self-appointed political function. His first two substantial speeches in the play are displays of confidence in his ability to 'plant Plantagenet, root him up who dares' (I.1.48); and after York's death he directs Edward's course as a superior rather than as a subject with near-royal powers. His defection to the Lancastrian side is but the decision of a moment, once he is convinced that he has been personally dishonoured by Edward's marriage to Lady Grey. The monstrous pride of the man is conveyed by the ego-rooted grammar and content of the lines which are his immediate reaction to the news:

> Did I forget that by the house of York
> My father came untimely to his death?
> Did I let pass th'abuse done to my niece?
> Did I impale him with the regal crown?
> Did I put Henry from his native right?
> And am I guerdoned at the last with shame?
>
> III.3.186–91

It is noticeable too that his support for Henry is couched in the same terminology that he used in connexion with York in the opening scene: this royal gardener will 're-plant Henry' in his personal plot of state, not because he pities Henry's misery but as he 'was the chief that raised

[Edward] to the crown' so will he 'be chief to bring him down again' (III.3.262–3). His death speech at Barnet field, for all its Alexandrian recognition that 'what is pomp, rule, reign, but earth and dust' (V.2.27), is primarily a lament for the loss of that special power for which history has nicknamed him:

> *For who lived king, but I could dig his grave?*
> *And who durst smile when Warwick bent his brow?*
>
> V.2.21–2

In a world peopled by men like Warwick, where force is right and wrong, where the crown is worn at the whim of the subject, Henry VI is obviously the least equipped of men to compete. After a few uncharacteristic attempts in the opening scenes to assert his monarchical authority, he ceases to be a part of the political world of the play. Margaret and Clifford send him away from the battles because they find they fare better when he is absent; he is defied by the power of Warwick, made to feel guilty in York's presence, lectured on how to be a king by his own son, and instructed on what he should have done to prevent rebellion by the man who is to be his successor as he stands at the head of an invading army. In view of his saintly character, it is hardly surprising that his resignation under the buffets of Fortune is even more striking and consistent than Edward's. In his famous speech at Towton he not only describes for us the unnatural and inconclusive tensions of the war but sets up in contrast to them a pastoral vision of the properly regulated rhythms possible in the life of a simple shepherd:

> *O God! Methinks it were a happy life*
> *To be no better than a homely swain;*
> *To sit upon a hill, as I do now;*
> *To carve out dials quaintly, point by point,*

Thereby to see the minutes how they run:
How many makes the hour full complete,
How many hours brings about the day,
How many days will finish up the year,
How many years a mortal man may live.
When this is known, then to divide the times:
So many hours must I tend my flock,
So many hours must I take my rest,
So many hours must I contemplate,
So many hours must I sport myself,
So many days my ewes have been with young,
So many weeks ere the poor fools will ean,
So many years ere I shall shear the fleece.
So minutes, hours, days, months, and years,
Passed over to the end they were created,
Would bring white hairs unto a quiet grave.

II.5.21–40

However, in the power-seeking reality of the play's world, such proportion is impossible for a shepherd-king. By means of dramatic juxtaposition, Shakespeare miniaturizes for the audience Henry's vision of service and social contract within the context that makes its realization impossible. Henry lists for Exeter, as they wait in the Bishop's palace, those qualities of his reign that should have prevailed in a sane land:

I have not stopped mine ears to their demands,
Nor posted off their suits with slow delays;
My pity hath been balm to heal their wounds,
My mildness hath allayed their swelling griefs,
My mercy dried their water-flowing tears;
I have not been desirous of their wealth,
Nor much oppressed them with great subsidies,
Nor forward of revenge, though they much erred.

IV.8.39–46

Immediately shouts are heard within and Edward and
Richard force their way in to bear away the 'shame-faced'
king. In a parallel scene (III.1) he is seized by his subjects
rather than his rivals; and the same ideas are explored in a
more leisurely, discursive fashion. Having wandered back
from exile in Scotland to see his kingdom once more,
Henry is captured by two gamekeepers; and his reaction
is a Socratic investigation into the nature of loyalty. The
two men claim that because they have sworn an oath of
allegiance to their new king, Edward, they must view
Henry as an enemy to the state. But, he asks them, did
they never swear an oath to him when he was their king,
which they are now breaking? No, they answer, 'we were
subjects but while you were king'. This reply draws to
itself all those other oaths – of York, Margaret, Warwick,
Edward, Richard, Clarence, Clifford – which were sworn
and broken in the service of dedicated self-interest. The
King's response can only be the sad perception of the
valueless, shifting realm he was called upon to rule:

> Why, am I dead? Do I not breathe a man?
> Ah, simple men, you know not what you swear!
> Look, as I blow this feather from my face,
> And as the air blows it to me again,
> Obeying with my wind when I do blow,
> And yielding to another when it blows,
> Commanded always by the greater gust;
> Such is the lightness of you common men.

III.1.81–8

It is ironical that Henry's realization takes the same form
as Jack Cade's bitter recognition of the fickleness of his
'subjects': 'Was ever feather so lightly blown to and fro
as this multitude? The name of Henry the Fifth hales
them to an hundred mischiefs, and makes them leave me
desolate' (2 Henry VI, IV.8.54–7).

Given the state of England and the character of Henry, there is only one crown he can effectively possess – one even more personal than that he tried to assure for himself in the opening scene:

> *My crown is in my heart, not on my head;*
> *Not decked with diamonds and Indian stones,*
> *Nor to be seen; my crown is called content;*
> *A crown it is that seldom kings enjoy.*   III.1.62–5

This balance in the private life, comparable with that of the shepherd's existence he envies, is what Henry settles for in a land where love of family produces a mad urge to destroy, where loyalty is equated with selfishness, where oaths are so many empty words, and where government means only the satisfaction of personal whim. There is not, nor can there be, in the play any dramatization of a better way of life; there can only be included a prophecy of it. This is the function of the scene of Henry's release from the Tower. By using the Tudor Myth for his own dramatic purposes, Shakespeare allows his failed Christian king to predict for the Elizabethan audience a future they knew to have come true. Henry places his hand on the shoulder of the boy who was to become Henry VII and promises the effective coming together of a nature framed to wear a crown and the rightful possession of it:

> *Come hither, England's hope. If secret powers*
> *Suggest but truth to my divining thoughts,*
> *This pretty lad will prove our country's bliss.*
> *His looks are full of peaceful majesty,*
> *His head by nature framed to wear a crown,*
> *His hand to wield a sceptre, and himself*
> *Likely in time to bless a regal throne.*   IV.6.68–74

Henry himself has to live out his inevitable end – death at the hands of the character in the play who sums up all the moral chaos. He falls uttering his second prophecy, of a time of outright tyranny which must intervene for England between his own wretched reign and the blessed time to be looked for under Henry Richmond:

> that many a thousand,
> Which now mistrust no parcel of my fear,
> And many an old man's sigh, and many a widow's,
> And many an orphan's water-standing eye –
> Men for their sons', wives for their husbands',
> And orphans for their parents' timeless death –
> Shall rue the hour that ever thou wast born.
>
> V.6.37–43

For his last words in this world, Henry slips out of his role of historical prophet and back into his Christian character to die with a prayer of forgiveness for himself and of pardon for the irredeemably damned: 'O, God forgive my sins, and pardon thee!' (V.6.60).

*

The scene in the Tower is clearly designed to bring together the moral extremes of the play and show the triumph of the worse. However, the violent contrast between Richard and Henry has been hinted at earlier. For example, after the Yorkist defeat at Tewkesbury, Richard asks whether Henry's way should be followed:

> But in this troublous time what's to be done?
> Shall we go throw away our coats of steel,
> And wrap our bodies in black mourning gowns,
> Numbering our Ave-Maries with our beads?

And he answers his own question:

> Or shall we on the helmets of our foes
> Tell our devotion with revengeful arms?
>
> II.1.158–61, 162–3

Later, in his first *credo* of evil (III.2.124–95), he echoes the 'crown of content' that Henry so prizes. Richard too can cry 'Content!' but for him it is not an indication of a mind at peace with itself, it is merely a mask to hide a far different inner state, like the smile on the face of a murderer.

Richard is much more than the polar opposite of a saintly king. He is also the summation of all the negative forces, obsessions, and attitudes manifested in the other characters. We have already noted the web of violations of the familial bond the play contains; and Richard is their culmination. Like Clifford he slaughters an innocent son, Prince Edward; like Margaret he toys with a captive grieving father, Henry, inflicting mental before final physical pain; like all the nobles he is driven by a revenge code that is crazed enough to want to pursue his enemy after death. But while these other characters are motivated, in even their most monstrous acts, by a family feeling pushed to mindless obsession, Richard by a kind of Machiavellian self-realization moves beyond the ordering standards imposed by kinship. The cold objectivity that enables him to see himself so clearly frees him from all human connexion: he is himself alone (V.6.83). This isolation permits him to contemplate without emotion Edward's death from venereal disease, to lay careful plans for Clarence's disgrace and murder, and promise his nephew's future destruction with a kiss. As we have seen in Clifford's case, this amoral pressure to destroy brings its own hell; and so with Richard the claustrophobia of violence is experienced:

> *And I – like one lost in a thorny wood,*
> *That rents the thorns and is rent with the thorns,*
> *Seeking a way and straying from the way,*

> *Not knowing how to find the open air,*
> *But toiling desperately to find it out –*
> *Torment myself to catch the English crown;*
> *And from that torment I will free myself,*
> *Or hew my way out with a bloody axe.*
>
> III.2.174–81

Like his father and brother, Richard also views the crown of England as the key to self-gratification; but his vision of possession is linked with the vocabulary of perversion. It is a 'misshaped trunk' that is to be topped with regal glory. The classical learning proper to a Renaissance prince is to provide him with the qualities necessary to pluck the crown from the hands of its owners: speech as fatal as the mermaid's song, the death-dealing glance of the basilisk, the cunning of Ulysses, the treachery of Sinon, the deception of Proteus, and the cynical ruthlessness of Machiavel (III.2.186–93). His confidence is persuasive; but it is less vivid than the energy with which he sums up the play's statement of the elusiveness of the crown for all such grabbers and overreachers:

> *Like one that stands upon a promontory*
> *And spies a far-off shore where he would tread,*
> *Wishing his foot were equal with his eye,*
> *And chides the sea that sunders him from thence,*
> *Saying he'll lade it dry to have his way;*
> *So do I wish the crown, being so far off;*
> *And so I chide the means that keeps me from it;*
> *And so I say I'll cut the causes off,*
> *Flattering me with impossibilities.*
>
> III.2.135–43

One of the qualities that make *Part Three* a more effective play than the two earlier parts is that Shakespeare appears to have learned during its composition to weave a dense poetic texture which works with rather than merely decorates the actions of the characters. Each of the main imagery patterns points to and finds fullest development in Richard. For example, the acted savagery is reinforced by vivid verbal pictures of malignant animals preying on helpless victims: Henry views York as 'an empty eagle' that will 'Tire on the flesh of me and of my son' (I.1.268–9); Clifford is a lion seizing Rutland 'to rend his limbs asunder' (I.3.15); Margaret is variously a tiger and a wolf. In the scene in the Tower, Richard becomes a human predatory animal before our eyes. He was born with teeth, which he assures us plainly signified that he 'should snarl and bite and play the dog' (V.6.77); and he is also the culmination of all those other cannibalistic actions, as he comes to make a bloody supper in the Tower. Henry perceives his own role, his son's and Richard's in terms of a preying world:

> So flies the reckless shepherd from the wolf;
> So first the harmless sheep doth yield his fleece,
> And next his throat unto the butcher's knife. . . .
> The bird that hath been limèd in a bush,
> With trembling wings misdoubteth every bush;
> And I, the hapless male to one sweet bird,
> Have now the fatal object in my eye
> Where my poor young was limed, was caught and killed.
>
> V.6.7–9, 13–17

By employing the fantastic lore about Richard's birth that he found in Sir Thomas More's biography *Ricardus Tertius*, and in the chronicles, Shakespeare fashioned him into the monstrous end-product of all the play's violations of love, procreation, primogeniture, and birth. Richard's description of his deformed being is an emblem of the disordered world: an England turned jungle has issued into this stigmatic, disproportionate in every part. However, at this point in his career, he constitutes only a threat; he is but an unshaped tyrant 'Like to a chaos, or an unlicked bear-whelp | That carries no impression like the dam' (III.2.161–2). As such he is also the embodiment of that elemental destructive energy that is linked throughout the play with images of overwhelming wind and sea power. Henry uses these natural forces as a metaphor for the battle at Towton. Warwick is 'Wind-changing' and 'moves both wind and tide' (V.1.57, III.3.48), but must finally submit himself to their power at Coventry. Margaret distributes among her enemies their destructive capacities:

> *And what is Edward but a ruthless sea?*
> *What Clarence but a quicksand of deceit?*
> *And Richard but a ragged fatal rock?*
>
> V.4.25–7

By the end of the play Richard is also the sea: in Henry's words he becomes the sea itself 'Whose envious gulf did swallow up' young Prince Edward's life – a prelude to all those other lives that are to be lost on his way to holding the throne as Richard III.

Most critics of the play have noticed the suddenness of Richard's emergence in III.2 as a character constructed on a different scale from all others. For the first half of the action there is little to differentiate him from the angry killers on both sides of the conflict. Like Clifford, Margaret, Warwick, York, and his brothers, he responds predictably to the events which force reaction upon him; and nothing prepares us for his revelation as a fully formed, credibly motivated, and acutely self-conscious villain. Some attempts have been made to account for this shift of character in psychological terms: that his father's death constitutes a spiritual turning-point in his life, transform-

34

ing him from loyal son into lonely hunter; or that his later
development is only an intensification of what he has
always been.

Certainly, the new creative power that has gone into the
portrayal of Richard in the latter half of the play encourages such theorizing about his character. There is a
vigour of utterance in his soliloquies found nowhere else,
which can encompass both the vividly pictured self-
loathing and the stark simplicity of his anti-human conclusions. When other characters speak alone – Henry at
Towton, or Warwick and Clifford at their deaths – their
speeches are but an extension of their public pronounce-
ments: they are orations without an audience. In Richard's
lines, however, there is a tension which persuades us that
he is attempting to give voice to thoughts that are in the
process of being formulated even as he speaks, that his
words are a means of making sense of his unique combination of ambition, deformity, wit, energy, and ruthless
calculation. Each of his major displays of himself grows
naturally out of something that has just been said: 'Ay,
Edward will use women honourably' (III.2.124), 'Indeed,
'tis true that Henry told me of' (V.6.69). And each leads
him into a believably conceived train of thought in which
he contemplates his being with frightening objectivity and
poses a series of questions that enable him to plan his
future course of action:

> *What other pleasure can the world afford? . . .*
> *And am I then a man to be beloved? . . .*
> *Can I do this, and cannot get a crown?*
>
> *Had I not reason, think ye, to make haste,*
> *And seek their ruin that usurped our right?*
>   III.2.147, 163, 194, V.6.72–3

35

Most remarkable of all is the idiom that Shakespeare invents for Richard. It already possesses some of the features that reflect his complex nature and are so striking in the later play he is to dominate: the grotesque comic relish –

> *The midwife wondered and the women cried*
> *'O, Jesus bless us, he is born with teeth!' –*
>
> V.6.74–5

a rough angularity of metre –

> *This shoulder was ordained so thick to heave;*
> *And heave it shall some weight or break my back.*
> *Work thou the way, and that shall execute –*
>
> V.7.23–5

the sharp movement from an observed fact to an outrageous immoral conclusion drawn from it –

> *Then, since the heavens have shaped my body so,*
> *Let hell make crooked my mind to answer it –*
>
> V.6.78–9

and a brusque confidence of phrasing derived from a knowledge of his ruthless capacities –

> *Can I do this, and cannot get a crown?*
> *Tut, were it farther off, I'll pluck it down.*
>
> III.2.194–5

Although Richard's dominance seems to have been due in part to the way his character stirred Shakespeare's imagination, we should not therefore assume that he unbalances the play. The figure emerges from and embodies the national chaos brought about by civil strife. As in orthodox Tudor historical theory, the terrible divisions of the Wars of the Roses produce their own monster to take advantage of the 'troublous times' and drain into his own tyrannous rule all England's ills. These in turn, in the person of Richard III, will be cut out of the body politic at Bosworth Field by God's own surgeon, Henry Richmond. But at the end of *Henry VI, Part Three*, all this lies ahead: here we have only Henry's prophecy of 'much more slaughter after this' (V.6.59) and Richard's promise of its fulfilment both in history and in another Shakespeare play, *The Life and Death of Richard III.*

FURTHER READING

GOOD surveys of scholarly and critical work done on the play are those by Harold Jenkins in *Shakespeare Survey 6* (Cambridge, 1953); by Ronald Berman in *A Reader's Guide to Shakespeare's Plays* (second edition, New York, 1973); and by A. R. Humphreys in *Shakespeare: Select Bibliographical Guides*, edited by Stanley Wells (Oxford, 1974).

Text, Date, and Authorship

The best reproduction of the text in the First Folio is in *The Norton Facsimile: The First Folio of Shakespeare*, prepared by Charlton Hinman (New York, 1968), and the most detailed analysis of it is in the same scholar's *The Printing and Proofreading of the First Folio of Shakespeare* (2 volumes, Oxford, 1963). A facsimile of the Octavo (Q1), *The True Tragedy of Richard Duke of York*, was prepared by W. W. Greg as Shakespeare Quarto Facsimile No. 11 (Oxford, 1958). In 1790 Edmond Malone claimed that Shakespeare had reworked this play into *3 Henry VI*, a view which was accepted until 1928–9, when Peter Alexander (*Shakespeare's 'Henry VI' and 'Richard III'*, 1929) and Madeleine Doran ('*Henry VI, 2 and 3*' in *University of Iowa Humanistic Studies*, VI, 4, 1928) proved it to be a corrupt reported version of Shakespeare's original play. Some scholars remained unconvinced by the work of Alexander and Doran; examples of the arguments against it may be found in J. Dover Wilson's New Cambridge edition of the play (Cambridge, 1952). There are valuable appraisals of the relationship between the two texts by W. W. Greg (*The Shakespeare First Folio*, Oxford, 1955), M. Mincoff (*English Studies* 42 (1961), 273–88), and Andrew S. Cairncross in his new Arden edition (London, 1964).

Adherents of the revision theory see the Folio text as being a mixture of the work of Shakespeare, Robert Greene, Thomas Nashe, and George Peele. The fullest treatment of the evidence for multiple authorship is found in Wilson's edition. Followers of Alexander and Doran view the play as totally by a young Shakespeare working under the influence of popular contemporary dramatists and gradually finding his own voice as he worked through the three parts. The play is variously dated between 1588 and 1592, according to the theories held about the authorship, the relationship between *The True Tragedy* and the Folio text, and the companies that probably acted them. The most recent clear presentation of the dating evidence is Hanspeter Born's article, 'The Date of *2, 3 Henry VI*' (*Shakespeare Quarterly* 25 (1974), 323–34).

Sources

The chronicles of Edward Hall, Raphael Holinshed, and Richard Grafton are available in early nineteenth-century reprints. For Hall and Holinshed the details are given at the head of the Commentary; Grafton's *A Chronicle at Large* (1569) was reprinted in 1809. There is a good general article on the use of the chronicles in all three parts of the play by R. A. Law in *Texas Studies in English* 33 (1955), 13–32. Geoffrey Bullough's introduction to his source selections in *Narrative and Dramatic Sources of Shakespeare* III (London, 1960), 157–71, is an invaluable balanced essay. In addition to his selections from the chronicles, Bullough also quotes the sections of *A Mirror for Magistrates* (1559) that Shakespeare probably used.

Criticism

A number of useful books supply accounts of Elizabethan attitudes to history. E. M. W. Tillyard's influential *Elizabethan World Picture* (1944) gives a summary of the official theory of government, and there are full studies of the history plays of the period in Irving Ribner's *The English History Play in the Age of Shakespeare* (Princeton, N.J., 1957; revised edition London, 1965) and David M. Bevington's *Tudor Drama and*

Politics: A Critical Approach to Topical Meaning (Cambridge, Mass., 1968).

Among studies of the history plays which see them as reflecting orthodox Elizabethan political beliefs are Tillyard's *Shakespeare's History Plays* (London, 1944), Lily B. Campbell's *Shakespeare's 'Histories': Mirrors of Elizabethan Policy* (San Marino, California, 1947), M. M. Reese's *The Cease of Majesty: A Study of Shakespeare's History Plays* (London, 1961), and S. C. Sen Gupta's *Shakespeare's Historical Plays* (Oxford, 1964). Recent critics have tended to find the plays less conservative in their political ideas. For example, Henry A. Kelly, in his *Divine Providence in the England of Shakespeare's Histories* (Cambridge, Mass., 1970), worked out freshly how Shakespeare treated the ideas he found in the chronicles; and Michael Manheim's *The Weak King Dilemma in the Shakespearean History Play* (Syracuse, N.Y., 1973) contains a penetrating sympathetic analysis of Henry VI as king and man.

There have been a number of full studies of the *Henry VI* sequence. R. B. Pierce examines the family–state correspondences in *Shakespeare's History Plays: The Family and the State* (Columbus, Ohio, 1971); E. W. Talbert's *Elizabethan Drama and Shakespeare's Early Plays* (Chapel Hill, North Carolina, 1963) shows a fine awareness of the problems of dramatizing history; David Riggs has some good comment on how the characters reflect political beliefs in *Shakespeare's Heroical Histories: 'Henry VI' and Its Literary Tradition* (Cambridge, Mass., 1971). Various studies emphasize particular aspects of the plays: Don M. Ricks in *Shakespeare's Emergent Form* (Logan, Utah, 1968) examines the structural principles; Robert Ornstein is perspicacious on character and style in *A Kingdom for a Stage: The Achievement of Shakespeare's History Plays* (Cambridge, Mass., 1972); Edward I. Berry's *Patterns of Decay: Shakespeare's Early Histories* (Charlottesville, Virginia, 1975) is a well-written exploration of the way central themes are embodied; and Robert Y. Turner's *Shakespeare's Apprenticeship* (Chicago, 1974) contains a subtle appreciation of aspects of the plays' dramaturgy. The most stimulating shorter essays on the sequence are J. P. Brockbank's in *Early Shakespeare* (Stratford-upon-Avon Studies No. 3), edited by J. R. Brown and Bernard Harris (London, 1961), and A. C. Hamilton's in his *The Early Shakespeare* (San Marino, California, 1967). The fullest treatment of the imagery patterns in the plays is C. M. Kay's essay in *Studies in the Literary Imagination* 1 (1972), 1–26.

Accounts of how the plays have fared on the stage can be found in C. B. Young's notes in Dover Wilson's editions and in Arthur Colby Sprague's *Shakespeare's Histories: Plays for the Stage* (London, 1964). Particular productions are discussed in Sir Barry Jackson's 'On Producing *Henry VI*', *Shakespeare Survey* 6 (1953), and John Russell Brown's analysis of Peter Hall's and John Barton's version, *The Wars of the Roses*, in *Shakespeare's Plays in Performance* (London, 1966).

THE THIRD PART OF
KING HENRY THE SIXTH

THE CHARACTERS IN THE PLAY

KING HENRY THE SIXTH
Margaret, QUEEN of England, daughter of King Reignier
Edward, PRINCE OF WALES, their son
DUKE OF EXETER ⎫
DUKE OF SOMERSET ⎪
EARL OF NORTHUMBERLAND ⎪
EARL OF WESTMORLAND ⎬ supporters of the house
EARL OF OXFORD ⎪ of Lancaster
LORD CLIFFORD ⎪
SIR JOHN SOMERVILLE ⎭

DUKE OF YORK, Richard Plantagenet
EDWARD, Earl of March, later Duke of ⎫
    York and King Edward IV ⎪
RICHARD, later Duke of Gloucester ⎬ sons of the Duke
GEORGE, later Duke of Clarence ⎪ of York
Edmund, EARL OF RUTLAND ⎭
SIR JOHN MORTIMER ⎫ uncles of the Duke of York
SIR HUGH MORTIMER ⎭
DUKE OF NORFOLK ⎫
MARQUESS OF MONTAGUE ⎪
EARL OF WARWICK ⎪
EARL OF PEMBROKE ⎬ supporters of the house
LORD HASTINGS ⎪ of York
LORD STAFFORD ⎪
SIR WILLIAM STANLEY ⎪
SIR JOHN MONTGOMERY ⎭

THE CHARACTERS IN THE PLAY

LADY ELIZABETH GREY, later wife of Edward IV and
  Queen of England
Prince Edward, her infant son
EARL RIVERS, brother of Lady Grey
Henry, Earl of Richmond
LEWIS THE ELEVENTH, King of France
LADY BONA, his sister

MESSENGERS
TUTOR of Edmund, Earl of Rutland
A SON that has killed his father ⎫
A FATHER that has killed his son ⎭ at the Battle of Towton
Two KEEPERS
A NOBLEMAN
POSTS
Three WATCHMEN
A HUNTSMAN
LIEUTENANT of the Tower of London
MAYOR of York

Soldiers, attendants, Admiral Bourbon, aldermen, Mayor
of Coventry, nurse to Prince Edward (infant son of
Edward IV)

Alarum. Enter York, Edward, Richard, Norfolk, I.1
Montague, Warwick, and soldiers, with white roses
in their hats

WARWICK

I wonder how the King escaped our hands?

YORK

While we pursued the horsemen of the north,
He slily stole away and left his men;
Whereat the great Lord of Northumberland,
Whose warlike ears could never brook retreat,
Cheered up the drooping army; and himself,
Lord Clifford, and Lord Stafford, all abreast,
Charged our main battle's front, and, breaking in,
Were by the swords of common soldiers slain.

EDWARD

Lord Stafford's father, Duke of Buckingham,   10
Is either slain or wounded dangerous;
I cleft his beaver with a downright blow.
That this is true, father, behold his blood.

MONTAGUE

And, brother, here's the Earl of Wiltshire's blood,
Whom I encountered as the battles joined.

RICHARD

Speak thou for me and tell them what I did.
    He throws down the Duke of Somerset's head

YORK

Richard hath best deserved of all my sons.
But is your grace dead, my lord of Somerset?

47

NORFOLK

Such hope have all the line of John of Gaunt!

RICHARD

20   Thus do I hope to shake King Henry's head.

WARWICK

And so do I. Victorious Prince of York,
Before I see thee seated in that throne
Which now the house of Lancaster usurps,
I vow by heaven these eyes shall never close.
This is the palace of the fearful King,
And this the regal seat; possess it, York;
For this is thine and not King Henry's heirs'.

YORK

Assist me then, sweet Warwick, and I will;
For hither we have broken in by force.

NORFOLK

30   We'll all assist you; he that flies shall die.

YORK

Thanks, gentle Norfolk; stay by me, my lords.
And, soldiers, stay and lodge by me this night.
    They go up

WARWICK

And when the King comes, offer him no violence,
Unless he seek to thrust you out perforce.

YORK

The Queen this day here holds her parliament,
But little thinks we shall be of her council;
By words or blows here let us win our right.

RICHARD

Armed as we are, let's stay within this house.

WARWICK

The bloody parliament shall this be called
40   Unless Plantagenet, Duke of York, be king,
And bashful Henry deposed, whose cowardice

Hath made us by-words to our enemies.

YORK

Then leave me not; my lords, be resolute;
I mean to take possession of my right.

WARWICK

Neither the King nor he that loves him best,
The proudest he that holds up Lancaster,
Dares stir a wing if Warwick shake his bells.
I'll plant Plantagenet, root him up who dares.
Resolve thee, Richard; claim the English crown.

> *Flourish. Enter King Henry, Clifford, North-*
> *umberland, Westmorland, Exeter, and soldiers, with*
> *red roses in their hats*

KING

My lords, look where the sturdy rebel sits,   50
Even in the chair of state! Belike he means,
Backed by the power of Warwick, that false peer,
To aspire unto the crown and reign as king.
Earl of Northumberland, he slew thy father,
And thine, Lord Clifford; and you both have vowed
          revenge
On him, his sons, his favourites, and his friends.

NORTHUMBERLAND

If I be not, heavens be revenged on me!

CLIFFORD

The hope thereof makes Clifford mourn in steel.

WESTMORLAND

What! Shall we suffer this? Let's pluck him down.
My heart for anger burns; I cannot brook it.   60

KING

Be patient, gentle Earl of Westmorland.

CLIFFORD

Patience is for poltroons, such as he;
He durst not sit there had your father lived.

My gracious lord, here in the parliament
Let us assail the family of York.

NORTHUMBERLAND
Well hast thou spoken, cousin; be it so.

KING
Ah, know you not the city favours them,
And they have troops of soldiers at their beck?

EXETER
But when the Duke is slain they'll quickly fly.

KING
70 Far be the thought of this from Henry's heart,
To make a shambles of the Parliament House!
Cousin of Exeter, frowns, words, and threats
Shall be the war that Henry means to use.
Thou factious Duke of York, descend my throne,
And kneel for grace and mercy at my feet;
I am thy sovereign.

YORK   I am thine.

EXETER
For shame, come down; he made thee Duke of York.

YORK
It was my inheritance, as the earldom was.

EXETER
Thy father was a traitor to the crown.

WARWICK
80 Exeter, thou art a traitor to the crown
In following this usurping Henry.

CLIFFORD
Whom should he follow but his natural king?

WARWICK
True, Clifford; that is Richard Duke of York.

KING
And shall I stand, and thou sit in my throne?

YORK
It must and shall be so; content thyself.

WARWICK

Be Duke of Lancaster; let him be king.

WESTMORLAND

He is both king and Duke of Lancaster;
And that the Lord of Westmorland shall maintain.

WARWICK

And Warwick shall disprove it. You forget
That we are those which chased you from the field   90
And slew your fathers, and with colours spread
Marched through the city to the palace gates.

NORTHUMBERLAND

Yes, Warwick, I remember it to my grief;
And, by his soul, thou and thy house shall rue it.

WESTMORLAND

Plantagenet, of thee and these thy sons,
Thy kinsmen, and thy friends, I'll have more lives
Than drops of blood were in my father's veins.

CLIFFORD

Urge it no more; lest that, instead of words,
I send thee, Warwick, such a messenger
As shall revenge his death before I stir.   100

WARWICK

Poor Clifford, how I scorn his worthless threats!

YORK

Will you we show our title to the crown?
If not, our swords shall plead it in the field.

KING

What title hast thou, traitor, to the crown?
Thy father was, as thou art, Duke of York;
Thy grandfather, Roger Mortimer, Earl of March.
I am the son of Henry the Fifth,
Who made the Dauphin and the French to stoop
And seized upon their towns and provinces.

WARWICK

Talk not of France, sith thou hast lost it all.   110

KING

The Lord Protector lost it, and not I.
When I was crowned I was but nine months old.

RICHARD

You are old enough now, and yet, methinks, you lose.
Father, tear the crown from the usurper's head.

EDWARD

Sweet father, do so; set it on your head.

MONTAGUE

Good brother, as thou lovest and honourest arms,
Let's fight it out and not stand cavilling thus.

RICHARD

Sound drums and trumpets, and the King will fly.

YORK

Sons, peace!

KING

120   Peace, thou! And give King Henry leave to
            speak.

WARWICK

Plantagenet shall speak first. Hear him, lords;
And be you silent and attentive too,
For he that interrupts him shall not live.

KING

Thinkest thou that I will leave my kingly throne,
Wherein my grandsire and my father sat?
No; first shall war unpeople this my realm;
Ay, and their colours, often borne in France,
And now in England to our hearts' great sorrow,
Shall be my winding-sheet. Why faint you, lords?

130   My title's good, and better far than his.

WARWICK

Prove it, Henry, and thou shalt be king.

KING

Henry the Fourth by conquest got the crown.

YORK

'Twas by rebellion against his king.

KING (*aside*)

I know not what to say; my title's weak. –
Tell me, may not a king adopt an heir?

YORK

What then?

KING

An if he may, then am I lawful king;
For Richard, in the view of many lords,
Resigned the crown to Henry the Fourth,
Whose heir my father was, and I am his.   140

YORK

He rose against him, being his sovereign,
And made him to resign his crown perforce.

WARWICK

Suppose, my lords, he did it unconstrained,
Think you 'twere prejudicial to his crown?

EXETER

No; for he could not so resign his crown
But that the next heir should succeed and reign.

KING

Art thou against us, Duke of Exeter?

EXETER

His is the right, and therefore pardon me.

YORK

Why whisper you, my lords, and answer not?

EXETER

My conscience tells me he is lawful king.   150

KING (*aside*)

All will revolt from me and turn to him.

NORTHUMBERLAND

Plantagenet, for all the claim thou layest,
Think not that Henry shall be so deposed.

53

WARWICK

Deposed he shall be, in despite of all.

NORTHUMBERLAND

Thou art deceived; 'tis not thy southern power
Of Essex, Norfolk, Suffolk, nor of Kent,
Which makes thee thus presumptuous and proud,
Can set the Duke up in despite of me.

CLIFFORD

King Henry, be thy title right or wrong,
160   Lord Clifford vows to fight in thy defence;
May that ground gape and swallow me alive,
Where I shall kneel to him that slew my father!

KING

O Clifford, how thy words revive my heart!

YORK

Henry of Lancaster, resign thy crown.
What mutter you, or what conspire you, lords?

WARWICK

Do right unto this princely Duke of York,
Or I will fill the house with armèd men,
And over the chair of state, where now he sits,
Write up his title with usurping blood.

*He stamps with his foot, and the soldiers show
themselves*

KING

170   My lord of Warwick, hear but one word;
Let me for this my lifetime reign as king.

YORK

Confirm the crown to me and to mine heirs,
And thou shalt reign in quiet while thou livest.

KING

I am content; Richard Plantagenet,
Enjoy the kingdom after my decease.

CLIFFORD
  What wrong is this unto the Prince your son!
WARWICK
  What good is this to England and himself!
WESTMORLAND
  Base, fearful, and despairing Henry!
CLIFFORD
  How hast thou injured both thyself and us!
WESTMORLAND
  I cannot stay to hear these articles.   180
NORTHUMBERLAND
  Nor I.
CLIFFORD
  Come, cousin, let us tell the Queen these news.
WESTMORLAND
  Farewell, faint-hearted and degenerate King,
  In whose cold blood no spark of honour bides.   *Exit*
NORTHUMBERLAND
  Be thou a prey unto the house of York,
  And die in bands for this unmanly deed!   *Exit*
CLIFFORD
  In dreadful war mayst thou be overcome,
  Or live in peace abandoned and despised!   *Exit*
WARWICK
  Turn this way, Henry, and regard them not.
EXETER
  They seek revenge and therefore will not yield.   190
KING
  Ah, Exeter!
WARWICK   Why should you sigh, my lord?
KING
  Not for myself, Lord Warwick, but my son,
  Whom I unnaturally shall disinherit.
  But be it as it may. (*To York*) I here entail

55

The crown to thee and to thine heirs for ever;
Conditionally that here thou take an oath
To cease this civil war; and, whilst I live,
To honour me as thy king and sovereign;
And neither by treason nor hostility
200 To seek to put me down and reign thyself.

YORK
This oath I willingly take and will perform.

WARWICK
Long live King Henry! Plantagenet, embrace him.

KING
And long live thou and these thy forward sons!

YORK
Now York and Lancaster are reconciled.

EXETER
Accursed be he that seeks to make them foes!
Sennet. Here they come down

YORK
Farewell, my gracious lord; I'll to my castle.

Exeunt York and his sons

WARWICK
And I'll keep London with my soldiers.   *Exit*

NORFOLK
And I to Norfolk with my followers.   *Exit*

MONTAGUE
And I unto the sea from whence I came.   *Exit*

KING
210 And I with grief and sorrow to the court.
Enter the Queen and the Prince of Wales

EXETER
Here comes the Queen, whose looks bewray her anger;
I'll steal away.

KING   Exeter, so will I.

QUEEN

Nay, go not from me, I will follow thee.

KING

Be patient, gentle Queen, and I will stay.

QUEEN

Who can be patient in such extremes?
Ah, wretched man! Would I had died a maid,
And never seen thee, never borne thee son,
Seeing thou hast proved so unnatural a father!
Hath he deserved to lose his birthright thus?
Hadst thou but loved him half so well as I,   220
Or felt that pain which I did for him once,
Or nourished him as I did with my blood,
Thou wouldst have left thy dearest heart-blood there,
Rather than have made that savage Duke thine heir
And disinherited thine only son.

PRINCE

Father, you cannot disinherit me;
If you be king, why should not I succeed?

KING

Pardon me, Margaret; pardon me, sweet son;
The Earl of Warwick and the Duke enforced me.

QUEEN

Enforced thee! Art thou king, and wilt be forced?   230
I shame to hear thee speak. Ah, timorous wretch!
Thou hast undone thyself, thy son, and me;
And given unto the house of York such head
As thou shalt reign but by their sufferance.
To entail him and his heirs unto the crown,
What is it but to make thy sepulchre,
And creep into it far before thy time?
Warwick is Chancellor and the Lord of Calais;
Stern Falconbridge commands the narrow seas;
The Duke is made Protector of the realm;   240

57

And yet shalt thou be safe? Such safety finds
The trembling lamb environèd with wolves.
Had I been there, which am a silly woman,
The soldiers should have tossed me on their pikes
Before I would have granted to that act.
But thou preferrest thy life before thine honour;
And, seeing thou dost, I here divorce myself
Both from thy table, Henry, and thy bed,
Until that act of parliament be repealed
250 Whereby my son is disinherited.
The northern lords that have forsworn thy colours
Will follow mine, if once they see them spread;
And spread they shall be, to thy foul disgrace
And utter ruin of the house of York.
Thus do I leave thee. Come, son, let's away.
Our army is ready; come, we'll after them.

KING

Stay, gentle Margaret, and hear me speak.

QUEEN

Thou hast spoke too much already; get thee gone.

KING

Gentle son Edward, thou wilt stay with me?

QUEEN

260 Ay, to be murdered by his enemies.

PRINCE

When I return with victory from the field,
I'll see your grace; till then I'll follow her.

QUEEN

Come, son, away; we may not linger thus.

                       Exeunt Queen and Prince

KING

Poor Queen! How love to me and to her son
Hath made her break out into terms of rage!
Revenged may she be on that hateful Duke,

Whose haughty spirit, wingèd with desire,
Will cost my crown, and like an empty eagle
Tire on the flesh of me and of my son!
The loss of those three lords torments my heart;   270
I'll write unto them and entreat them fair.
Come, cousin, you shall be the messenger.

EXETER
And I, I hope, shall reconcile them all.

Flourish. Exeunt

Enter Richard, Edward, and Montague   I.2

RICHARD
Brother, though I be youngest, give me leave.

EDWARD
No, I can better play the orator.

MONTAGUE
But I have reasons strong and forcible.
Enter the Duke of York

YORK
Why, how now, sons and brother! At a strife?
What is your quarrel? How began it first?

EDWARD
No quarrel, but a slight contention.

YORK
About what?

RICHARD
About that which concerns your grace and us –
The crown of England, father, which is yours.

YORK
Mine, boy? Not till King Henry be dead.   10

RICHARD
Your right depends not on his life or death.

59

EDWARD

Now you are heir; therefore enjoy it now.
By giving the house of Lancaster leave to breathe,
It will outrun you, father, in the end.

YORK

I took an oath that he should quietly reign.

EDWARD

But for a kingdom any oath may be broken;
I would break a thousand oaths to reign one year.

RICHARD

No; God forbid your grace should be forsworn.

YORK

I shall be, if I claim by open war.

RICHARD

20   I'll prove the contrary, if you'll hear me speak.

YORK

Thou canst not, son; it is impossible.

RICHARD

An oath is of no moment, being not took
Before a true and lawful magistrate
That hath authority over him that swears;
Henry had none, but did usurp the place.
Then, seeing 'twas he that made you to depose,
Your oath, my lord, is vain and frivolous.
Therefore to arms! And, father, do but think
How sweet a thing it is to wear a crown;
30   Within whose circuit is Elysium
And all that poets feign of bliss and joy.
Why do we linger thus? I cannot rest
Until the white rose that I wear be dyed
Even in the lukewarm blood of Henry's heart.

YORK

Richard, enough! I will be king or die.
Brother, thou shalt to London presently,

And whet on Warwick to this enterprise.
Thou, Richard, shalt to the Duke of Norfolk
And tell him privily of our intent.
You, Edward, shall unto my Lord Cobham,   40
With whom the Kentishmen will willingly rise;
In them I trust, for they are soldiers,
Witty, courteous, liberal, full of spirit.
While you are thus employed, what resteth more
But that I seek occasion how to rise,
And yet the King not privy to my drift,
Nor any of the house of Lancaster?
          Enter a Messenger
But stay; what news? Why comest thou in such post?

MESSENGER
The Queen with all the northern earls and lords
Intend here to besiege you in your castle.   50
She is hard by with twenty thousand men;
And therefore fortify your hold, my lord.

YORK
Ay, with my sword. What! Thinkest thou that we fear
          them?
Edward and Richard, you shall stay with me;
My brother Montague shall post to London.
Let noble Warwick, Cobham, and the rest,
Whom we have left protectors of the King,
With powerful policy strengthen themselves,
And trust not simple Henry nor his oaths.

MONTAGUE
Brother, I go; I'll win them, fear it not;   60
And thus most humbly I do take my leave.   *Exit*
          Enter Sir John Mortimer and Sir Hugh Mortimer,
          his brother

YORK
Sir John and Sir Hugh Mortimer, mine uncles,

You are come to Sandal in a happy hour;
The army of the Queen mean to besiege us.

SIR JOHN

She shall not need; we'll meet her in the field.

YORK

What, with five thousand men?

RICHARD

Ay, with five hundred, father, for a need.
A woman's general; what should we fear?
            A march afar off

EDWARD

I hear their drums; let's set our men in order,
70   And issue forth and bid them battle straight.

YORK

Five men to twenty! Though the odds be great,
I doubt not, uncle, of our victory.
Many a battle have I won in France
When as the enemy hath been ten to one;
Why should I not now have the like success? *Exeunt*

I.3   *Alarum. Enter Rutland and his Tutor*

RUTLAND

Ah, whither shall I fly to 'scape their hands?
Ah, tutor, look where bloody Clifford comes!
            Enter Clifford and soldiers

CLIFFORD

Chaplain, away! Thy priesthood saves thy life.
As for the brat of this accursèd duke,
Whose father slew my father, he shall die.

TUTOR

And I, my lord, will bear him company.

CLIFFORD

Soldiers, away with him!

TUTOR

Ah, Clifford, murder not this innocent child,
Lest thou be hated both of God and man.

Exit, dragged off by soldiers

CLIFFORD

How now? Is he dead already? Or is it fear   10
That makes him close his eyes? I'll open them.

RUTLAND

So looks the pent-up lion o'er the wretch
That trembles under his devouring paws;
And so he walks, insulting o'er his prey,
And so he comes, to rend his limbs asunder.
Ah, gentle Clifford, kill me with thy sword,
And not with such a cruel threatening look!
Sweet Clifford, hear me speak before I die.
I am too mean a subject for thy wrath;
Be thou revenged on men, and let me live.   20

CLIFFORD

In vain thou speakest, poor boy; my father's blood
Hath stopped the passage where thy words should enter.

RUTLAND

Then let my father's blood open it again;
He is a man, and, Clifford, cope with him.

CLIFFORD

Had I thy brethren here, their lives and thine
Were not revenge sufficient for me;
No, if I digged up thy forefathers' graves
And hung their rotten coffins up in chains,
It could not slake mine ire nor ease my heart.
The sight of any of the house of York   30
Is as a fury to torment my soul;
And till I root out their accursèd line
And leave not one alive, I live in hell.
Therefore –

63

He lifts his sword

RUTLAND

O, let me pray before I take my death!
To thee I pray; sweet Clifford, pity me!

CLIFFORD

Such pity as my rapier's point affords.

RUTLAND

I never did thee harm; why wilt thou slay me?

CLIFFORD

Thy father hath.

RUTLAND   But 'twas ere I was born.
40 Thou hast one son; for his sake pity me,
Lest in revenge thereof, sith God is just,
He be as miserably slain as I.
Ah, let me live in prison all my days;
And when I give occasion of offence,
Then let me die, for now thou hast no cause.

CLIFFORD

No cause?
Thy father slew my father; therefore die.

He stabs Rutland

RUTLAND

Di faciant laudis summa sit ista tuae.   *He dies*

CLIFFORD

Plantagenet! I come, Plantagenet!
50 And this thy son's blood cleaving to my blade
Shall rust upon my weapon, till thy blood,
Congealed with this, do make me wipe off both.   *Exit*

I.4   *Alarum. Enter Richard Duke of York*

YORK

The army of the Queen hath got the field;
My uncles both are slain in rescuing me;

And all my followers to the eager foe
Turn back and fly, like ships before the wind
Or lambs pursued by hunger-starvèd wolves.
My sons, God knows what hath bechancèd them;
But this I know, they have demeaned themselves
Like men born to renown by life or death.
Three times did Richard make a lane to me,
And thrice cried 'Courage, father! Fight it out!'   10
And full as oft came Edward to my side,
With purple falchion, painted to the hilt
In blood of those that had encountered him.
And when the hardiest warriors did retire,
Richard cried 'Charge! And give no foot of ground!'
And cried 'A crown, or else a glorious tomb!
A sceptre or an earthly sepulchre!'
With this we charged again; but, out, alas!
We budged again; as I have seen a swan
With bootless labour swim against the tide   20
And spend her strength with overmatching waves.
    A short alarum within
Ah, hark! The fatal followers do pursue,
And I am faint and cannot fly their fury;
And were I strong, I would not shun their fury.
The sands are numbered that makes up my life;
Here must I stay, and here my life must end.
    Enter the Queen, Clifford, Northumberland, the
    young Prince, and soldiers
Come, bloody Clifford, rough Northumberland,
I dare your quenchless fury to more rage;
I am your butt, and I abide your shot.

NORTHUMBERLAND
  Yield to our mercy, proud Plantagenet.   30

CLIFFORD
  Ay, to such mercy as his ruthless arm

With downright payment showed unto my father.
Now Phaethon hath tumbled from his car,
And made an evening at the noontide prick.

YORK

My ashes, as the phoenix, may bring forth
A bird that will revenge upon you all;
And in that hope I throw mine eyes to heaven,
Scorning whate'er you can afflict me with.
Why come you not? What! Multitudes, and fear?

CLIFFORD

40 So cowards fight when they can fly no further;
So doves do peck the falcon's piercing talons;
So desperate thieves, all hopeless of their lives,
Breathe out invectives 'gainst the officers.

YORK

O Clifford, but bethink thee once again,
And in thy thought o'errun my former time;
And, if thou canst for blushing, view this face,
And bite thy tongue, that slanders him with cowardice
Whose frown hath made thee faint and fly ere this!

CLIFFORD

I will not bandy with thee word for word,
50 But buckler with thee blows, twice two for one.

He draws his sword

QUEEN

Hold, valiant Clifford! For a thousand causes
I would prolong awhile the traitor's life.
Wrath makes him deaf; speak thou, Northumberland.

NORTHUMBERLAND

Hold, Clifford! Do not honour him so much
To prick thy finger, though to wound his heart.
What valour were it, when a cur doth grin,
For one to thrust his hand between his teeth,
When he might spurn him with his foot away?

It is war's prize to take all vantages;
And ten to one is no impeach of valour. 60
They fight and York is taken

CLIFFORD
Ay, ay, so strives the woodcock with the gin.

NORTHUMBERLAND
So doth the cony struggle in the net.

YORK
So triumph thieves upon their conquered booty;
So true men yield, with robbers so o'ermatched.

NORTHUMBERLAND
What would your grace have done unto him now?

QUEEN
Brave warriors, Clifford and Northumberland,
Come, make him stand upon this molehill here
That raught at mountains with outstretchèd arms,
Yet parted but the shadow with his hand.
What! Was it you that would be England's king? 70
Was't you that revelled in our parliament
And made a preachment of your high descent?
Where are your mess of sons to back you now?
The wanton Edward, and the lusty George?
And where's that valiant crook-back prodigy,
Dicky your boy, that with his grumbling voice
Was wont to cheer his dad in mutinies?
Or, with the rest, where is your darling Rutland?
Look, York, I stained this napkin with the blood
That valiant Clifford, with his rapier's point, 80
Made issue from the bosom of the boy;
And if thine eyes can water for his death,
I give thee this to dry thy cheeks withal.
Alas, poor York! But that I hate thee deadly,
I should lament thy miserable state.
I prithee grieve, to make me merry, York.

What! Hath thy fiery heart so parched thine entrails
That not a tear can fall for Rutland's death?
Why art thou patient, man? Thou shouldst be mad;
And I, to make thee mad, do mock thee thus.
Stamp, rave, and fret, that I may sing and dance.
Thou wouldst be fee'd, I see, to make me sport;
York cannot speak, unless he wear a crown.
A crown for York! And, lords, bow low to him;
Hold you his hands whilst I do set it on.
She puts a paper crown on York's head
Ay, marry, sir, now looks he like a king!
Ay, this is he that took King Henry's chair;
And this is he was his adopted heir.
But how is it that great Plantagenet
Is crowned so soon, and broke his solemn oath?
As I bethink me, you should not be king
Till our King Henry had shook hands with Death.
And will you pale your head in Henry's glory,
And rob his temples of the diadem,
Now in his life, against your holy oath?
O, 'tis a fault too too unpardonable!
Off with the crown; and, with the crown, his head;
And, whilst we breathe, take time to do him dead.

CLIFFORD

That is my office, for my father's sake.

QUEEN

Nay, stay; let's hear the orisons he makes.

YORK

She-wolf of France, but worse than wolves of France,
Whose tongue more poisons than the adder's tooth!
How ill-beseeming is it in thy sex
To triumph, like an Amazonian trull,
Upon their woes whom Fortune captivates!
But that thy face is vizard-like, unchanging,

Made impudent with use of evil deeds,
I would assay, proud Queen, to make thee blush.
To tell thee whence thou camest, of whom derived,
Were shame enough to shame thee, wert thou not shame-
     less.   120
Thy father bears the type of King of Naples,
Of both the Sicils and Jerusalem,
Yet not so wealthy as an English yeoman.
Hath that poor monarch taught thee to insult?
It needs not, nor it boots thee not, proud Queen;
Unless the adage must be verified,
That beggars mounted run their horse to death.
'Tis beauty that doth oft make women proud,
But, God He knows, thy share thereof is small.
'Tis virtue that doth make them most admired;   130
The contrary doth make thee wondered at.
'Tis government that makes them seem divine;
The want thereof makes thee abominable.
Thou art as opposite to every good
As the Antipodes are unto us,
Or as the south to the Septentrion.
O tiger's heart wrapped in a woman's hide!
How couldst thou drain the lifeblood of the child,
To bid the father wipe his eyes withal,
And yet be seen to bear a woman's face?   140
Women are soft, mild, pitiful, and flexible;
Thou stern, obdurate, flinty, rough, remorseless.
Biddest thou me rage? Why, now thou hast thy wish;
Wouldst have me weep? Why, now thou hast thy will;
For raging wind blows up incessant showers,
And when the rage allays, the rain begins.
These tears are my sweet Rutland's obsequies,
And every drop cries vengeance for his death
'Gainst thee, fell Clifford, and thee, false Frenchwoman.

NORTHUMBERLAND

150   Beshrew me, but his passions moves me so
   That hardly can I check my eyes from tears.

YORK

   That face of his the hungry cannibals
   Would not have touched, would not have stained with
         blood;
   But you are more inhuman, more inexorable,
   O, ten times more, than tigers of Hyrcania.
   See, ruthless Queen, a hapless father's tears;
   This cloth thou dipped'st in blood of my sweet boy,
   And I with tears do wash the blood away.
   Keep thou the napkin, and go boast of this;
160   And if thou tellest the heavy story right,
   Upon my soul, the hearers will shed tears;
   Yea, even my foes will shed fast-falling tears,
   And say 'Alas, it was a piteous deed!'
   There, take the crown, and with the crown my
         curse;
   And in thy need such comfort come to thee
   As now I reap at thy too cruel hand!
   Hard-hearted Clifford, take me from the world;
   My soul to heaven, my blood upon your heads!

NORTHUMBERLAND

   Had he been slaughter-man to all my kin,
170   I should not for my life but weep with him,
   To see how inly sorrow gripes his soul.

QUEEN

   What, weeping-ripe, my Lord Northumberland?
   Think but upon the wrong he did us all,
   And that will quickly dry thy melting tears.

CLIFFORD

   Here's for my oath, here's for my father's death.
     He stabs York

QUEEN

    And here's to right our gentle-hearted King.
       She stabs York

YORK

    Open Thy gate of mercy, gracious God!
    My soul flies through these wounds to seek out Thee.
                            He dies

QUEEN

    Off with his head, and set it on York gates;
    So York may overlook the town of York.   180
                    Flourish. Exeunt

*

    A march. Enter Edward, Richard, and their power II.1

EDWARD

    I wonder how our princely father 'scaped,
    Or whether he be 'scaped away or no
    From Clifford's and Northumberland's pursuit.
    Had he been ta'en, we should have heard the news;
    Had he been slain, we should have heard the news;
    Or had he 'scaped, methinks we should have heard
    The happy tidings of his good escape.
    How fares my brother? Why is he so sad?

RICHARD

    I cannot joy, until I be resolved
    Where our right valiant father is become.   10
    I saw him in the battle range about,
    And watched him how he singled Clifford forth.
    Methought he bore him in the thickest troop
    As doth a lion in a herd of neat;
    Or as a bear encompassed round with dogs,
    Who having pinched a few and made them cry,
    The rest stand all aloof and bark at him.

II.1

So fared our father with his enemies;
So fled his enemies my warlike father.
20 Methinks 'tis prize enough to be his son.
See how the morning opes her golden gates,
And takes her farewell of the glorious sun!
How well resembles it the prime of youth,
Trimmed like a younker prancing to his love!

EDWARD

Dazzle mine eyes, or do I see three suns?

RICHARD

Three glorious suns, each one a perfect sun;
Not separated with the racking clouds,
But severed in a pale clear-shining sky.
See, see! They join, embrace, and seem to kiss,
30 As if they vowed some league inviolable;
Now are they but one lamp, one light, one sun.
In this the heaven figures some event.

EDWARD

'Tis wondrous strange, the like yet never heard of.
I think it cites us, brother, to the field,
That we, the sons of brave Plantagenet,
Each one already blazing by our meeds,
Should notwithstanding join our lights together
And over-shine the earth as this the world.
Whate'er it bodes, henceforward will I bear
40 Upon my target three fair-shining suns.

RICHARD

Nay, bear three daughters; by your leave I speak it,
You love the breeder better than the male.

Enter a Messenger, blowing a horn

But what art thou, whose heavy looks foretell
Some dreadful story hanging on thy tongue?

MESSENGER

Ah, one that was a woeful looker-on

72

When as the noble Duke of York was slain,
Your princely father and my loving lord.

EDWARD

O, speak no more, for I have heard too much.

RICHARD

Say how he died, for I will hear it all.

MESSENGER

Environèd he was with many foes, 50
And stood against them, as the hope of Troy
Against the Greeks that would have entered Troy.
But Hercules himself must yield to odds;
And many strokes, though with a little axe,
Hews down and fells the hardest-timbered oak.
By many hands your father was subdued;
But only slaughtered by the ireful arm
Of unrelenting Clifford and the Queen,
Who crowned the gracious Duke in high despite,
Laughed in his face; and when with grief he wept, 60
The ruthless Queen gave him to dry his cheeks
A napkin steepèd in the harmless blood
Of sweet young Rutland, by rough Clifford slain;
And after many scorns, many foul taunts,
They took his head, and on the gates of York
They set the same; and there it doth remain,
The saddest spectacle that e'er I viewed.

EDWARD

Sweet Duke of York, our prop to lean upon,
Now thou art gone, we have no staff, no stay.
O Clifford, boisterous Clifford! Thou hast slain 70
The flower of Europe for his chivalry;
And treacherously hast thou vanquished him,
For hand to hand he would have vanquished thee.
Now my soul's palace is become a prison;
Ah, would she break from hence, that this my body

73

Might in the ground be closèd up in rest!
For never henceforth shall I joy again;
Never, O never, shall I see more joy!

RICHARD

I cannot weep, for all my body's moisture
80 Scarce serves to quench my furnace-burning heart;
Nor can my tongue unload my heart's great burden;
For self-same wind that I should speak withal
Is kindling coals that fires all my breast,
And burns me up with flames that tears would quench.
To weep is to make less the depth of grief;
Tears then for babes, blows and revenge for me!
Richard, I bear thy name; I'll venge thy death,
Or die renownèd by attempting it.

EDWARD

His name that valiant Duke hath left with thee;
90 His dukedom and his chair with me is left.

RICHARD

Nay, if thou be that princely eagle's bird,
Show thy descent by gazing 'gainst the sun:
For 'chair and dukedom', 'throne and kingdom' say;
Either that is thine, or else thou wert not his.

*March. Enter Warwick, the Marquess of Montague,
and their army*

WARWICK

How now, fair lords! What fare? What news abroad?

RICHARD

Great Lord of Warwick, if we should recompt
Our baleful news, and at each word's deliverance
Stab poniards in our flesh till all were told,
The words would add more anguish than the wounds.
100 O valiant lord, the Duke of York is slain!

EDWARD

O Warwick, Warwick! That Plantagenet,

Which held thee dearly as his soul's redemption,
Is by the stern Lord Clifford done to death.

WARWICK

Ten days ago I drowned these news in tears;
And now, to add more measure to your woes,
I come to tell you things sith then befallen.
After the bloody fray at Wakefield fought,
Where your brave father breathed his latest gasp,
Tidings, as swiftly as the posts could run,
Were brought me of your loss and his depart.   110
I, then in London, keeper of the King,
Mustered my soldiers, gathered flocks of friends,
Marched toward Saint Albans to intercept the Queen,
Bearing the King in my behalf along;
For by my scouts I was advertisèd
That she was coming with a full intent
To dash our late decree in parliament
Touching King Henry's oath and your succession.
Short tale to make, we at Saint Albans met,
Our battles joined, and both sides fiercely fought;   120
But whether 'twas the coldness of the King,
Who looked full gently on his warlike Queen,
That robbed my soldiers of their heated spleen;
Or whether 'twas report of her success,
Or more than common fear of Clifford's rigour,
Who thunders to his captives blood and death,
I cannot judge; but, to conclude with truth,
Their weapons like to lightning came and went;
Our soldiers', like the night-owl's lazy flight,
Or like a lazy thresher with a flail,   130
Fell gently down, as if they struck their friends.
I cheered them up with justice of our cause,
With promise of high pay and great rewards;
But all in vain; they had no heart to fight,

And we in them no hope to win the day;
So that we fled; the King unto the Queen;
Lord George your brother, Norfolk, and myself
In haste, post-haste, are come to join with you;
For in the Marches here we heard you were,
140   Making another head to fight again.

EDWARD

Where is the Duke of Norfolk, gentle Warwick?
And when came George from Burgundy to England?

WARWICK

Some six miles off the Duke is with the soldiers;
And for your brother, he was lately sent
From your kind aunt, Duchess of Burgundy,
With aid of soldiers to this needful war.

RICHARD

'Twas odds, belike, when valiant Warwick fled;
Oft have I heard his praises in pursuit,
But ne'er till now his scandal of retire.

WARWICK

150   Nor now my scandal, Richard, dost thou hear;
For thou shalt know this strong right hand of mine
Can pluck the diadem from faint Henry's head,
And wring the awful sceptre from his fist,
Were he as famous and as bold in war
As he is famed for mildness, peace, and prayer.

RICHARD

I know it well, Lord Warwick; blame me not:
'Tis love I bear thy glories makes me speak.
But in this troublous time what's to be done?
Shall we go throw away our coats of steel,
160   And wrap our bodies in black mourning gowns,
Numbering our Ave-Maries with our beads?
Or shall we on the helmets of our foes
Tell our devotion with revengeful arms?

If for the last, say ay, and to it, lords.

WARWICK

Why, therefore Warwick came to seek you out,
And therefore comes my brother Montague.
Attend me, lords. The proud insulting Queen,
With Clifford and the haught Northumberland,
And of their feather many moe proud birds,
Have wrought the easy-melting King like wax.   170
He swore consent to your succession,
His oath enrollèd in the parliament;
And now to London all the crew are gone,
To frustrate both his oath and what beside
May make against the house of Lancaster.
Their power, I think, is thirty thousand strong.
Now, if the help of Norfolk and myself,
With all the friends that thou, brave Earl of March,
Amongst the loving Welshmen canst procure,
Will but amount to five and twenty thousand,   180
Why, via! To London will we march amain,
And once again bestride our foaming steeds,
And once again cry 'Charge!' upon our foes;
But never once again turn back and fly.

RICHARD

Ay, now methinks I hear great Warwick speak.
Ne'er may he live to see a sunshine day
That cries 'Retire!' if Warwick bid him stay.

EDWARD

Lord Warwick, on thy shoulder will I lean;
And when thou failest – as God forbid the hour! –
Must Edward fall, which peril heaven forfend!   190

WARWICK

No longer Earl of March, but Duke of York;
The next degree is England's royal throne;
For King of England shalt thou be proclaimed

77

In every borough as we pass along;
And he that throws not up his cap for joy
Shall for the fault make forfeit of his head.
King Edward, valiant Richard, Montague,
Stay we no longer, dreaming of renown,
But sound the trumpets, and about our task.

RICHARD

200   Then Clifford, were thy heart as hard as steel,
As thou hast shown it flinty by thy deeds,
I come to pierce it, or to give thee mine.

EDWARD

Then strike up drums; God and Saint George for us!

Enter a Messenger

WARWICK

How now! What news?

MESSENGER

The Duke of Norfolk sends you word by me
The Queen is coming with a puissant host,
And craves your company for speedy counsel.

WARWICK

Why then it sorts, brave warriors; let's away.

Exeunt

II.2   *Flourish. Enter the King, Queen, Clifford, North-*
umberland, and the young Prince, with drum and
trumpets

QUEEN

Welcome, my lord, to this brave town of York.
Yonder's the head of that arch-enemy
That sought to be encompassed with your crown.
Doth not the object cheer your heart, my lord?

KING

Ay, as the rocks cheer them that fear their wrack;

To see this sight, it irks my very soul.
Withhold revenge, dear God! 'Tis not my fault,
Nor wittingly have I infringed my vow.

CLIFFORD

My gracious liege, this too much lenity
And harmful pity must be laid aside.   10
To whom do lions cast their gentle looks?
Not to the beast that would usurp their den.
Whose hand is that the forest bear doth lick?
Not his that spoils her young before her face.
Who 'scapes the lurking serpent's mortal sting?
Not he that sets his foot upon her back.
The smallest worm will turn, being trodden on,
And doves will peck in safeguard of their brood.
Ambitious York did level at thy crown,
Thou smiling while he knit his angry brows;   20
He, but a duke, would have his son a king,
And raise his issue like a loving sire;
Thou, being a king, blessed with a goodly son,
Didst yield consent to disinherit him,
Which argued thee a most unloving father.
Unreasonable creatures feed their young;
And though man's face be fearful to their eyes,
Yet, in protection of their tender ones,
Who hath not seen them, even with those wings
Which sometime they have used with fearful flight,   30
Make war with him that climbed unto their nest,
Offering their own lives in their young's defence?
For shame, my liege, make them your precedent!
Were it not pity that this goodly boy
Should lose his birthright by his father's fault,
And long hereafter say unto his child
'What my great-grandfather and grandsire got
My careless father fondly gave away'?

79

Ah, what a shame were this! Look on the boy;
40   And let his manly face, which promiseth
Successful fortune, steel thy melting heart
To hold thine own and leave thine own with him.

KING

Full well hath Clifford played the orator,
Inferring arguments of mighty force.
But, Clifford, tell me, didst thou never hear
That things ill got had ever bad success?
And happy always was it for that son
Whose father for his hoarding went to hell?
I'll leave my son my virtuous deeds behind;
50   And would my father had left me no more!
For all the rest is held at such a rate
As brings a thousand-fold more care to keep
Than in possession any jot of pleasure.
Ah, cousin York! Would thy best friends did know
How it doth grieve me that thy head is here!

QUEEN

My lord, cheer up your spirits; our foes are nigh,
And this soft courage makes your followers faint.
You promised knighthood to our forward son;
Unsheathe your sword and dub him presently.
60   Edward, kneel down.

KING

Edward Plantagenet, arise a knight;
And learn this lesson: draw thy sword in right.

PRINCE

My gracious father, by your kingly leave,
I'll draw it as apparent to the crown,
And in that quarrel use it to the death.

CLIFFORD

Why, that is spoken like a toward prince.
    Enter a Messenger

MESSENGER

    Royal commanders, be in readiness;
    For with a band of thirty thousand men
    Comes Warwick, backing of the Duke of York;
    And in the towns, as they do march along,   70
    Proclaims him king, and many fly to him.
    Darraign your battle, for they are at hand.

CLIFFORD

    I would your highness would depart the field;
    The Queen hath best success when you are absent.

QUEEN

    Ay, good my lord, and leave us to our fortune.

KING

    Why, that's my fortune too; therefore I'll stay.

NORTHUMBERLAND

    Be it with resolution then to fight.

PRINCE

    My royal father, cheer these noble lords,
    And hearten those that fight in your defence;
    Unsheathe your sword, good father; cry 'Saint George!' 80
        March. Enter Edward, Warwick, Richard, George,
        Norfolk, Montague, and soldiers

EDWARD

    Now, perjured Henry, wilt thou kneel for grace,
    And set thy diadem upon my head;
    Or bide the mortal fortune of the field?

QUEEN

    Go, rate thy minions, proud insulting boy!
    Becomes it thee to be thus bold in terms
    Before thy sovereign and thy lawful king?

EDWARD

    I am his king, and he should bow his knee.
    I was adopted heir by his consent;
    Since when, his oath is broke; for, as I hear,

90   You, that are king, though he do wear the crown,
Have caused him by new act of parliament
To blot out me, and put his own son in.

CLIFFORD

And reason too;
Who should succeed the father but the son?

RICHARD

Are you there, butcher? O, I cannot speak!

CLIFFORD

Ay, crook-back, here I stand to answer thee,
Or any he the proudest of thy sort.

RICHARD

'Twas you that killed young Rutland, was it not?

CLIFFORD

Ay, and old York, and yet not satisfied.

RICHARD

100   For God's sake, lords, give signal to the fight.

WARWICK

What sayst thou, Henry? Wilt thou yield the crown?

QUEEN

Why, how now, long-tongued Warwick! Dare you
    speak?
When you and I met at Saint Albans last,
Your legs did better service than your hands.

WARWICK

Then 'twas my turn to fly, and now 'tis thine.

CLIFFORD

You said so much before, and yet you fled.

WARWICK

'Twas not your valour, Clifford, drove me thence.

NORTHUMBERLAND

No, nor your manhood that durst make you stay.

RICHARD

Northumberland, I hold thee reverently.

Break off the parley; for scarce I can refrain   110
The execution of my big-swollen heart
Upon that Clifford, that cruel child-killer.

CLIFFORD

I slew thy father; callest thou him a child?

RICHARD

Ay, like a dastard and a treacherous coward,
As thou didst kill our tender brother Rutland;
But ere sun set I'll make thee curse the deed.

KING

Have done with words, my lords, and hear me
       speak.

QUEEN

Defy them then, or else hold close thy lips.

KING

I prithee give no limits to my tongue;
I am a king and privileged to speak.   120

CLIFFORD

My liege, the wound that bred this meeting here
Cannot be cured by words; therefore be still.

RICHARD

Then, executioner, unsheathe thy sword.
By Him that made us all, I am resolved
That Clifford's manhood lies upon his tongue.

EDWARD

Say, Henry, shall I have my right or no?
A thousand men have broke their fasts today,
That ne'er shall dine unless thou yield the crown.

WARWICK

If thou deny, their blood upon thy head;
For York in justice puts his armour on.   130

PRINCE

If that be right which Warwick says is right,
There is no wrong, but everything is right.

RICHARD

    Whoever got thee, there thy mother stands;
    For, well I wot, thou hast thy mother's tongue.

QUEEN

    But thou art neither like thy sire nor dam;
    But like a foul misshapen stigmatic,
    Marked by the destinies to be avoided,
    As venom toads or lizards' dreadful stings.

RICHARD

    Iron of Naples hid with English gilt,
140   Whose father bears the title of a king –
    As if a channel should be called the sea –
    Shamest thou not, knowing whence thou art extraught,
    To let thy tongue detect thy base-born heart?

EDWARD

    A wisp of straw were worth a thousand crowns
    To make this shameless callet know herself.
    Helen of Greece was fairer far than thou,
    Although thy husband may be Menelaus;
    And ne'er was Agamemnon's brother wronged
    By that false woman, as this king by thee.
150   His father revelled in the heart of France,
    And tamed the King, and made the Dauphin stoop;
    And had he matched according to his state,
    He might have kept that glory to this day.
    But when he took a beggar to his bed
    And graced thy poor sire with his bridal day,
    Even then that sunshine brewed a shower for him
    That washed his father's fortunes forth of France,
    And heaped sedition on his crown at home.
    For what hath broached this tumult but thy pride?
160   Hadst thou been meek, our title still had slept;
    And we, in pity for the gentle King,
    Had slipped our claim until another age.

GEORGE

  But when we saw our sunshine made thy spring,
  And that thy summer bred us no increase,
  We set the axe to thy usurping root;
  And though the edge hath something hit ourselves,
  Yet know thou, since we have begun to strike,
  We'll never leave till we have hewn thee down,
  Or bathed thy growing with our heated bloods.

EDWARD

  And in this resolution I defy thee;   170
  Not willing any longer conference,
  Since thou deniest the gentle King to speak.
  Sound trumpets! Let our bloody colours wave!
  And either victory, or else a grave!

QUEEN

  Stay, Edward.

EDWARD

  No, wrangling woman, we'll no longer stay:
  These words will cost ten thousand lives this day.

                            Exeunt

    Alarum. Excursions. Enter Warwick   II.3

WARWICK

  Forspent with toil, as runners with a race,
  I lay me down a little while to breathe;
  For strokes received, and many blows repaid,
  Have robbed my strong-knit sinews of their strength,
  And, spite of spite, needs must I rest a while.

    Enter Edward, running

EDWARD

  Smile, gentle heaven, or strike, ungentle death!
  For this world frowns, and Edward's sun is clouded.

WARWICK

How now, my lord! What hap? What hope of good?
Enter George

GEORGE

Our hap is loss, our hope but sad despair;
10   Our ranks are broke, and ruin follows us.
What counsel give you? Whither shall we fly?

EDWARD

Bootless is flight; they follow us with wings,
And weak we are and cannot shun pursuit.
Enter Richard

RICHARD

Ah, Warwick, why hast thou withdrawn thyself?
Thy brother's blood the thirsty earth hath drunk,
Broached with the steely point of Clifford's lance;
And in the very pangs of death he cried,
Like to a dismal clangour heard from far,
'Warwick, revenge! Brother, revenge my death!'
20   So, underneath the belly of their steeds,
That stained their fetlocks in his smoking blood,
The noble gentleman gave up the ghost.

WARWICK

Then let the earth be drunken with our blood;
I'll kill my horse, because I will not fly.
Why stand we like soft-hearted women here,
Wailing our losses, whiles the foe doth rage;
And look upon, as if the tragedy
Were played in jest by counterfeiting actors?
Here on my knee I vow to God above
30   I'll never pause again, never stand still,
Till either death hath closed these eyes of mine
Or fortune given me measure of revenge.

EDWARD

O Warwick, I do bend my knee with thine;
And in this vow do chain my soul to thine!

And, ere my knee rise from the earth's cold face,
I throw my hands, mine eyes, my heart to Thee,
Thou setter-up and plucker-down of kings,
Beseeching Thee, if with Thy will it stands
That to my foes this body must be prey,
Yet that Thy brazen gates of heaven may ope 40
And give sweet passage to my sinful soul!
Now, lords, take leave until we meet again,
Where'er it be, in heaven or in earth.

RICHARD

Brother, give me thy hand; and, gentle Warwick,
Let me embrace thee in my weary arms.
I, that did never weep, now melt with woe
That winter should cut off our spring-time so.

WARWICK

Away, away! Once more, sweet lords, farewell.

GEORGE

Yet let us all together to our troops,
And give them leave to fly that will not stay; 50
And call them pillars that will stand to us;
And, if we thrive, promise them such rewards
As victors wear at the Olympian games.
This may plant courage in their quailing breasts;
For yet is hope of life and victory.
Forslow no longer; make we hence amain. *Exeunt*

Excursions. Enter Richard and Clifford II.4

RICHARD

Now, Clifford, I have singled thee alone.
Suppose this arm is for the Duke of York,
And this for Rutland, both bound to revenge,
Wert thou environed with a brazen wall.

CLIFFORD

Now, Richard, I am with thee here alone.

This is the hand that stabbed thy father York,
And this the hand that slew thy brother Rutland,
And here's the heart that triumphs in their death
And cheers these hands that slew thy sire and brother
10 To execute the like upon thyself;
And so, have at thee!

They fight. Warwick comes. Clifford flies

RICHARD

Nay, Warwick, single out some other chase;
For I myself will hunt this wolf to death.

Exeunt

II.5 *Alarum. Enter King Henry alone*

KING

This battle fares like to the morning's war,
When dying clouds contend with growing light,
What time the shepherd, blowing of his nails,
Can neither call it perfect day nor night.
Now sways it this way, like a mighty sea
Forced by the tide to combat with the wind;
Now sways it that way, like the self-same sea
Forced to retire by fury of the wind.
Sometime the flood prevails, and then the wind;
10 Now one the better, then another best;
Both tugging to be victors, breast to breast,
Yet neither conqueror nor conquerèd;
So is the equal poise of this fell war.
Here on this molehill will I sit me down.
To whom God will, there be the victory!
For Margaret my Queen, and Clifford too,
Have chid me from the battle, swearing both
They prosper best of all when I am thence.
Would I were dead, if God's good will were so!

20 For what is in this world but grief and woe?
    O God! Methinks it were a happy life
    To be no better than a homely swain;
    To sit upon a hill, as I do now;
    To carve out dials quaintly, point by point,
    Thereby to see the minutes how they run:
    How many makes the hour full complete,
    How many hours brings about the day,
    How many days will finish up the year,
    How many years a mortal man may live.
    When this is known, then to divide the times: 30
    So many hours must I tend my flock,
    So many hours must I take my rest,
    So many hours must I contemplate,
    So many hours must I sport myself,
    So many days my ewes have been with young,
    So many weeks ere the poor fools will ean,
    So many years ere I shall shear the fleece.
    So minutes, hours, days, months, and years,
    Passed over to the end they were created,
    Would bring white hairs unto a quiet grave.   40
    Ah, what a life were this! How sweet! How lovely!
    Gives not the hawthorn bush a sweeter shade
    To shepherds looking on their silly sheep
    Than doth a rich embroidered canopy
    To kings that fear their subjects' treachery?
    O yes, it doth; a thousand-fold it doth.
    And to conclude, the shepherd's homely curds,
    His cold thin drink out of his leather bottle,
    His wonted sleep under a fresh tree's shade,
    All which secure and sweetly he enjoys,   50
    Is far beyond a prince's delicates,
    His viands sparkling in a golden cup,
    His body couchèd in a curious bed,

When care, mistrust, and treason waits on him.

Alarum. Enter at one door a Son that hath killed his
father, with the dead body in his arms

SON

Ill blows the wind that profits nobody.
This man whom hand to hand I slew in fight
May be possessèd with some store of crowns;
And I, that haply take them from him now,
May yet ere night yield both my life and them
60   To some man else, as this dead man doth me. –
Who's this? O God! It is my father's face,
Whom in this conflict I, unwares, have killed.
O, heavy times, begetting such events!
From London by the King was I pressed forth;
My father, being the Earl of Warwick's man,
Came on the part of York, pressed by his master;
And I, who at his hands received my life,
Have by my hands of life bereavèd him.
Pardon me, God, I knew not what I did!
70   And pardon, father, for I knew not thee!
My tears shall wipe away these bloody marks;
And no more words till they have flowed their fill.

KING

O, piteous spectacle! O, bloody times!
Whiles lions war and battle for their dens,
Poor harmless lambs abide their enmity.
Weep, wretched man; I'll aid thee tear for tear;
And let our hearts and eyes, like civil war,
Be blind with tears, and break o'ercharged with grief.

Enter at another door a Father that hath killed his
son, with the dead body in his arms

FATHER

Thou that so stoutly hath resisted me,
80   Give me thy gold, if thou hast any gold;

For I have bought it with an hundred blows.
But let me see: is this our foeman's face?
Ah, no, no, no, it is mine only son!
Ah, boy, if any life be left in thee,
Throw up thine eye! See, see what showers arise,
Blown with the windy tempest of my heart,
Upon thy wounds, that kills mine eye and heart!
O, pity, God, this miserable age!
What stratagems, how fell, how butcherly,
Erroneous, mutinous, and unnatural,   90
This deadly quarrel daily doth beget!
O boy, thy father gave thee life too soon,
And hath bereft thee of thy life too late!

KING

Woe above woe! Grief more than common grief!
O that my death would stay these ruthful deeds!
O, pity, pity, gentle heaven, pity!
The red rose and the white are on his face,
The fatal colours of our striving houses;
The one his purple blood right well resembles;
The other his pale cheeks, methinks, presenteth.   100
Wither one rose, and let the other flourish;
If you contend, a thousand lives must wither.

SON

How will my mother for a father's death
Take on with me and ne'er be satisfied!

FATHER

How will my wife for slaughter of my son
Shed seas of tears and ne'er be satisfied!

KING

How will the country for these woeful chances
Misthink the King and not be satisfied!

SON

Was ever son so rued a father's death?

FATHER

110   Was ever father so bemoaned his son?

KING

Was ever king so grieved for subjects' woe?
Much is your sorrow; mine ten times so much.

SON

I'll bear thee hence, where I may weep my fill.

Exit with the body of his father

FATHER

These arms of mine shall be thy winding-sheet;
My heart, sweet boy, shall be thy sepulchre,
For from my heart thine image ne'er shall go;
My sighing breast shall be thy funeral bell;
And so obsequious will thy father be,
Even for the loss of thee, having no more,
120   As Priam was for all his valiant sons.
I'll bear thee hence; and let them fight that will,
For I have murdered where I should not kill.

Exit with the body of his son

KING

Sad-hearted men, much overgone with care,
Here sits a king more woeful than you are.

*Alarums. Excursions. Enter the Queen, Prince, and
Exeter*

PRINCE

Fly, father, fly! For all your friends are fled,
And Warwick rages like a chafèd bull.
Away! For death doth hold us in pursuit.

QUEEN

Mount you, my lord; towards Berwick post amain.
Edward and Richard, like a brace of greyhounds
130   Having the fearful flying hare in sight,
With fiery eyes sparkling for very wrath,
And bloody steel grasped in their ireful hands,

Are at our backs; and therefore hence amain.
EXETER

Away! For vengeance comes along with them;
Nay, stay not to expostulate, make speed;
Or else come after; I'll away before.
KING

Nay, take me with thee, good sweet Exeter;
Not that I fear to stay, but love to go
Whither the Queen intends. Forward! Away!

Exeunt

A loud alarum. Enter Clifford, wounded   II.6
CLIFFORD

Here burns my candle out; ay, here it dies,
Which, whiles it lasted, gave King Henry light.
O Lancaster, I fear thy overthrow
More than my body's parting with my soul!
My love and fear glued many friends to thee;
And, now I fall, thy tough commixture melts,
Impairing Henry, strengthening misproud York.
The common people swarm like summer flies;
And whither fly the gnats but to the sun?
And who shines now but Henry's enemies?   10
O Phoebus, hadst thou never given consent
That Phaethon should check thy fiery steeds,
Thy burning car never had scorched the earth!
And, Henry, hadst thou swayed as kings should do,
Or as thy father and his father did,
Giving no ground unto the house of York,
They never then had sprung like summer flies;
I and ten thousand in this luckless realm
Had left no mourning widows for our death;
And thou this day hadst kept thy chair in peace.   20

93

For what doth cherish weeds but gentle air?
And what makes robbers bold but too much lenity?
Bootless are plaints, and cureless are my wounds;
No way to fly, nor strength to hold out flight;
The foe is merciless and will not pity,
For at their hands I have deserved no pity.
The air hath got into my deadly wounds,
And much effuse of blood doth make me faint.
Come, York and Richard, Warwick and the rest;
30 I stabbed your fathers' bosoms; split my breast.
> *He faints*
> *Alarum and retreat. Enter Edward, Richard, George,*
> *Warwick, Montague, and soldiers*

EDWARD
Now breathe we, lords; good fortune bids us pause,
And smooth the frowns of war with peaceful looks.
Some troops pursue the bloody-minded Queen,
That led calm Henry, though he were a king,
As doth a sail, filled with a fretting gust,
Command an argosy to stem the waves.
But think you, lords, that Clifford fled with them?

WARWICK
No, 'tis impossible he should escape;
For, though before his face I speak the words,
40 Your brother Richard marked him for the grave;
And wheresoe'er he is, he's surely dead.
> *Clifford groans and then dies*

RICHARD
Whose soul is that which takes her heavy leave?
A deadly groan, like life and death's departing.

EDWARD
See who it is; and, now the battle's ended,
If friend or foe, let him be gently used.

RICHARD
Revoke that doom of mercy, for 'tis Clifford;

Who not contented that he lopped the branch
In hewing Rutland when his leaves put forth,
But set his murdering knife unto the root
From whence that tender spray did sweetly spring: 50
I mean our princely father, Duke of York.

WARWICK

From off the gates of York fetch down the head,
Your father's head, which Clifford placèd there;
Instead whereof let this supply the room:
Measure for measure must be answerèd.

EDWARD

Bring forth that fatal screech-owl to our house,
That nothing sung but death to us and ours;
Now death shall stop his dismal threatening sound
And his ill-boding tongue no more shall speak.

WARWICK

I think his understanding is bereft.   60
Speak, Clifford, dost thou know who speaks to thee?
Dark cloudy death o'ershades his beams of life,
And he nor sees nor hears us what we say.

RICHARD

O, would he did! And so perhaps he doth;
'Tis but his policy to counterfeit,
Because he would avoid such bitter taunts
Which in the time of death he gave our father.

GEORGE

If so thou thinkest, vex him with eager words.

RICHARD

Clifford, ask mercy and obtain no grace.

EDWARD

Clifford, repent in bootless penitence.   70

WARWICK

Clifford, devise excuses for thy faults.

GEORGE

While we devise fell tortures for thy faults.

RICHARD

Thou didst love York, and I am son to York.

EDWARD

Thou pitied'st Rutland; I will pity thee.

GEORGE

Where's Captain Margaret to fence you now?

WARWICK

They mock thee, Clifford; swear as thou wast wont.

RICHARD

What! Not an oath? Nay, then the world goes hard
When Clifford cannot spare his friends an oath.
I know by that he's dead; and, by my soul,
80 If this right hand would buy two hours' life,
That I in all despite might rail at him,
This hand should chop it off, and with the issuing blood
Stifle the villain whose unstanchèd thirst
York and young Rutland could not satisfy.

WARWICK

Ay, but he's dead. Off with the traitor's head,
And rear it in the place your father's stands.
And now to London with triumphant march,
There to be crownèd England's royal king;
From whence shall Warwick cut the sea to France,
90 And ask the Lady Bona for thy queen.
So shalt thou sinew both these lands together;
And, having France thy friend, thou shalt not dread
The scattered foe that hopes to rise again;
For though they cannot greatly sting to hurt,
Yet look to have them buzz to offend thine ears.
First will I see the coronation,
And then to Brittany I'll cross the sea
To effect this marriage, so it please my lord.

EDWARD

Even as thou wilt, sweet Warwick, let it be;

For in thy shoulder do I build my seat,   100
And never will I undertake the thing
Wherein thy counsel and consent is wanting.
Richard, I will create thee Duke of Gloucester,
And George, of Clarence; Warwick, as ourself,
Shall do and undo as him pleaseth best.

RICHARD

Let me be Duke of Clarence, George of Gloucester;
For Gloucester's dukedom is too ominous.

WARWICK

Tut, that's a foolish observation;
Richard, be Duke of Gloucester. Now to London,
To see these honours in possession. .   *Exeunt* 110

*

Enter two Keepers, with cross-bows in their hands   III.1

FIRST KEEPER

Under this thick-grown brake we'll shroud ourselves;
For through this laund anon the deer will come,
And in this covert will we make our stand,
Culling the principal of all the deer.

SECOND KEEPER

I'll stay above the hill, so both may shoot.

FIRST KEEPER

That cannot be; the noise of thy cross-bow
Will scare the herd, and so my shoot is lost.
Here stand we both, and aim we at the best;
And for the time shall not seem tedious,
I'll tell thee what befell me on a day   10
In this self place where now we mean to stand.

SECOND KEEPER

Here comes a man; let's stay till he be past.

Enter King Henry, disguised, with a prayer-book

97

III.1

KING

    From Scotland am I stolen, even of pure love,
    To greet mine own land with my wishful sight.
    No, Harry, Harry, 'tis no land of thine;
    Thy place is filled, thy sceptre wrung from thee,
    Thy balm washed off wherewith thou wast anointed;
    No bending knee will call thee Caesar now,
    No humble suitors press to speak for right,
20   No, not a man comes for redress of thee;
    For how can I help them and not myself?

FIRST KEEPER

    Ay, here's a deer whose skin's a keeper's fee:
    This is the quondam king; let's seize upon him.

KING

    Let me embrace thee, sour adversity,
    For wise men say it is the wisest course.

SECOND KEEPER

    Why linger we? Let us lay hands upon him.

FIRST KEEPER

    Forbear awhile; we'll hear a little more.

KING

    My Queen and son are gone to France for aid;
    And, as I hear, the great commanding Warwick
30   Is thither gone to crave the French King's sister
    To wife for Edward. If this news be true,
    Poor Queen and son, your labour is but lost;
    For Warwick is a subtle orator,
    And Lewis a prince soon won with moving words.
    By this account then Margaret may win him;
    For she's a woman to be pitied much.
    Her sighs will make a battery in his breast;
    Her tears will pierce into a marble heart;
    The tiger will be mild whiles she doth mourn;
40   And Nero will be tainted with remorse,

To hear and see her plaints, her brinish tears.
Ay, but she's come to beg, Warwick to give;
She, on his left side, craving aid for Henry,
He, on his right, asking a wife for Edward.
She weeps, and says her Henry is deposed;
He smiles, and says his Edward is installed;
That she, poor wretch, for grief can speak no more;
Whiles Warwick tells his title, smooths the wrong,
Inferreth arguments of mighty strength,
And in conclusion wins the King from her,   50
With promise of his sister, and what else,
To strengthen and support King Edward's place.
O Margaret, thus 'twill be; and thou, poor soul,
Art then forsaken, as thou wentest forlorn!

SECOND KEEPER
Say, what art thou that talkest of kings and queens?

KING
More than I seem, and less than I was born to:
A man at least, for less I should not be;
And men may talk of kings, and why not I?

SECOND KEEPER
Ay, but thou talkest as if thou wert a king.

KING
Why, so I am, in mind, and that's enough.   60

SECOND KEEPER
But if thou be a king, where is thy crown?

KING
My crown is in my heart, not on my head;
Not decked with diamonds and Indian stones,
Nor to be seen; my crown is called content;
A crown it is that seldom kings enjoy.

SECOND KEEPER
Well, if you be a king crowned with content,
Your crown content and you must be contented

To go along with us; for, as we think,
You are the king King Edward hath deposed;
And we his subjects, sworn in all allegiance,
Will apprehend you as his enemy.

KING

But did you never swear, and break an oath?

SECOND KEEPER

No, never such an oath, nor will not now.

KING

Where did you dwell when I was King of England?

SECOND KEEPER

Here in this country, where we now remain.

KING

I was anointed king at nine months old;
My father and my grandfather were kings,
And you were sworn true subjects unto me;
And tell me, then, have you not broke your oaths?

FIRST KEEPER

No, for we were subjects but while you were king.

KING

Why, am I dead? Do I not breathe a man?
Ah, simple men, you know not what you swear!
Look, as I blow this feather from my face,
And as the air blows it to me again,
Obeying with my wind when I do blow,
And yielding to another when it blows,
Commanded always by the greater gust;
Such is the lightness of you common men.
But do not break your oaths; for of that sin
My mild entreaty shall not make you guilty.
Go where you will, the King shall be commanded;
And be you kings, command, and I'll obey.

FIRST KEEPER

We are true subjects to the King, King Edward.

KING

　So would you be again to Henry,
　If he were seated as King Edward is.

FIRST KEEPER

　We charge you in God's name, and the King's,
　To go with us unto the officers.

KING

　In God's name, lead; your king's name be obeyed;
　And what God will, that let your king perform;
　And what he will, I humbly yield unto.　　　　　100

　　　　　　　　　　　　　　　　　Exeunt

Enter King Edward. Richard Duke of Gloucester, III.2
　　George Duke of Clarence, and Lady Grey

EDWARD

　Brother of Gloucester, at Saint Albans field
　This lady's husband, Sir Richard Grey, was slain,
　His lands then seized on by the conqueror.
　Her suit is now to repossess those lands;
　Which we in justice cannot well deny,
　Because in quarrel of the house of York
　The worthy gentleman did lose his life.

RICHARD

　Your highness shall do well to grant her suit;
　It were dishonour to deny it her.

EDWARD

　It were no less; but yet I'll make a pause.　　　　10

RICHARD (*aside to George*)

　Yea, is it so?
　I see the lady hath a thing to grant
　Before the King will grant her humble suit.

GEORGE (*aside to Richard*)

　He knows the game; how true he keeps the wind!

III.2

RICHARD (*aside to George*)
  Silence!

EDWARD
  Widow, we will consider of your suit;
  And come some other time to know our mind.

LADY GREY
  Right gracious lord, I cannot brook delay;
  May it please your highness to resolve me now,
20 And what your pleasure is shall satisfy me.

RICHARD (*aside to George*)
  Ay, widow? Then I'll warrant you all your lands,
  An if what pleases him shall pleasure you.
  Fight closer, or, good faith, you'll catch a blow.

GEORGE (*aside to Richard*)
  I fear her not unless she chance to fall.

RICHARD (*aside to George*)
  God forbid that! For he'll take vantages.

EDWARD
  How many children hast thou, widow? Tell me.

GEORGE (*aside to Richard*)
  I think he means to beg a child of her.

RICHARD (*aside to George*)
  Nay then, whip me; he'll rather give her two.

LADY GREY
  Three, my most gracious lord.

RICHARD (*aside to George*)
30 You shall have four, if you'll be ruled by him.

EDWARD
  'Twere pity they should lose their father's lands.

LADY GREY
  Be pitiful, dread lord, and grant it then.

EDWARD
  Lords, give us leave; I'll try this widow's wit.

RICHARD (*aside to George*)
  Ay, good leave have you; for you will have leave,

Till youth take leave and leave you to the crutch.
Richard and George go out of earshot

EDWARD
Now tell me, madam, do you love your children?

LADY GREY
Ay, full as dearly as I love myself.

EDWARD
And would you not do much to do them good?

LADY GREY
To do them good I would sustain some harm.

EDWARD
Then get your husband's lands, to do them good.   40

LADY GREY
Therefore I came unto your majesty.

EDWARD
I'll tell you how these lands are to be got.

LADY GREY
So shall you bind me to your highness' service.

EDWARD
What service wilt thou do me, if I give them?

LADY GREY
What you command, that rests in me to do.

EDWARD
But you will take exceptions to my boon.

LADY GREY
No, gracious lord, except I cannot do it.

EDWARD
Ay, but thou canst do what I mean to ask.

LADY GREY
Why, then I will do what your grace commands.

RICHARD (*aside to George*)
He plies her hard; and much rain wears the marble.   50

GEORGE (*aside to Richard*)
As red as fire! Nay, then her wax must melt.

LADY GREY

Why stops my lord? Shall I not hear my task?

EDWARD

An easy task; 'tis but to love a king.

LADY GREY

That's soon performed, because I am a subject.

EDWARD

Why, then, thy husband's lands I freely give thee.

LADY GREY

I take my leave with many thousand thanks.

RICHARD (*aside to George*)

The match is made; she seals it with a curtsy.

EDWARD

But stay thee; 'tis the fruits of love I mean.

LADY GREY

The fruits of love I mean, my loving liege.

EDWARD

60 Ay, but I fear me in another sense.

What love, thinkest thou, I sue so much to get?

LADY GREY

My love till death, my humble thanks, my prayers;

That love which virtue begs and virtue grants.

EDWARD

No, by my troth, I did not mean such love.

LADY GREY

Why, then you mean not as I thought you did.

EDWARD

But now you partly may perceive my mind.

LADY GREY

My mind will never grant what I perceive

Your highness aims at, if I aim aright.

EDWARD

To tell thee plain, I aim to lie with thee.

LADY GREY

70 To tell you plain, I had rather lie in prison.

EDWARD
Why, then thou shalt not have thy husband's lands.

LADY GREY
Why, then mine honesty shall be my dower;
For by that loss I will not purchase them.

EDWARD
Therein thou wrongest thy children mightily.

LADY GREY
Herein your highness wrongs both them and me.
But, mighty lord, this merry inclination
Accords not with the sadness of my suit:
Please you dismiss me, either with ay or no.

EDWARD
Ay, if thou wilt say 'ay' to my request;
No, if thou dost say 'no' to my demand. 80

LADY GREY
Then, no, my lord. My suit is at an end.

RICHARD (*aside to George*)
The widow likes him not; she knits her brows.

GEORGE (*aside to Richard*)
He is the bluntest wooer in Christendom.

EDWARD (*aside*)
Her looks doth argue her replete with modesty;
Her words doth show her wit incomparable;
All her perfections challenge sovereignty.
One way or other, she is for a king;
And she shall be my love or else my queen.
(*To Lady Grey*)
Say that King Edward take thee for his queen?

LADY GREY
'Tis better said than done, my gracious lord. 90
I am a subject fit to jest withal,
But far unfit to be a sovereign.

EDWARD
Sweet widow, by my state I swear to thee

I speak no more than what my soul intends;
And that is, to enjoy thee for my love.

LADY GREY

And that is more than I will yield unto.
I know I am too mean to be your queen,
And yet too good to be your concubine.

EDWARD

You cavil, widow; I did mean my queen.

LADY GREY

'Twill grieve your grace my sons should call you
100   father.

EDWARD

No more than when my daughters call thee mother.
Thou art a widow and thou hast some children;
And, by God's mother, I, being but a bachelor,
Have other some; why, 'tis a happy thing
To be the father unto many sons.
Answer no more, for thou shalt be my queen.

RICHARD (*aside to George*)

The ghostly father now hath done his shrift.

GEORGE (*aside to Richard*)

When he was made a shriver, 'twas for shift.

EDWARD

Brothers, you muse what chat we two have had.

RICHARD

110 The widow likes it not, for she looks very sad.

EDWARD

You'd think it strange if I should marry her.

GEORGE

To who, my lord?

EDWARD   Why, Clarence, to myself.

RICHARD

That would be ten days' wonder at the least.

GEORGE
  That's a day longer than a wonder lasts.

RICHARD
  By so much is the wonder in extremes.

EDWARD
  Well, jest on, brothers; I can tell you both
  Her suit is granted for her husband's lands.
      Enter a Nobleman

NOBLEMAN
  My gracious lord, Henry your foe is taken,
  And brought your prisoner to your palace gate.

EDWARD
  See that he be conveyed unto the Tower;   120
  And go we, brothers, to the man that took him,
  To question of his apprehension.
  Widow, go you along. Lords, use her honourably.
                              Exeunt all but Richard

RICHARD
  Ay, Edward will use women honourably.
  Would he were wasted, marrow, bones, and all,
  That from his loins no hopeful branch may spring,
  To cross me from the golden time I look for!
  And yet, between my soul's desire and me –
  The lustful Edward's title burièd –
  Is Clarence, Henry, and his son young Edward,   130
  And all the unlooked-for issue of their bodies,
  To take their rooms, ere I can place myself:
  A cold premeditation for my purpose!
  Why then, I do but dream on sovereignty;
  Like one that stands upon a promontory
  And spies a far-off shore where he would tread,
  Wishing his foot were equal with his eye,
  And chides the sea that sunders him from thence,
  Saying he'll lade it dry to have his way;

140 So do I wish the crown, being so far off;
  And so I chide the means that keeps me from it;
  And so I say I'll cut the causes off,
  Flattering me with impossibilities.
  My eye's too quick, my heart o'erweens too much,
  Unless my hand and strength could equal them.
  Well, say there is no kingdom then for Richard,
  What other pleasure can the world afford?
  I'll make my heaven in a lady's lap,
  And deck my body in gay ornaments,
150 And 'witch sweet ladies with my words and looks.
  O, miserable thought! And more unlikely
  Than to accomplish twenty golden crowns!
  Why, love forswore me in my mother's womb;
  And, for I should not deal in her soft laws,
  She did corrupt frail nature with some bribe
  To shrink mine arm up like a withered shrub;
  To make an envious mountain on my back,
  Where sits deformity to mock my body;
  To shape my legs of an unequal size;
160 To disproportion me in every part,
  Like to a chaos, or an unlicked bear-whelp
  That carries no impression like the dam.
  And am I then a man to be beloved?
  O, monstrous fault, to harbour such a thought!
  Then, since this earth affords no joy to me
  But to command, to check, to o'erbear such
  As are of better person than myself,
  I'll make my heaven to dream upon the crown,
  And, whiles I live, t'account this world but hell,
170 Until my misshaped trunk that bears this head
  Be round impalèd with a glorious crown.
  And yet I know not how to get the crown,
  For many lives stand between me and home;

And I – like one lost in a thorny wood,
That rents the thorns and is rent with the thorns,
Seeking a way and straying from the way,
Not knowing how to find the open air,
But toiling desperately to find it out –
Torment myself to catch the English crown;
And from that torment I will free myself,   180
Or hew my way out with a bloody axe.
Why, I can smile, and murder whiles I smile,
And cry 'Content!' to that which grieves my heart,
And wet my cheeks with artificial tears,
And frame my face to all occasions.
I'll drown more sailors than the mermaid shall;
I'll slay more gazers than the basilisk;
I'll play the orator as well as Nestor,
Deceive more slily than Ulysses could,
And, like a Sinon, take another Troy.   190
I can add colours to the chameleon,
Change shapes with Proteus for advantages,
And set the murderous Machiavel to school.
Can I do this, and cannot get a crown?
Tut, were it farther off, I'll pluck it down.   *Exit*

Flourish. Enter Lewis the French King, his sister III.3
Bona, his admiral, called Bourbon; Prince Edward,
Queen Margaret, and the Earl of Oxford. Lewis sits
and riseth up again

LEWIS
Fair Queen of England, worthy Margaret,
Sit down with us; it ill befits thy state
And birth that thou shouldst stand while Lewis doth sit.
QUEEN
No, mighty King of France; now Margaret

Must strike her sail and learn awhile to serve
Where kings command. I was, I must confess,
Great Albion's Queen in former golden days;
But now mischance hath trod my title down,
And with dishonour laid me on the ground;
Where I must take like seat unto my fortune
And to my humble seat conform myself.

LEWIS

Why, say, fair Queen, whence springs this deep despair?

QUEEN

From such a cause as fills mine eyes with tears
And stops my tongue, while heart is drowned in cares.

LEWIS

Whate'er it be, be thou still like thyself,
And sit thee by our side.

He seats her by him

Yield not thy neck
To Fortune's yoke, but let thy dauntless mind
Still ride in triumph over all mischance.
Be plain, Queen Margaret, and tell thy grief;
It shall be eased, if France can yield relief.

QUEEN

Those gracious words revive my drooping thoughts
And give my tongue-tied sorrows leave to speak.
Now, therefore, be it known to noble Lewis
That Henry, sole possessor of my love,
Is of a king become a banished man,
And forced to live in Scotland a forlorn;
While proud ambitious Edward Duke of York
Usurps the regal title and the seat
Of England's true-anointed lawful King.
This is the cause that I, poor Margaret,
With this my son, Prince Edward, Henry's heir,
Am come to crave thy just and lawful aid;

And if thou fail us, all our hope is done.
Scotland hath will to help, but cannot help;
Our people and our peers are both misled,
Our treasure seized, our soldiers put to flight,
And, as thou seest, ourselves in heavy plight.

LEWIS

Renownèd Queen, with patience calm the storm,
While we bethink a means to break it off.

QUEEN

The more we stay, the stronger grows our foe.   40

LEWIS

The more I stay, the more I'll succour thee.

QUEEN

O, but impatience waiteth on true sorrow.
And see where comes the breeder of my sorrow!
    Enter Warwick

LEWIS

What's he approacheth boldly to our presence?

QUEEN

Our Earl of Warwick, Edward's greatest friend.

LEWIS

Welcome, brave Warwick. What brings thee to France?
    He descends. She ariseth

QUEEN

Ay, now begins a second storm to rise,
For this is he that moves both wind and tide.

WARWICK

From worthy Edward, King of Albion,
My lord and sovereign, and thy vowèd friend,   50
I come, in kindness and unfeignèd love,
First, to do greetings to thy royal person;
And then to crave a league of amity;
And lastly to confirm that amity
With nuptial knot, if thou vouchsafe to grant

That virtuous Lady Bona, thy fair sister,
To England's King in lawful marriage.

QUEEN (*aside*)

If that go forward, Henry's hope is done.

WARWICK (*to Bona*)

And, gracious madam, in our king's behalf,
60 I am commanded, with your leave and favour,
Humbly to kiss your hand, and with my tongue
To tell the passion of my sovereign's heart;
Where fame, late entering at his heedful ears,
Hath placed thy beauty's image and thy virtue.

QUEEN

King Lewis and Lady Bona, hear me speak,
Before you answer Warwick. His demand
Springs not from Edward's well-meant honest love,
But from deceit bred by necessity;
For how can tyrants safely govern home,
70 Unless abroad they purchase great alliance?
To prove him tyrant this reason may suffice,
That Henry liveth still; but were he dead,
Yet here Prince Edward stands, King Henry's son.
Look, therefore, Lewis, that by this league and marriage
Thou draw not on thy danger and dishonour;
For though usurpers sway the rule awhile,
Yet heavens are just, and time suppresseth wrongs.

WARWICK

Injurious Margaret!

PRINCE   And why not 'Queen'?

WARWICK

Because thy father Henry did usurp;
80 And thou no more art prince than she is queen.

OXFORD

Then Warwick disannuls great John of Gaunt,
Which did subdue the greatest part of Spain;

And, after John of Gaunt, Henry the Fourth,
Whose wisdom was a mirror to the wisest;
And, after that wise prince, Henry the Fifth,
Who by his prowess conquerèd all France –
From these our Henry lineally descends.

WARWICK

Oxford, how haps it in this smooth discourse
You told not how Henry the Sixth hath lost
All that which Henry the Fifth had gotten?   90
Methinks these peers of France should smile at that.
But for the rest, you tell a pedigree
Of threescore and two years – a silly time
To make prescription for a kingdom's worth.

OXFORD

Why, Warwick, canst thou speak against thy liege,
Whom thou obeyèd'st thirty and six years,
And not bewray thy treason with a blush?

WARWICK

Can Oxford, that did ever fence the right,
Now buckler falsehood with a pedigree?
For shame! Leave Henry, and call Edward king.   100

OXFORD

Call him my king by whose injurious doom
My elder brother, the Lord Aubrey Vere,
Was done to death? And more than so, my father,
Even in the downfall of his mellowed years,
When nature brought him to the door of death?
No, Warwick, no; while life upholds this arm,
This arm upholds the house of Lancaster.

WARWICK

And I the house of York.

LEWIS

Queen Margaret, Prince Edward, and Oxford,
Vouchsafe, at our request, to stand aside   110

While I use further conference with Warwick.
> *They stand aloof*

QUEEN (*aside*)
Heavens grant that Warwick's words bewitch him not!

LEWIS
Now, Warwick, tell me even upon thy conscience,
Is Edward your true king? For I were loath
To link with him that were not lawful chosen.

WARWICK
Thereon I pawn my credit and mine honour.

LEWIS
But is he gracious in the people's eye?

WARWICK
The more that Henry was unfortunate.

LEWIS
Then further, all dissembling set aside,
120 Tell me for truth the measure of his love
Unto our sister Bona.

WARWICK   Such it seems
As may beseem a monarch like himself.
Myself have often heard him say and swear
That this his love was an eternal plant,
Whereof the root was fixed in virtue's ground,
The leaves and fruit maintained with beauty's sun,
Exempt from envy, but not from disdain,
Unless the Lady Bona quit his pain.

LEWIS
Now, sister, let us hear your firm resolve.

BONA
130 Your grant, or your denial, shall be mine;
(*To Warwick*) Yet I confess that often ere this day,
When I have heard your king's desert recounted,
Mine ear hath tempted judgement to desire.

LEWIS
Then, Warwick, thus: our sister shall be Edward's;

And now forthwith shall articles be drawn
Touching the jointure that your king must make,
Which with her dowry shall be counterpoised.
Draw near, Queen Margaret, and be a witness
That Bona shall be wife to the English king.

PRINCE

To Edward, but not to the English king.   140

QUEEN

Deceitful Warwick! It was thy device
By this alliance to make void my suit;
Before thy coming Lewis was Henry's friend.

LEWIS

And still is friend to him and Margaret;
But if your title to the crown be weak,
As may appear by Edward's good success,
Then 'tis but reason that I be released
From giving aid which late I promisèd.
Yet shall you have all kindness at my hand
That your estate requires and mine can yield.   150

WARWICK

Henry now lives in Scotland at his ease,
Where having nothing, nothing can he lose.
And as for you yourself, our quondam queen,
You have a father able to maintain you,
And better 'twere you troubled him than France.

QUEEN

Peace, impudent and shameless Warwick, peace,
Proud setter-up and puller-down of kings!
I will not hence till, with my talk and tears,
Both full of truth, I make King Lewis behold
Thy sly conveyance and thy lord's false love;   160
For both of you are birds of self-same feather.
        Post blowing a horn within

LEWIS

Warwick, this is some post to us or thee.

III.3

Enter the Post

POST (*to Warwick*)

My lord ambassador, these letters are for you,
Sent from your brother, Marquess Montague;
(*To Lewis*)
These from our King unto your majesty;
(*To Queen*)
And, madam, these for you, from whom I know not.
They all read their letters

OXFORD

I like it well that our fair Queen and mistress
Smiles at her news, while Warwick frowns at his.

PRINCE

Nay, mark how Lewis stamps as he were nettled;
170   I hope all's for the best.

LEWIS

Warwick, what are thy news? And yours, fair Queen?

QUEEN

Mine, such as fill my heart with unhoped joys.

WARWICK

Mine, full of sorrow and heart's discontent.

LEWIS

What! Has your king married the Lady Grey?
And now, to soothe your forgery and his,
Sends me a paper to persuade me patience?
Is this th'alliance that he seeks with France?
Dare he presume to scorn us in this manner?

QUEEN

I told your majesty as much before:
180   This proveth Edward's love and Warwick's honesty!

WARWICK

King Lewis, I here protest in sight of heaven,
And by the hope I have of heavenly bliss,
That I am clear from this misdeed of Edward's,
No more my king, for he dishonours me,

But most himself, if he could see his shame.
Did I forget that by the house of York
My father came untimely to his death?
Did I let pass th'abuse done to my niece?
Did I impale him with the regal crown?
Did I put Henry from his native right?   190
And am I guerdoned at the last with shame?
Shame on himself! For my desert is honour;
And to repair my honour lost for him,
I here renounce him and return to Henry.
My noble Queen, let former grudges pass,
And henceforth I am thy true servitor.
I will revenge his wrong to Lady Bona
And replant Henry in his former state.

QUEEN
Warwick, these words have turned my hate to love;
And I forgive and quite forget old faults,   200
And joy that thou becomest King Henry's friend.

WARWICK
So much his friend, ay, his unfeignèd friend,
That if King Lewis vouchsafe to furnish us
With some few bands of chosen soldiers,
I'll undertake to land them on our coast
And force the tyrant from his seat by war.
'Tis not his new-made bride shall succour him;
And as for Clarence, as my letters tell me,
He's very likely now to fall from him
For matching more for wanton lust than honour,   210
Or than for strength and safety of our country.

BONA
Dear brother, how shall Bona be revenged
But by thy help to this distressèd Queen?

QUEEN
Renownèd Prince, how shall poor Henry live
Unless thou rescue him from foul despair?

BONA

My quarrel and this English Queen's are one.

WARWICK

And mine, fair Lady Bona, joins with yours.

LEWIS

And mine with hers, and thine, and Margaret's.
Therefore at last I firmly am resolved:
220 You shall have aid.

QUEEN

Let me give humble thanks for all at once.

LEWIS

Then, England's messenger, return in post
And tell false Edward, thy supposèd king,
That Lewis of France is sending over masquers
To revel it with him and his new bride;
Thou seest what's passed, go fear thy king withal.

BONA

Tell him, in hope he'll prove a widower shortly,
I'll wear the willow garland for his sake.

QUEEN

Tell him my mourning weeds are laid aside,
230 And I am ready to put armour on.

WARWICK

Tell him from me that he hath done me wrong,
And therefore I'll uncrown him ere't be long.
There's thy reward; be gone.   *Exit Post*

LEWIS   But, Warwick,
Thou and Oxford, with five thousand men,
Shall cross the seas and bid false Edward battle;
And, as occasion serves, this noble Queen
And Prince shall follow with a fresh supply.
Yet, ere thou go, but answer me one doubt:
What pledge have we of thy firm loyalty?

WARWICK

240 This shall assure my constant loyalty:

That if our Queen and this young Prince agree,
I'll join mine eldest daughter and my joy
To him forthwith in holy wedlock bands.

QUEEN

Yes, I agree, and thank you for your motion.
Son Edward, she is fair and virtuous;
Therefore delay not, give thy hand to Warwick;
And, with thy hand, thy faith irrevocable
That only Warwick's daughter shall be thine.

PRINCE

Yes, I accept her, for she well deserves it;
And here, to pledge my vow, I give my hand.   250
     He gives his hand to Warwick

LEWIS

Why stay we now? These soldiers shall be levied,
And thou, Lord Bourbon, our High Admiral,
Shalt waft them over with our royal fleet.
I long till Edward fall by war's mischance,
For mocking marriage with a dame of France.
                              Exeunt all but Warwick

WARWICK

I came from Edward as ambassador,
But I return his sworn and mortal foe;
Matter of marriage was the charge he gave me,
But dreadful war shall answer his demand.
Had he none else to make a stale but me?   260
Then none but I shall turn his jest to sorrow.
I was the chief that raised him to the crown,
And I'll be chief to bring him down again;
Not that I pity Henry's misery,
But seek revenge on Edward's mockery.   *Exit*

*

Enter Richard, George, Somerset, and Montague

RICHARD

Now tell me, brother Clarence, what think you
Of this new marriage with the Lady Grey?
Hath not our brother made a worthy choice?

GEORGE

Alas, you know, 'tis far from hence to France;
How could he stay till Warwick made return?

SOMERSET

My lords, forbear this talk; here comes the King.

*Flourish. Enter Edward, attended; Lady Grey, as
queen; Pembroke, Stafford, Hastings, and other
courtiers. Four stand on one side and four on the
other*

RICHARD

And his well-chosen bride.

GEORGE

I mind to tell him plainly what I think.

EDWARD

Now, brother of Clarence, how like you our choice,
10 That you stand pensive, as half-malcontent?

GEORGE

As well as Lewis of France, or the Earl of Warwick,
Which are so weak of courage and in judgement
That they'll take no offence at our abuse.

EDWARD

Suppose they take offence without a cause,
They are but Lewis and Warwick; I am Edward,
Your king and Warwick's, and must have my will.

RICHARD

And shall have your will, because our king;
Yet hasty marriage seldom proveth well.

EDWARD

Yea, brother Richard, are you offended too?

RICHARD
    Not I;   20
    No, God forbid that I should wish them severed
    Whom God hath joined together; ay, and 'twere pity
    To sunder them that yoke so well together.

EDWARD
    Setting your scorns and your mislike aside,
    Tell me some reason why the Lady Grey
    Should not become my wife and England's queen.
    And you too, Somerset and Montague,
    Speak freely what you think.

GEORGE
    Then this is mine opinion: that King Lewis
    Becomes your enemy, for mocking him   30
    About the marriage of the Lady Bona.

RICHARD
    And Warwick, doing what you gave in charge,
    Is now dishonourèd by this new marriage.

EDWARD
    What if both Lewis and Warwick be appeased
    By such invention as I can devise?

MONTAGUE
    Yet, to have joined with France in such alliance
    Would more have strengthened this our commonwealth
    'Gainst foreign storms than any home-bred marriage.

HASTINGS
    Why, knows not Montague that of itself
    England is safe, if true within itself?   40

MONTAGUE
    But the safer when 'tis backed with France.

HASTINGS
    'Tis better using France than trusting France;
    Let us be backed with God and with the seas
    Which He hath given for fence impregnable,

And with their helps only defend ourselves;
In them and in ourselves our safety lies.

GEORGE

For this one speech Lord Hastings well deserves
To have the heir of the Lord Hungerford.

EDWARD

Ay, what of that? It was my will and grant;
50 And for this once my will shall stand for law.

RICHARD

And yet methinks your grace hath not done well
To give the heir and daughter of Lord Scales
Unto the brother of your loving bride.
She better would have fitted me or Clarence;
But in your bride you bury brotherhood.

GEORGE

Or else you would not have bestowed the heir
Of the Lord Bonville on your new wife's son,
And leave your brothers to go speed elsewhere.

EDWARD

Alas, poor Clarence! Is it for a wife
60 That thou art malcontent? I will provide thee.

GEORGE

In choosing for yourself, you showed your judgement;
Which being shallow, you shall give me leave
To play the broker in mine own behalf;
And to that end I shortly mind to leave you.

EDWARD

Leave me, or tarry. Edward will be king,
And not be tied unto his brother's will.

LADY GREY

My lords, before it pleased his majesty
To raise my state to title of a queen,
Do me but right, and you must all confess
70 That I was not ignoble of descent;

And meaner than myself have had like fortune.
But as this title honours me and mine,
So your dislikes, to whom I would be pleasing,
Doth cloud my joys with danger and with sorrow.

EDWARD

My love, forbear to fawn upon their frowns;
What danger or what sorrow can befall thee,
So long as Edward is thy constant friend,
And their true sovereign, whom they must obey?
Nay, whom they shall obey, and love thee too,
Unless they seek for hatred at my hands;   80
Which if they do, yet will I keep thee safe,
And they shall feel the vengeance of my wrath.

RICHARD (aside)

I hear, yet say not much, but think the more.
        Enter a Post

EDWARD

Now, messenger, what letters or what news
From France?

POST

My sovereign liege, no letters; and few words,
But such as I, without your special pardon,
Dare not relate.

EDWARD

Go to, we pardon thee; therefore, in brief,
Tell me their words as near as thou canst guess them.   90
What answer makes King Lewis unto our letters?

POST

At my depart, these were his very words:
'Go tell false Edward, thy supposèd king,
That Lewis of France is sending over masquers
To revel it with him and his new bride.'

EDWARD

Is Lewis so brave? Belike he thinks me Henry.

IV.1

But what said Lady Bona to my marriage?

POST

These were her words, uttered with mild disdain:
'Tell him, in hope he'll prove a widower shortly,
I'll wear the willow garland for his sake.'

EDWARD

I blame not her, she could say little less;
She had the wrong. But what said Henry's queen?
For I have heard that she was there in place.

POST

'Tell him,' quoth she, 'my mourning weeds are done,
And I am ready to put armour on.'

EDWARD

Belike she minds to play the Amazon.
But what said Warwick to these injuries?

POST

He, more incensed against your majesty
Than all the rest, discharged me with these words:
'Tell him from me that he hath done me wrong,
And therefore I'll uncrown him ere't be long.'

EDWARD

Ha! Durst the traitor breathe out so proud words?
Well, I will arm me, being thus forewarned;
They shall have wars and pay for their presumption.
But say, is Warwick friends with Margaret?

POST

Ay, gracious sovereign; they are so linked in friendship,
That young Prince Edward marries Warwick's daughter.

GEORGE

Belike the elder; Clarence will have the younger.
Now, brother King, farewell, and sit you fast,
For I will hence to Warwick's other daughter;
That, though I want a kingdom, yet in marriage
I may not prove inferior to yourself.
You that love me and Warwick, follow me.

Exit George, and Somerset follows

RICHARD (*aside*)

    Not I; my thoughts aim at a further matter.

    I stay not for the love of Edward, but the crown.

EDWARD

    Clarence and Somerset both gone to Warwick!

    Yet am I armed against the worst can happen;

    And haste is needful in this desperate case.

    Pembroke and Stafford, you in our behalf

    Go levy men, and make prepare for war;   130

    They are already, or quickly will be, landed;

    Myself in person will straight follow you.

               Exeunt Pembroke and Stafford

    But, ere I go, Hastings and Montague,

    Resolve my doubt. You twain, of all the rest,

    Are near to Warwick by blood and by alliance;

    Tell me if you love Warwick more than me.

    If it be so, then both depart to him;

    I rather wish you foes than hollow friends.

    But if you mind to hold your true obedience,

    Give me assurance with some friendly vow,   140

    That I may never have you in suspect.

MONTAGUE

    So God help Montague as he proves true!

HASTINGS

    And Hastings as he favours Edward's cause!

EDWARD

    Now, brother Richard, will you stand by us?

RICHARD

    Ay, in despite of all that shall withstand you.

EDWARD

    Why, so. Then I am sure of victory.

    Now therefore let us hence, and lose no hour

    Till we meet Warwick with his foreign power.

                      Exeunt

Enter Warwick and Oxford in England, with
              French soldiers

WARWICK

Trust me, my lord, all hitherto goes well;
The common people by numbers swarm to us.
          Enter George and Somerset
But see where Somerset and Clarence comes!
Speak suddenly, my lords, are we all friends?

GEORGE

Fear not that, my lord.

WARWICK

Then, gentle Clarence, welcome unto Warwick;
And welcome, Somerset. I hold it cowardice
To rest mistrustful where a noble heart
Hath pawned an open hand in sign of love;
10   Else might I think that Clarence, Edward's brother,
Were but a feignèd friend to our proceedings;
But welcome, sweet Clarence; my daughter shall be
          thine.
And now what rests but, in night's coverture,
Thy brother being carelessly encamped,
His soldiers lurking in the towns about,
And but attended by a simple guard,
We may surprise and take him at our pleasure?
Our scouts have found the adventure very easy;
That, as Ulysses and stout Diomede
20   With sleight and manhood stole to Rhesus' tents,
And brought from thence the Thracian fatal steeds,
So we, well covered with the night's black mantle,
At unawares may beat down Edward's guard
And seize himself; I say not 'slaughter him',
For I intend but only to surprise him.
You that will follow me to this attempt,
Applaud the name of Henry with your leader.

They all cry 'Henry!'
Why, then, let's on our way in silent sort;
For Warwick and his friends, God and Saint George!

Exeunt

Enter three Watchmen, to guard King Edward's IV.3
tent

FIRST WATCHMAN
  Come on, my masters; each man take his stand.
  The King by this is set him down to sleep.

SECOND WATCHMAN What, will he not to bed?

FIRST WATCHMAN
  Why, no; for he hath made a solemn vow
  Never to lie and take his natural rest
  Till Warwick or himself be quite suppressed.

SECOND WATCHMAN
  Tomorrow then belike shall be the day,
  If Warwick be so near as men report.

THIRD WATCHMAN
  But say, I pray, what nobleman is that
  That with the King here resteth in his tent?   10

FIRST WATCHMAN
  'Tis the Lord Hastings, the King's chiefest friend.

THIRD WATCHMAN
  O, is it so? But why commands the King
  That his chief followers lodge in towns about him,
  While he himself keeps in the cold field?

SECOND WATCHMAN
  'Tis the more honour, because more dangerous.

THIRD WATCHMAN
  Ay, but give me worship and quietness;
  I like it better than a dangerous honour.
  If Warwick knew in what estate he stands,

'Tis to be doubted he would waken him.

FIRST WATCHMAN
20 Unless our halberds did shut up his passage.

SECOND WATCHMAN
Ay, wherefore else guard we his royal tent,
But to defend his person from night-foes?

> *Enter Warwick, George, Oxford, Somerset, and
> French soldiers, silent all*

WARWICK
This is his tent; and see where stand his guard.
Courage, my masters! Honour now or never!
But follow me, and Edward shall be ours.

FIRST WATCHMAN Who goes there?

SECOND WATCHMAN Stay, or thou diest!

> *Warwick and the rest cry all 'Warwick! Warwick!'
> and set upon the guard, who fly, crying 'Arm! Arm!',
> Warwick and the rest following them
> The drum playing and trumpet sounding, enter
> Warwick, Somerset, and the rest, bringing King
> Edward out in his gown, sitting in a chair. Richard
> and Hastings fly over the stage*

SOMERSET What are they that fly there?

WARWICK Richard and Hastings; let them go. Here is the
30 Duke.

EDWARD
'The Duke'! Why, Warwick, when we parted,
Thou called'st me king.

WARWICK   Ay, but the case is altered:
When you disgraced me in my embassade,
Then I degraded you from being king,
And come now to create you Duke of York.
Alas! How should you govern any kingdom,
That know not how to use ambassadors,
Nor how to be contented with one wife,

Nor how to use your brothers brotherly,
Nor how to study for the people's welfare,   40
Nor how to shroud yourself from enemies?

EDWARD

Yea, brother of Clarence, art thou here too?
Nay, then I see that Edward needs must down.
Yet, Warwick, in despite of all mischance,
Of thee thyself and all thy complices,
Edward will always bear himself as king.
Though Fortune's malice overthrow my state,
My mind exceeds the compass of her wheel.

WARWICK

Then, for his mind, be Edward England's king.
        He takes off Edward's crown
But Henry now shall wear the English crown,   50
And be true king indeed, thou but the shadow.
My lord of Somerset, at my request,
See that forthwith Duke Edward be conveyed
Unto my brother, Archbishop of York.
When I have fought with Pembroke and his fellows,
I'll follow you, and tell what answer
Lewis and the Lady Bona send to him.
Now for a while farewell, good Duke of York.

EDWARD

What fates impose, that men must needs abide;
It boots not to resist both wind and tide.   60
                        They lead him out forcibly

OXFORD

What now remains, my lords, for us to do
But march to London with our soldiers?

WARWICK

Ay, that's the first thing that we have to do;
To free King Henry from imprisonment
And see him seated in the regal throne.   *Exeunt*

RIVERS

   Madam, what makes you in this sudden change?

LADY GREY

   Why, brother Rivers, are you yet to learn

   What late misfortune is befallen King Edward?

RIVERS

   What! Loss of some pitched battle against Warwick?

LADY GREY

   No, but the loss of his own royal person.

RIVERS

   Then is my sovereign slain?

LADY GREY

   Ay, almost slain, for he is taken prisoner,

   Either betrayed by falsehood of his guard

   Or by his foe surprised at unawares;

10   And, as I further have to understand,

   Is new committed to the Bishop of York,

   Fell Warwick's brother and by that our foe.

RIVERS

   These news, I must confess, are full of grief;

   Yet, gracious madam, bear it as you may;

   Warwick may lose, that now hath won the day.

LADY GREY

   Till then fair hope must hinder life's decay;

   And I the rather wean me from despair

   For love of Edward's offspring in my womb.

   This is it that makes me bridle passion

20   And bear with mildness my misfortune's cross;

   Ay, ay, for this I draw in many a tear

   And stop the rising of blood-sucking sighs,

   Lest with my sighs or tears I blast or drown

   King Edward's fruit, true heir to th'English crown.

RIVERS

   But, madam, where is Warwick then become?

LADY GREY

  I am informèd that he comes towards London,
  To set the crown once more on Henry's head.
  Guess thou the rest: King Edward's friends must down.
  But to prevent the tyrant's violence –
  For trust not him that hath once broken faith –   30
  I'll hence forthwith unto the sanctuary,
  To save at least the heir of Edward's right.
  There shall I rest secure from force and fraud.
  Come, therefore, let us fly while we may fly;
  If Warwick take us, we are sure to die.

                    Exeunt

    Enter Richard, Hastings, and Sir William Stanley   IV.5

RICHARD

  Now, my Lord Hastings and Sir William Stanley,
  Leave off to wonder why I drew you hither
  Into this chiefest thicket of the park.
  Thus stands the case: you know our King, my brother,
  Is prisoner to the Bishop here, at whose hands
  He hath good usage and great liberty,
  And, often but attended with weak guard,
  Comes hunting this way to disport himself.
  I have advertised him by secret means
  That if about this hour he make this way   10
  Under the colour of his usual game,
  He shall here find his friends with horse and men
  To set him free from his captivity.

    Enter King Edward and a Huntsman with him

HUNTSMAN

  This way, my lord; for this way lies the game.

EDWARD

  Nay, this way, man; see where the huntsmen stand.
  Now, brother of Gloucester, Lord Hastings, and the rest,

Stand you thus close to steal the Bishop's deer?

RICHARD

Brother, the time and case requireth haste;
Your horse stands ready at the park corner.

EDWARD

But whither shall we then?

20 HASTINGS   To Lynn, my lord.
And ship from thence to Flanders?

RICHARD

Well guessed, believe me; for that was my meaning.

EDWARD

Stanley, I will requite thy forwardness.

RICHARD

But wherefore stay we? 'Tis no time to talk.

EDWARD

Huntsman, what sayst thou? Wilt thou go along?

HUNTSMAN

Better do so than tarry and be hanged.

RICHARD

Come then, away; let's ha' no more ado.

EDWARD

Bishop, farewell; shield thee from Warwick's frown;
And pray that I may repossess the crown.

Exeunt

IV.6   *Flourish. Enter King Henry the Sixth, George, War-*
            wick, Somerset, young Henry Richmond, Oxford,
            Montague, and the Lieutenant of the Tower

KING

Master Lieutenant, now that God and friends
Have shaken Edward from the regal seat,
And turned my captive state to liberty,
My fear to hope, my sorrows unto joys,

At our enlargement what are thy due fees?

LIEUTENANT

Subjects may challenge nothing of their sovereigns;
But if an humble prayer may prevail,
I then crave pardon of your majesty.

KING

For what, Lieutenant? For well using me?
Nay, be thou sure I'll well requite thy kindness,　　10
For that it made my imprisonment a pleasure;
Ay, such a pleasure as incagèd birds
Conceive when, after many moody thoughts,
At last by notes of household harmony
They quite forget their loss of liberty.
But, Warwick, after God, thou settest me free,
And chiefly therefore I thank God and thee;
He was the author, thou the instrument.
Therefore, that I may conquer Fortune's spite
By living low, where Fortune cannot hurt me,　　20
And that the people of this blessèd land
May not be punished with my thwarting stars,
Warwick, although my head still wear the crown,
I here resign my government to thee,
For thou art fortunate in all thy deeds.

WARWICK

Your grace hath still been famed for virtuous;
And now may seem as wise as virtuous
By spying and avoiding Fortune's malice,
For few men rightly temper with the stars.
Yet in this one thing let me blame your grace,　　30
For choosing me when Clarence is in place.

GEORGE

No, Warwick, thou art worthy of the sway,
To whom the heavens in thy nativity
Adjudged an olive branch and laurel crown,

As likely to be blessed in peace and war;
And therefore I yield thee my free consent.

WARWICK

And I choose Clarence only for Protector.

KING

Warwick and Clarence, give me both your hands.
Now join your hands, and with your hands your hearts,
40 That no dissension hinder government;
I make you both Protectors of this land,
While I myself will lead a private life
And in devotion spend my latter days,
To sin's rebuke and my Creator's praise.

WARWICK

What answers Clarence to his sovereign's will?

GEORGE

That he consents, if Warwick yield consent;
For on thy fortune I repose myself.

WARWICK

Why then, though loath, yet must I be content;
We'll yoke together, like a double shadow
50 To Henry's body, and supply his place;
I mean, in bearing weight of government,
While he enjoys the honour and his ease.
And, Clarence, now then it is more than needful
Forthwith that Edward be pronounced a traitor,
And all his lands and goods be confiscate.

GEORGE

What else? And that succession be determined.

WARWICK

Ay, therein Clarence shall not want his part.

KING

But with the first of all your chief affairs,
Let me entreat – for I command no more –
60 That Margaret your Queen and my son Edward
Be sent for, to return from France with speed;

For, till I see them here, by doubtful fear
My joy of liberty is half eclipsed.

GEORGE

It shall be done, my sovereign, with all speed.

KING

My lord of Somerset, what youth is that,
Of whom you seem to have so tender care?

SOMERSET

My liege, it is young Henry Earl of Richmond.

KING

Come hither, England's hope.

He lays his hand on his head

                          If secret powers
Suggest but truth to my divining thoughts,
This pretty lad will prove our country's bliss.   70
His looks are full of peaceful majesty,
His head by nature framed to wear a crown,
His hand to wield a sceptre, and himself
Likely in time to bless a regal throne.
Make much of him, my lords, for this is he
Must help you more than you are hurt by me.

Enter a Post

WARWICK

What news, my friend?

POST

That Edward is escapèd from your brother
And fled, as he hears since, to Burgundy.

WARWICK

Unsavoury news! But how made he escape?   80

POST

He was conveyed by Richard Duke of Gloucester
And the Lord Hastings, who attended him
In secret ambush on the forest side
And from the Bishop's huntsmen rescued him;
For hunting was his daily exercise.

WARWICK

My brother was too careless of his charge;
But let us hence, my sovereign, to provide
A salve for any sore that may betide.

Exeunt all but Somerset, Richmond,
and Oxford

SOMERSET

My lord, I like not of this flight of Edward's;
90   For doubtless Burgundy will yield him help,
And we shall have more wars before't be long.
As Henry's late presaging prophecy
Did glad my heart with hope of this young Richmond,
So doth my heart misgive me, in these conflicts,
What may befall him, to his harm and ours.
Therefore, Lord Oxford, to prevent the worst,
Forthwith we'll send him hence to Brittany,
Till storms be past of civil enmity.

OXFORD

Ay, for if Edward repossess the crown,
100   'Tis like that Richmond with the rest shall down.

SOMERSET

It shall be so; he shall to Brittany.
Come, therefore, let's about it speedily.

Exeunt

IV.7   *Flourish. Enter Edward, Richard, Hastings, and sol-*
diers

EDWARD

Now, brother Richard, Lord Hastings, and the rest,
Yet thus far Fortune maketh us amends,
And says that once more I shall interchange
My wanèd state for Henry's regal crown.
Well have we passed and now repassed the seas

And brought desirèd help from Burgundy.
What then remains, we being thus arrived
From Ravenspurgh haven before the gates of York,
But that we enter, as into our dukedom?

RICHARD

The gates made fast! Brother, I like not this;　　　10
For many men that stumble at the threshold
Are well foretold that danger lurks within.

EDWARD

Tush, man, abodements must not now affright us;
By fair or foul means we must enter in,
For hither will our friends repair to us.

HASTINGS

My liege, I'll knock once more to summon them.
　　Enter, on the walls, the Mayor of York and his
　　brethren

MAYOR

My lords, we were forewarnèd of your coming,
And shut the gates for safety of ourselves;
For now we owe allegiance unto Henry.

EDWARD

But, master Mayor, if Henry be your king,　　　20
Yet Edward at the least is Duke of York.

MAYOR

True, my good lord, I know you for no less.

EDWARD

Why, and I challenge nothing but my dukedom,
As being well content with that alone.

RICHARD (*aside*)

But when the fox hath once got in his nose,
He'll soon find means to make the body follow.

HASTINGS

Why, master Mayor, why stand you in a doubt?
Open the gates; we are King Henry's friends.

MAYOR

Ay, say you so? The gates shall then be opened.
He descends

RICHARD

30   A wise stout captain, and soon persuaded!

HASTINGS

The good old man would fain that all were well,
So 'twere not 'long of him; but being entered,
I doubt not, I, but we shall soon persuade
Both him and all his brothers unto reason.
Enter the Mayor and two aldermen, below

EDWARD

So, master Mayor: these gates must not be shut
But in the night or in the time of war.
What! Fear not, man, but yield me up the keys;
  (*He takes his keys*)
For Edward will defend the town and thee,
And all those friends that deign to follow me.
*March. Enter Sir John Montgomery with drum and
soldiers*

RICHARD

40   Brother, this is Sir John Montgomery,
Our trusty friend, unless I be deceived.

EDWARD

Welcome, Sir John! But why come you in arms?

MONTGOMERY

To help King Edward in his time of storm,
As every loyal subject ought to do.

EDWARD

Thanks, good Montgomery; but we now forget
Our title to the crown, and only claim
Our dukedom till God please to send the rest.

MONTGOMERY

Then fare you well, for I will hence again;

I came to serve a king and not a duke.
Drummer, strike up, and let us march away.   50
   The drum begins to march

EDWARD
  Nay, stay, Sir John, a while, and we'll debate
  By what safe means the crown may be recovered.

MONTGOMERY
  What talk you of debating? In few words,
  If you'll not here proclaim yourself our king,
  I'll leave you to your fortune and be gone
  To keep them back that come to succour you.
  Why shall we fight, if you pretend no title?

RICHARD
  Why, brother, wherefore stand you on nice points?

EDWARD
  When we grow stronger, then we'll make our claim;
  Till then, 'tis wisdom to conceal our meaning.   60

HASTINGS
  Away with scrupulous wit! Now arms must rule.

RICHARD
  And fearless minds climb soonest unto crowns.
  Brother, we will proclaim you out of hand;
  The bruit thereof will bring you many friends.

EDWARD
  Then be it as you will; for 'tis my right,
  And Henry but usurps the diadem.

MONTGOMERY
  Ay, now my sovereign speaketh like himself;
  And now will I be Edward's champion.

HASTINGS
  Sound trumpet; Edward shall be here proclaimed.
  Come, fellow soldier, make thou proclamation.   70
   Flourish. Sound

SOLDIER Edward the Fourth, by the grace of God,

King of England and France, and Lord of Ireland, *etc.*

MONTGOMERY

And whosoe'er gainsays King Edward's right,
By this I challenge him to single fight.

He throws down his gauntlet

ALL

Long live Edward the Fourth!

EDWARD

Thanks, brave Montgomery, and thanks unto you all;
If fortune serve me, I'll requite this kindness.
Now, for this night, let's harbour here in York;
And when the morning sun shall raise his car
80 Above the border of this horizon,
We'll forward towards Warwick and his mates;
For well I wot that Henry is no soldier.
Ah, froward Clarence! How evil it beseems thee
To flatter Henry and forsake thy brother!
Yet, as we may, we'll meet both thee and Warwick.
Come on, brave soldiers; doubt not of the day,
And, that once gotten, doubt not of large pay. *Exeunt*

IV.8   *Flourish. Enter King Henry, Warwick, Montague,*
              George, and Oxford

WARWICK

What counsel, lords? Edward from Belgia,
With hasty Germans and blunt Hollanders,
Hath passed in safety through the narrow seas,
And with his troops doth march amain to London;
And many giddy people flock to him.

KING

Let's levy men and beat him back again.

GEORGE

A little fire is quickly trodden out;

Which, being suffered, rivers cannot quench.

WARWICK

In Warwickshire I have true-hearted friends,
Not mutinous in peace, yet bold in war;   10
Those will I muster up; and thou, son Clarence,
Shalt stir up in Suffolk, Norfolk, and in Kent,
The knights and gentlemen to come with thee.
Thou, brother Montague, in Buckingham,
Northampton, and in Leicestershire, shalt find
Men well inclined to hear what thou commandest.
And thou, brave Oxford, wondrous well-beloved
In Oxfordshire, shalt muster up thy friends.
My sovereign, with the loving citizens,
Like to his island girt in with the ocean,   20
Or modest Dian circled with her nymphs,
Shall rest in London till we come to him.
Fair lords, take leave and stand not to reply.
Farewell, my sovereign.

KING

Farewell, my Hector and my Troy's true hope.

GEORGE

In sign of truth, I kiss your highness' hand.

KING

Well-minded Clarence, be thou fortunate!

MONTAGUE

Comfort, my lord; and so I take my leave.

OXFORD

And thus I seal my truth and bid adieu.

KING

Sweet Oxford, and my loving Montague,   30
And all at once, once more a happy farewell.

WARWICK

Farewell, sweet lords; let's meet at Coventry.

Exeunt

Enter King Henry and Exeter

KING

Here at the palace will I rest a while.
Cousin of Exeter, what thinks your lordship?
Methinks the power that Edward hath in field
Should not be able to encounter mine.

EXETER

The doubt is that he will seduce the rest.

KING

That's not my fear. My meed hath got me fame;
I have not stopped mine ears to their demands,
40   Nor posted off their suits with slow delays;
My pity hath been balm to heal their wounds,
My mildness hath allayed their swelling griefs,
My mercy dried their water-flowing tears;
I have not been desirous of their wealth,
Nor much oppressed them with great subsidies,
Nor forward of revenge, though they much erred.
Then why should they love Edward more than me?
No, Exeter, these graces challenge grace;
And when the lion fawns upon the lamb,
50   The lamb will never cease to follow him.
    Shout within 'À York! À York!'

EXETER

Hark, hark, my lord! What shouts are these?
    Enter Edward, Richard, and their soldiers

EDWARD

Seize on the shame-faced Henry, bear him hence;
And once again proclaim us King of England.
You are the fount that makes small brooks to flow;
Now stops thy spring; my sea shall suck them dry,
And swell so much the higher by their ebb.
Hence with him to the Tower; let him not speak.
    Exeunt some soldiers with King Henry

And, lords, towards Coventry bend we our course,
Where peremptory Warwick now remains.
The sun shines hot; and, if we use delay,   60
Cold biting winter mars our hoped-for hay.

RICHARD
Away betimes, before his forces join,
And take the great-grown traitor unawares.
Brave warriors, march amain towards Coventry.

Exeunt

✳

Enter Warwick, the Mayor of Coventry, two Mes-   V.1
sengers, and others upon the walls

WARWICK
Where is the post that came from valiant Oxford? –
How far hence is thy lord, mine honest fellow?

FIRST MESSENGER
By this at Dunsmore, marching hitherward.

WARWICK
How far off is our brother Montague?
Where is the post that came from Montague?

SECOND MESSENGER
By this at Daintry, with a puissant troop.
    Enter Sir John Somerville

WARWICK
Say, Somerville, what says my loving son?
And, by thy guess, how nigh is Clarence now?

SOMERVILLE
At Southam I did leave him with his forces,
And do expect him here some two hours hence.   10
    A drum is heard

WARWICK
Then Clarence is at hand; I hear his drum.

143

SOMERVILLE

It is not his, my lord. Here Southam lies;
The drum your honour hears marcheth from Warwick.

WARWICK

Who should that be? Belike, unlooked-for friends.

SOMERVILLE

They are at hand, and you shall quickly know.

March. Flourish. Enter Edward, Richard, and soldiers

EDWARD

Go, trumpet, to the walls and sound a parle.

RICHARD

See how the surly Warwick mans the wall!

WARWICK

O, unbid spite! Is sportful Edward come?
Where slept our scouts, or how are they seduced,
20   That we could hear no news of his repair?

EDWARD

Now, Warwick, wilt thou ope the city gates,
Speak gentle words, and humbly bend thy knee,
Call Edward king, and at his hands beg mercy?
And he shall pardon thee these outrages.

WARWICK

Nay, rather, wilt thou draw thy forces hence,
Confess who set thee up and plucked thee down,
Call Warwick patron, and be penitent?
And thou shalt still remain the Duke of York.

RICHARD

I thought at least he would have said 'the King'.
30   Or did he make the jest against his will?

WARWICK

Is not a dukedom, sir, a goodly gift?

RICHARD

Ay, by my faith, for a poor earl to give;
I'll do thee service for so good a gift.

WARWICK

'Twas I that gave the kingdom to thy brother.

EDWARD

Why then, 'tis mine, if but by Warwick's gift.

WARWICK

Thou art no Atlas for so great a weight;
And, weakling, Warwick takes his gift again;
And Henry is my king, Warwick his subject.

EDWARD

But Warwick's king is Edward's prisoner;
And, gallant Warwick, do but answer this: 40
What is the body when the head is off?

RICHARD

Alas, that Warwick had no more forecast,
But whiles he thought to steal the single ten,
The king was slily fingered from the deck!
You left poor Henry at the Bishop's palace,
And ten to one you'll meet him in the Tower.

EDWARD

'Tis even so, yet you are Warwick still.

RICHARD

Come, Warwick, take the time; kneel down, kneel down.
Nay, when? Strike now, or else the iron cools.

WARWICK

I had rather chop this hand off at a blow,   50
And with the other fling it at thy face,
Than bear so low a sail to strike to thee.

EDWARD

Sail how thou canst, have wind and tide thy friend,
This hand, fast wound about thy coal-black hair,
Shall, whiles thy head is warm and new cut off,
Write in the dust this sentence with thy blood:
'Wind-changing Warwick now can change no more.'

Enter Oxford, with drum and colours

145

WARWICK

O, cheerful colours! See where Oxford comes!

OXFORD

Oxford, Oxford, for Lancaster!
He leads his forces into the city

RICHARD

60   The gates are open; let us enter too.

EDWARD

So other foes may set upon our backs.
Stand we in good array, for they no doubt
Will issue out again and bid us battle;
If not, the city being but of small defence,
We'll quickly rouse the traitors in the same.

WARWICK

O, welcome, Oxford, for we want thy help.
Enter Montague, with drum and colours

MONTAGUE

Montague, Montague, for Lancaster!
He leads his forces into the city

RICHARD

Thou and thy brother both shall buy this treason
Even with the dearest blood your bodies bear.

EDWARD

70   The harder matched, the greater victory;
My mind presageth happy gain and conquest.
Enter Somerset, with drum and colours

SOMERSET

Somerset, Somerset, for Lancaster!
He leads his forces into the city

RICHARD

Two of thy name, both Dukes of Somerset,
Have sold their lives unto the house of York,
And thou shalt be the third, if this sword hold.
Enter George, with drum and colours

WARWICK

    And lo, where George of Clarence sweeps along,
    Of force enough to bid his brother battle;
    With whom an upright zeal to right prevails
    More than the nature of a brother's love!
    Come, Clarence, come; thou wilt, if Warwick call.   80

GEORGE

    Father of Warwick, know you what this means?
        He takes his red rose out of his hat and throws it at
        Warwick
    Look here, I throw my infamy at thee.
    I will not ruinate my father's house,
    Who gave his blood to lime the stones together,
    And set up Lancaster. Why, trowest thou, Warwick,
    That Clarence is so harsh, so blunt, unnatural,
    To bend the fatal instruments of war
    Against his brother and his lawful king?
    Perhaps thou wilt object my holy oath;
    To keep that oath were more impiety   90
    Than Jephthah, when he sacrificed his daughter.
    I am so sorry for my trespass made
    That, to deserve well at my brother's hands,
    I here proclaim myself thy mortal foe,
    With resolution, wheresoe'er I meet thee –
    As I will meet thee, if thou stir abroad –
    To plague thee for thy foul misleading me.
    And so, proud-hearted Warwick, I defy thee,
    And to my brother turn my blushing cheeks.
    Pardon me, Edward, I will make amends;   100
    And, Richard, do not frown upon my faults,
    For I will henceforth be no more unconstant.

EDWARD

    Now welcome more, and ten times more beloved,
    Than if thou never hadst deserved our hate.

RICHARD

Welcome, good Clarence; this is brother-like.

WARWICK

O passing traitor, perjured and unjust!

EDWARD

What, Warwick, wilt thou leave the town and fight?
Or shall we beat the stones about thine ears?

WARWICK

Alas, I am not cooped here for defence!
110 I will away towards Barnet presently,
And bid thee battle, Edward, if thou darest.

EDWARD

Yes, Warwick, Edward dares, and leads the way.
Lords, to the field; Saint George and victory!

Exeunt Edward and his company
March. Warwick and his company follow

V.2 *Alarum and excursions. Enter Edward, bringing forth*
Warwick wounded

EDWARD

So, lie thou there; die thou, and die our fear;
For Warwick was a bug that feared us all.
Now, Montague, sit fast; I seek for thee,
That Warwick's bones may keep thine company. *Exit*

WARWICK

Ah, who is nigh? Come to me, friend or foe,
And tell me who is victor, York or Warwick?
Why ask I that? My mangled body shows,
My blood, my want of strength, my sick heart shows,
That I must yield my body to the earth,
10 And, by my fall, the conquest to my foe.
Thus yields the cedar to the axe's edge,
Whose arms gave shelter to the princely eagle,

148

Under whose shade the ramping lion slept,
Whose top branch over-peered Jove's spreading tree
And kept low shrubs from winter's powerful wind.
These eyes, that now are dimmed with death's black veil,
Have been as piercing as the midday sun,
To search the secret treasons of the world;
The wrinkles in my brows, now filled with blood,
Were likened oft to kingly sepulchres;   20
For who lived king, but I could dig his grave?
And who durst smile when Warwick bent his brow?
Lo, now my glory smeared in dust and blood!
My parks, my walks, my manors that I had,
Even now forsake me, and of all my lands
Is nothing left me but my body's length.
Why, what is pomp, rule, reign, but earth and dust?
And, live we how we can, yet die we must.
        Enter Oxford and Somerset

SOMERSET
  Ah, Warwick, Warwick! Wert thou as we are,
  We might recover all our loss again.   30
  The Queen from France hath brought a puissant power;
  Even now we heard the news. Ah, couldst thou fly!

WARWICK
  Why, then I would not fly. Ah, Montague,
  If thou be there, sweet brother, take my hand,
  And with thy lips keep in my soul a while!
  Thou lovest me not; for, brother, if thou didst,
  Thy tears would wash this cold congealèd blood
  That glues my lips and will not let me speak.
  Come quickly, Montague, or I am dead.

SOMERSET
  Ah, Warwick! Montague hath breathed his last;   40
  And to the latest gasp cried out for Warwick,
  And said 'Commend me to my valiant brother.'

And more he would have said, and more he spoke,
Which sounded like a cannon in a vault,
That mought not be distinguished; but at last
I well might hear, deliverèd with a groan,
'O, farewell, Warwick!'

WARWICK

Sweet rest his soul! Fly, lords, and save yourselves;
For Warwick bids you all farewell, to meet in heaven.

He dies

OXFORD

50   Away, away, to meet the Queen's great power.

Here they bear away his body. Exeunt

V.3   *Flourish. Enter King Edward in triumph, with Rich-*
       ard, George, and the rest

EDWARD

Thus far our fortune keeps an upward course,
And we are graced with wreaths of victory.
But, in the midst of this bright-shining day,
I spy a black, suspicious, threatening cloud,
That will encounter with our glorious sun
Ere he attain his easeful western bed;
I mean, my lords, those powers that the Queen
Hath raised in Gallia have arrived our coast,
And, as we hear, march on to fight with us.

GEORGE

10   A little gale will soon disperse that cloud
And blow it to the source from whence it came;
Thy very beams will dry those vapours up,
For every cloud engenders not a storm.

RICHARD

The Queen is valued thirty thousand strong,
And Somerset, with Oxford, fled to her;

If she have time to breathe, be well assured
Her faction will be full as strong as ours.

EDWARD

We are advertised by our loving friends
That they do hold their course toward Tewkesbury.
We, having now the best at Barnet field,   20
Will thither straight, for willingness rids way;
And, as we march, our strength will be augmented
In every county as we go along.
Strike up the drum; cry 'Courage!' and away!

Exeunt

Flourish. March. Enter the Queen, Prince Edward **V.4**
Somerset, Oxford, and soldiers

QUEEN

Great lords, wise men ne'er sit and wail their loss,
But cheerly seek how to redress their harms.
What though the mast be now blown overboard,
The cable broke, the holding-anchor lost,
And half our sailors swallowed in the flood?
Yet lives our pilot still. Is't meet that he
Should leave the helm and, like a fearful lad,
With tearful eyes add water to the sea,
And give more strength to that which hath too much,
Whiles, in his moan, the ship splits on the rock,   10
Which industry and courage might have saved?
Ah, what a shame! Ah, what a fault were this!
Say Warwick was our anchor; what of that?
And Montague our topmast; what of him?
Our slaughtered friends the tackles; what of these?
Why, is not Oxford here another anchor?
And Somerset another goodly mast?
The friends of France our shrouds and tacklings?

And, though unskilful, why not Ned and I
20 For once allowed the skilful pilot's charge?
We will not from the helm to sit and weep,
But keep our course, though the rough wind say no,
From shelves and rocks that threaten us with wrack.
As good to chide the waves as speak them fair.
And what is Edward but a ruthless sea?
What Clarence but a quicksand of deceit?
And Richard but a ragged fatal rock?
All these the enemies to our poor bark.
Say you can swim; alas, 'tis but a while!
30 Tread on the sand; why, there you quickly sink.
Bestride the rock; the tide will wash you off,
Or else you famish; that's a threefold death.
This speak I, lords, to let you understand,
If case some one of you would fly from us,
That there's no hoped-for mercy with the brothers
More than with ruthless waves, with sands and rocks.
Why, courage then! What cannot be avoided
'Twere childish weakness to lament or fear.

PRINCE

Methinks a woman of this valiant spirit
40 Should, if a coward heard her speak these words,
Infuse his breast with magnanimity,
And make him, naked, foil a man at arms.
I speak not this as doubting any here;
For did I but suspect a fearful man,
He should have leave to go away betimes,
Lest in our need he might infect another
And make him of like spirit to himself.
If any such be here – as God forbid! –
Let him depart before we need his help.

OXFORD

50 Women and children of so high a courage,

And warriors faint! Why, 'twere perpetual shame.
O brave young Prince! Thy famous grandfather
Doth live again in thee; long mayst thou live
To bear his image and renew his glories!

SOMERSET

And he that will not fight for such a hope,
Go home to bed, and like the owl by day,
If he arise, be mocked and wondered at.

QUEEN

Thanks, gentle Somerset; sweet Oxford, thanks.

PRINCE

And take his thanks that yet hath nothing else.
Enter a Messenger

MESSENGER

Prepare you, lords, for Edward is at hand, 60
Ready to fight; therefore be resolute.

OXFORD

I thought no less; it is his policy
To haste thus fast to find us unprovided.

SOMERSET

But he's deceived; we are in readiness.

QUEEN

This cheers my heart, to see your forwardness.

OXFORD

Here pitch our battle; hence we will not budge.
*Flourish and march. Enter Edward, Richard, George,
and soldiers*

EDWARD

Brave followers, yonder stands the thorny wood,
Which, by the heavens' assistance and your strength,
Must by the roots be hewn up yet ere night.
I need not add more fuel to your fire, 70
For well I wot ye blaze to burn them out.
Give signal to the fight, and to it, lords!

QUEEN

> Lords, knights, and gentlemen, what I should say
> My tears gainsay; for every word I speak,
> Ye see I drink the water of my eye.
> Therefore, no more but this: Henry, your sovereign,
> Is prisoner to the foe; his state usurped,
> His realm a slaughter-house, his subjects slain,
> His statutes cancelled, and his treasure spent;
> 80 And yonder is the wolf that makes this spoil.
> You fight in justice; then in God's name, lords,
> Be valiant, and give signal to the fight.

Alarums, retreat, excursions. Exeunt

V.5 *Flourish. Enter Edward, Richard, George, and their army, with the Queen, Oxford, and Somerset, prisoners*

EDWARD

> Now here a period of tumultuous broils.
> Away with Oxford to Hames Castle straight;
> For Somerset, off with his guilty head.
> Go, bear them hence; I will not hear them speak.

OXFORD

> For my part I'll not trouble thee with words.

SOMERSET

> Nor I, but stoop with patience to my fortune.

Exeunt Oxford and Somerset, guarded

QUEEN

> So part we sadly in this troublous world,
> To meet with joy in sweet Jerusalem.

EDWARD

> Is proclamation made that who finds Edward
> 10 Shall have a high reward, and he his life?

154

RICHARD

  It is; and lo, where youthful Edward comes!
    Enter the Prince, guarded

EDWARD

  Bring forth the gallant; let us hear him speak.
  What! Can so young a thorn begin to prick?
  Edward, what satisfaction canst thou make
  For bearing arms, for stirring up my subjects,
  And all the trouble thou hast turned me to?

PRINCE

  Speak like a subject, proud ambitious York!
  Suppose that I am now my father's mouth;
  Resign thy chair, and where I stand kneel thou,
  Whilst I propose the self-same words to thee,   20
  Which, traitor, thou wouldst have me answer to.

QUEEN

  Ah, that thy father had been so resolved!

RICHARD

  That you might still have worn the petticoat
  And ne'er have stolen the breech from Lancaster.

PRINCE

  Let Aesop fable in a winter's night;
  His currish riddles sorts not with this place.

RICHARD

  By heaven, brat, I'll plague ye for that word.

QUEEN

  Ay, thou wast born to be a plague to men.

RICHARD

  For God's sake, take away this captive scold.

PRINCE

  Nay, take away this scolding crook-back rather.   30

EDWARD

  Peace, wilful boy, or I will charm your tongue.

GEORGE

Untutored lad, thou art too malapert.

PRINCE

I know my duty; you are all undutiful.
Lascivious Edward, and thou perjured George,
And thou misshapen Dick, I tell ye all
I am your better, traitors as ye are;
And thou usurpest my father's right and mine.

EDWARD

Take that, the likeness of this railer here.
He stabs him

RICHARD

Sprawlest thou? Take that, to end thy agony.
He stabs him

GEORGE

40 And there's for twitting me with perjury.
He stabs him

QUEEN

O, kill me too!

RICHARD

Marry, and shall.
He offers to kill her

EDWARD

Hold, Richard, hold; for we have done too much.

RICHARD

Why should she live to fill the world with words?

EDWARD

What! Doth she swoon? Use means for her recovery.

RICHARD

Clarence, excuse me to the King my brother;
I'll hence to London on a serious matter.
Ere ye come there, be sure to hear some news.

GEORGE

What? What?

RICHARD

    The Tower, the Tower.   *Exit* 50

QUEEN

    O Ned, sweet Ned, speak to thy mother, boy!

    Canst thou not speak? O traitors! Murderers!

    They that stabbed Caesar shed no blood at all,

    Did not offend, nor were not worthy blame,

    If this foul deed were by to equal it.

    He was a man; this, in respect, a child;

    And men ne'er spend their fury on a child.

    What's worse than murderer, that I may name it?

    No, no, my heart will burst an if I speak;

    And I will speak that so my heart may burst.   60

    Butchers and villains! Bloody cannibals!

    How sweet a plant have you untimely cropped!

    You have no children, butchers; if you had,

    The thought of them would have stirred up remorse.

    But if you ever chance to have a child,

    Look in his youth to have him so cut off

    As, deathsmen, you have rid this sweet young Prince!

EDWARD

    Away with her; go, bear her hence perforce.

QUEEN

    Nay, never bear me hence, dispatch me here;

    Here sheathe thy sword; I'll pardon thee my death.   70

    What! Wilt thou not? Then, Clarence, do it thou.

GEORGE

    By heaven, I will not do thee so much ease.

QUEEN

    Good Clarence, do; sweet Clarence, do thou do it.

GEORGE

    Didst thou not hear me swear I would not do it?

QUEEN

    Ay, but thou usest to forswear thyself,

'Twas sin before, but now 'tis charity.
What! Wilt thou not? Where is that devil's butcher
    Richard?
Hard-favoured Richard; Richard, where art thou?
Thou art not here; murder is thy alms-deed;
80 Petitioners for blood thou ne'er puttest back.

EDWARD

Away, I say; I charge ye, bear her hence.

QUEEN

So come to you and yours as to this Prince!

                     Exit, guarded

EDWARD

Where's Richard gone?

GEORGE

To London all in post; and, as I guess,
To make a bloody supper in the Tower.

EDWARD

He's sudden if a thing comes in his head.
Now march we hence; discharge the common sort
With pay and thanks, and let's away to London,
And see our gentle Queen how well she fares;
90 By this, I hope, she hath a son for me.   *Exeunt*

V.6   *Enter King Henry the Sixth and Richard below, with
           the Lieutenant of the Tower on the walls*

RICHARD

Good day, my lord. What! At your book so hard?

KING

Ay, my good lord – 'my lord', I should say rather.
'Tis sin to flatter; 'good' was little better.
'Good Gloucester' and 'good devil' were alike,
And both preposterous; therefore, not 'good lord'.

RICHARD

Sirrah, leave us to ourselves; we must confer.

Exit Lieutenant

KING

So flies the reckless shepherd from the wolf;
So first the harmless sheep doth yield his fleece,
And next his throat unto the butcher's knife.
What scene of death hath Roscius now to act? 10

RICHARD

Suspicion always haunts the guilty mind;
The thief doth fear each bush an officer.

KING

The bird that hath been limèd in a bush,
With trembling wings misdoubteth every bush;
And I, the hapless male to one sweet bird,
Have now the fatal object in my eye
Where my poor young was limed, was caught and killed.

RICHARD

Why, what a peevish fool was that of Crete,
That taught his son the office of a fowl!
And yet, for all his wings, the fool was drowned. 20

KING

I, Daedalus; my poor boy, Icarus;
Thy father, Minos, that denied our course;
The sun that seared the wings of my sweet boy,
Thy brother Edward, and thyself, the sea
Whose envious gulf did swallow up his life.
Ah, kill me with thy weapon, not with words!
My breast can better brook thy dagger's point
Than can my ears that tragic history.
But wherefore dost thou come? Is't for my life?

RICHARD

Thinkest thou I am an executioner? 30

159

KING

> A persecutor I am sure thou art;
> If murdering innocents be executing,
> Why, then thou art an executioner.

RICHARD

> Thy son I killed for his presumption.

KING

> Hadst thou been killed when first thou didst presume,
> Thou hadst not lived to kill a son of mine.
> And thus I prophesy, that many a thousand,
> Which now mistrust no parcel of my fear,
> And many an old man's sigh, and many a widow's,
40 > And many an orphan's water-standing eye –
> Men for their sons', wives for their husbands',
> And orphans for their parents' timeless death –
> Shall rue the hour that ever thou wast born.
> The owl shrieked at thy birth, an evil sign;
> The night-crow cried, aboding luckless time;
> Dogs howled, and hideous tempests shook down trees;
> The raven rooked her on the chimney's top,
> And chattering pies in dismal discords sung.
> Thy mother felt more than a mother's pain,
50 > And yet brought forth less than a mother's hope,
> To wit, an indigested and deformèd lump,
> Not like the fruit of such a goodly tree.
> Teeth hadst thou in thy head when thou wast born,
> To signify thou camest to bite the world;
> And if the rest be true which I have heard,
> Thou camest –

RICHARD

> I'll hear no more; die, prophet, in thy speech!
> *He stabs him*
> For this, amongst the rest, was I ordained.

KING

  Ay, and for much more slaughter after this.
  O, God forgive my sins, and pardon thee!   *He dies* 60

RICHARD

  What! Will the aspiring blood of Lancaster
  Sink in the ground? I thought it would have mounted.
  See how my sword weeps for the poor King's death!
  O, may such purple tears be alway shed
  From those that wish the downfall of our house!
  If any spark of life be yet remaining,
  Down, down to hell; and say I sent thee thither,
     (*He stabs him again*)
  I that have neither pity, love, nor fear.
  Indeed, 'tis true that Henry told me of;
  For I have often heard my mother say   70
  I came into the world with my legs forward.
  Had I not reason, think ye, to make haste,
  And seek their ruin that usurped our right?
  The midwife wondered and the women cried
  'O, Jesus bless us, he is born with teeth!'
  And so I was, which plainly signified
  That I should snarl and bite and play the dog.
  Then, since the heavens have shaped my body so,
  Let hell make crooked my mind to answer it.
  I have no brother, I am like no brother;   80
  And this word 'love', which greybeards call divine,
  Be resident in men like one another
  And not in me; I am myself alone.
  Clarence, beware; thou keepest me from the light.
  But I will sort a pitchy day for thee;
  For I will buzz abroad such prophecies
  That Edward shall be fearful of his life,
  And then, to purge his fear, I'll be thy death.

King Henry and the Prince his son are gone;
90   Clarence, thy turn is next, and then the rest,
Counting myself but bad till I be best.
I'll throw thy body in another room
And triumph, Henry, in thy day of doom.

Exit with the body

V.7   *Flourish. Enter Edward and Lady Grey, as king and*
      queen, George, Richard, Hastings, a nurse carrying
      the infant prince, and attendants

EDWARD

Once more we sit in England's royal throne,
Repurchased with the blood of enemies.
What valiant foemen, like to autumn's corn,
Have we mowed down in tops of all their pride!
Three Dukes of Somerset, threefold renowned
For hardy and undoubted champions;
Two Cliffords, as the father and the son;
And two Northumberlands – two braver men
Ne'er spurred their coursers at the trumpet's sound;
10   With them, the two brave bears, Warwick and Montague,
That in their chains fettered the kingly lion
And made the forest tremble when they roared.
Thus have we swept suspicion from our seat
And made our footstool of security.
Come hither, Bess, and let me kiss my boy.
Young Ned, for thee, thine uncles and myself
Have in our armours watched the winter's night,
Went all afoot in summer's scalding heat,
That thou mightst repossess the crown in peace;
20   And of our labours thou shalt reap the gain.

RICHARD (*aside*)

I'll blast his harvest, if your head were laid;

For yet I am not looked on in the world.
This shoulder was ordained so thick to heave;
And heave it shall some weight or break my back.
Work thou the way, and that shall execute.

EDWARD

Clarence and Gloucester, love my lovely Queen;
And kiss your princely nephew, brothers both.

GEORGE

The duty that I owe unto your majesty
I seal upon the lips of this sweet babe.

LADY GREY

Thanks, noble Clarence; worthy brother, thanks.   30

RICHARD

And that I love the tree from whence thou sprangest,
Witness the loving kiss I give the fruit.
(*Aside*) To say the truth, so Judas kissed his master,
And cried 'All hail!' when as he meant all harm.

EDWARD

Now am I seated as my soul delights,
Having my country's peace and brothers' loves.

GEORGE

What will your grace have done with Margaret?
Reignier, her father, to the King of France
Hath pawned the Sicils and Jerusalem,
And hither have they sent it for her ransom.   40

EDWARD

Away with her and waft her hence to France.
And now what rests but that we spend the time
With stately triumphs, mirthful comic shows,
Such as befits the pleasure of the court?
Sound drums and trumpets! Farewell, sour annoy!
For here, I hope, begins our lasting joy.   *Exeunt*

COMMENTARY

The chief sources of the play are the chronicles of Edward Hall, Richard Grafton, and Raphael Holinshed. In this Commentary, Hall is quoted where all the chroniclers agree, Holinshed where special use seems to have been made of him. References are to the following editions: Hall's *The Union of the Two Noble and Illustre Families of Lancaster and York* (1548–50), the reprint of 1809; Holinshed's *The Chronicles of England, Scotland, and Ireland* (Volume III, 2nd ed., 1587), the reprint of 1808. Biblical quotations are from the Bishops' Bible (1568 etc.), the official English translation of Elizabeth's reign. Quotations are normally given in modernized spelling and punctuation, with the exception of those from the 1595 edition of *The true Tragedie of Richard Duke of York* (referred to as 'Q1') and from the first Folio, 1623 (referred to as 'F').

The Characters in the Play
For the family relationships between the principal characters, see the Genealogical Tables; and for the regularization of names in this edition, see the Collations, pages 287–90. Biographical facts about each character are given in the Commentary at his or her first appearance in the play or mention in the text.

I.1   The scene takes place in the Parliament House in London. The talk of the battle and York's regrets at not capturing Henry VI imply a continuation of *Part Two*, which ended on the field of the first Battle of Saint Albans (1455). Historically York did not lay claim to the throne after this battle, but mounted the throne and proclaimed his right in the parliament of 1460, which followed the Battle of Northampton. As can be seen from the quotations from Hall throughout the Commentary, Shakespeare has telescoped time to avail himself of events taking place at both dates.

(stage direction) *Alarum* (trumpet call to arms)

York. Richard Plantagenet (1411–60) was the only son of Richard Earl of Cambridge, and thus the grandson of Edmund Langley, the fifth son of Edward III. He became the third Duke of York in 1415 and was Henry VI's lieutenant in France from 1440 to 1445. He was proclaimed Protector after the defeat of the King at the first Battle of Saint Albans (1455). He returned from exile in Ireland after Warwick's victory at the Battle of Northampton (1460), when he was again made Protector. He died after being besieged in Wakefield Castle in 1460.

Edward. Eldest son of the Duke of York, he was born at Rouen in 1442. After defeating the Lancastrians at the Battle of Towton he proclaimed himself king and was crowned Edward IV in 1461. He died in 1483.

Richard. The youngest son of the Duke of York, born at Fotheringay in 1452. His brother Edward created him Duke of Gloucester in 1461. Parliament proclaimed him Richard III in 1483 and he was slain at Bosworth Field in 1485.

Norfolk. John Mowbray (1415–61), third Duke and hereditary Earl Marshal of England, succeeded his father in 1432. York was his uncle by marriage. He shared Warwick's defeat at the second Battle of Saint Albans in 1461 and fought with Edward at Towton.

Montague. John Nevil (d. 1471) was the son of Richard, first Earl of Salisbury, and thus the brother of Warwick and nephew of York. After Edward's coronation he was created Lord Montague; later he was made Marquess and in 1465 Baron Montague. He was imprisoned at York after the second Battle of Saint Albans (1461), but was liberated by Edward IV after the Battle of Towton (1461). He later joined the Lancastrians and was killed at the Battle of Barnet (1471).

Warwick. Richard Nevil (1428–71), 'The Kingmaker', was the son of Richard, first Earl of Salisbury. He succeeded to the earldom of Warwick in 1449 by the right of his wife, Anne Beauchamp. He was the real ruler of England during the first three years of Edward IV's reign. Later he joined the Lancastrian cause and was slain by Edward at the Battle of Barnet.

white roses (the badge of the house of York. For Shakespeare's version of the origin of the roses as badges of the rival houses, see *Part One*, II.4.)

1   *I wonder how*. This is really the equivalent of 'how did'.

the King escaped our hands. This is Shakespeare's invention. After the Battle of Northampton (1460), at which York was not present, the King was 'kept and ordered at his pleasure' (Hall, page 245). After the first Battle of Saint Albans (1455) 'the Duke of York . . . , using all lenity, mercy, and bounteousness, would not once touch or apprehend the body of King Henry . . . but . . . conveyed him to London and so to Westminster' (Hall, page 233).

2   *the horsemen of the north* (the supporters of Henry VI's adherent nobles; see the notes to lines 155 and 251 below)

3   *He slily stole away and left his men*. This seems to have been suggested by Hall's words about Henry after the Battle of Northampton (1460): 'the King himself left alone and disconsolate' (page 244).

4–15   *Whereat the great Lord . . . the battles joined*. This is based upon Hall's account of the slain at the first Battle of Saint Albans (1455): 'there died, under the Sign of the Castle, Edmund Duke of Somerset ... and beside him lay Henry, the second Earl of Northumberland, Humphrey Earl of Stafford, son to the Duke of Buckingham, John Lord Clifford, and eight thousand men and more. Humphrey Duke of Buckingham, being wounded, and James Butler, Earl of Wiltshire and Ormonde, seeing Fortune's louring chance, left the King post alone and with a great number fled away' (page 233).

4   *Lord of Northumberland*. Henry Percy (1394–1455) was the son and heir of Hotspur and second Earl. He was appointed to the council of the Regency after the death of Henry V and was a bitter enemy of Warwick and Salisbury. He joined the royal forces after York took up arms in 1455 and died at the first Battle of Saint Albans (1455).

5   *brook retreat* bear to hear the trumpet signalling withdrawal from battle

7–9   *Lord Clifford ... by the swords of common soldiers slain*. This is based on Hall (page 233), who simply lists Old Clifford among the slain at Saint Albans (1455). However, it contradicts *Part Two*, V.2.27, where York kills Old Clifford, and also the references later in *Part Three* (I.1.55 and 162, I.3.5 and 47, and I.4.31-2 and 175). York's responsibility for Old Clifford's death is based upon Hall's report of young Clifford's words as he stabs the Earl of Rutland: 'By God's blood, thy father slew mine, and so will I do thee and all thy kin' (page 251).

7   *Lord Clifford*. Thomas de Clifford (1414–55), twelfth Baron Clifford and eighth Baron of Westmorland, was the son-in-law of Hotspur and one of the staunchest supporters of the house of Lancaster.

     Lord Stafford. Humphrey Stafford, eldest son of the first Duke of Buckingham, married Margaret, daughter of the second Duke of Somerset. He was severely wounded at the first Battle of Saint Albans (1455) and died not long after, although he is listed by Hall as being killed during the battle (page 233).

8   *our main battle* the principal body of our forces

10   *Duke of Buckingham.* Humphrey Stafford (1402–60), first Duke, was the grandson of Thomas of Woodstock, the sixth son of Edward III. He accompanied Henry VI abroad in 1430 and was created Duke in 1444. He was a strong supporter of the Queen and was slain on the eve of the Battle of Northampton (1460) by a Kentish follower of the Yorkists.

11   *dangerous* dangerously, mortally

12   *beaver* (technically the movable lower portion of the faceguard of a helmet, but here used to mean the helmet itself)

       downright administered vertically (and thus with one's full force)

14   *brother*. Here and at line 116 and I.2.4, 36, 55, and 60 Montague is erroneously taken to be York's brother. He was actually Warwick's brother, as which he appears at II.1.166 and for the rest of the play.

       Earl of Wiltshire. James Butler (1420–61) was the eldest son of James, fourth Earl of Ormonde. He was a zealous Lancastrian, was Viceroy of Ireland in 1453 and Treasurer of England in 1455. He fought at the first Battle of Saint Albans, where he was wounded by Montague, and at Wakefield. He was taken prisoner and beheaded at Towton. See the quotation from Hall in the note to lines 4–15.

15   *battles joined* battalions fell to combat

16   (stage direction) *Duke of Somerset.* Edmund Beaufort (d. 1455), second Duke, was the nephew of Cardinal Beaufort. It was during his Regency that most of the English possessions in France were lost. On York's appointment as Protector in 1455, Somerset was imprisoned in the Tower. He died at the first Battle

of Saint Albans. See the quotation from Hall in the note to lines 4–15 and *Part Two*, V.2, where his death and the prophecy connected with it are dramatized.

17   *Richard hath best deserved.* Historically Richard was eight years old at the date of the Battle of Northampton and three at the time of the first Battle of Saint Albans.
best deserved earned the greatest credit

19   *Such hope have* may such be the expectation of. Some editors emend *hope* to 'hap', believing that Richard puns on 'hap'/'hope' in line 20.
line of John of Gaunt descendants of John of Gaunt. Somerset was the grandson of Gaunt and Catherine Swynford.

20   *shake* cause to totter. Richard possibly picks the head up here and makes his action a visual quibble.

23   *the house of Lancaster usurps.* The reference is to Henry IV's usurpation of the crown of Richard II.

25–44 *This is the palace ... my right.* After the first Battle of Saint Albans (1455), York made no claim to the throne but was appointed Protector. It was following the Battle of Northampton (1460) that York, 'with a bold countenance, entered into the chamber of the peers and sat down in the throne royal under the cloth of estate (which is the king's peculiar seat), and in the presence as well of the nobility as of the spirituality, after a pause made, said these words in effect: "My singular good lords and very indifferent friends, in whose power and authority consisteth the peise and the stay of this noble realm of England ... I declare and publish to you that here I sit, as in the place to me by very justice lawfully belonging; and here I rest, as he to whom this chair of right appertaineth"' (Hall, page 245).

25   *fearful* timorous

31   *gentle* noble

32   *lodge* remain
(stage direction) *They go up.* There was presumably a throne upon a dais on the stage.

33   *offer him no violence* do not attack him. This is
      probably an echo of Hall; see the quotation in the
      note to line 1.

34   *perforce* by violent means

36   *of her council* members of her council (with a quibble on
      'give her advice')

40   *be* become

41   *bashful* easily intimidated

42   *by-words* objects of scorn, types of cowardice. Compare
      Psalm 44.15: 'Thou makest us to be a by-word among
      the heathen'.

44   *I mean to take possession of my right.* York concludes
      his oration to the 1460 parliament with the words
      'according to my just and true title, I have and do
      take possession of this royal throne' (Hall, page 247).

46   *proudest he* most courageous man
      holds up supports

47   *Dares stir a wing if Warwick shake his bells.* Warwick
      pictures himself as a hunting falcon which terrifies
      birds merely by the sound of the bells attached to its
      feet. Compare *The Rape of Lucrece*, 511: 'With
      trembling fear, as fowl hear falcons' bells.'

48   *plant* install (in the throne)

49   *Resolve thee* take the decision
      (stage direction) *Flourish* (fanfare of trumpets)
      Henry. Born in 1421, Henry VI succeeded his father,
      Henry V, in 1422 under the Protectorship of the
      Duke of Bedford. He married Margaret of Anjou in
      1445, and a son, Edward, was born to them in 1453.
      Clifford. John (1435?–1461), 'Young Clifford' of
      Part Two, was the thirteenth Baron Clifford and
      ninth Baron of Westmorland. He was a strong
      Lancastrian and was nicknamed 'The Butcher'
      after killing Rutland at Wakefield. He was slain six
      weeks after the second Battle of Saint Albans on the
      eve of the Battle of Towton.
      Northumberland. Henry Percy (1421–61) was the
      third Earl, succeeding his father (see the note to

line 4 above) in 1455. He defeated and slew the Duke of York at Wakefield (1460) and assisted the Queen to conquer Warwick at the second Battle of Saint Albans. He died at the Battle of Towton.

49   *Westmorland.* Ralph Nevil (d. 1484) succeeded as second Earl in 1425. He was married to Elizabeth Percy, the daughter of Hotspur. Historically he left the active support of Henry VI to his younger brother John, who was killed at the Battle of Towton (1461). Hall mistakenly lists him as being slain in the battle (page 256).

    Exeter. Henry Holland (d. 1473), although married to Edward IV's sister, Anne Plantagenet, remained faithful to Henry VI, fighting for him at Wakefield, Towton, and Barnet. He was attainted by Edward IV and died in poverty.

    red roses (the badge of the house of Lancaster)

50   *sturdy* confident of his strength

51   *chair of state* throne

    Belike apparently

52   *Backed* supported

    power troops

54–5   *Earl of Northumberland, he slew thy father, | And thine, Lord Clifford.* Compare Hall: 'the Earl of Northumberland and the Lord Clifford, whose fathers were slain at Saint Albans' (page 237).

56   *favourites* supporters (those who favour him)

57   *not* not avenged

58   *steel* armour (instead of conventional mourning clothes)

59   *suffer* permit

60   *for* with

    brook endure

62   *poltroons* cowards

63   *durst not* would not have dared

    your father (Henry V)

66, 72   *cousin* kinsman

67   *the city favours them.* The opposite is asserted in

Part Two, V.2.81; but this is in line with Hall, who notes that York 'had too many friends about the city of London' (page 232) and that the Queen 'well perceived the Duke of York to be had in more estimation among the citizens and commonality than the King' (page 236).

68   *at their beck* on call

71   *shambles* slaughter-house

74   *factious* rebellious

77   *he* (Henry VI; see *Part One*, III.1, where the investiture of York is dramatized)

78   *earldom* (earldom of March, which York held in the right of his mother, Anne Mortimer)

79   *Thy father* (Richard Earl of Cambridge, executed as a traitor by Henry V at Southampton in 1415; see *Henry V*, II.2)

82   *natural* legitimate (by right of birth)

91   *colours* battle-flags

94, 100   *his* my father's

97   *my father*. Historically Westmorland's father, John Nevil, was not slain in battle and died in 1423; see the note to the stage direction at line 49.

98   *Urge it* press the argument

     lest that lest. ('That' was often added after words such as 'if', 'after', 'when'.)

102-3   *Will you we show . . . field*. Compare York's oration to parliament in 1460: 'So that of fine force I am compelled to use power instead of prayer and force instead of request' (Hall, page 246).

102   *Will you we* do you wish us to

103   *plead* give arguments for

105   *Thy father was, as thou art, Duke of York*. In fact York's father was Richard Earl of Cambridge; it was from his father's older brother, Edward, that York inherited the dukedom.

106   *Thy grandfather* (York's maternal grandfather, the fourth Earl)

108   *Who made the Dauphin and the French to stoop.*
       Edward echoes this at II.2.151.
       the Dauphin (Charles VII, who became King of
       France in 1422. However, the Dauphin Shakespeare
       has as a character in *Henry V* is Louis, the eldest son
       of Charles VI.)
       stoop submit

110   *Talk not of France, sith thou hast lost it all.* The loss
       of the English possessions in France is one of the
       themes of *Part One*, and is repeatedly referred to in
       Part Two, particularly in connexion with Henry's
       agreeing, on his marriage to Margaret, to give Anjou
       and Maine to her father, Reignier.
       sith since

111   *The Lord Protector* (Humphrey Duke of Gloucester;
       see *Part Two*)

112–13 *When I was crowned ... lose.* Compare York's
       oration to parliament in 1460: 'although [Henry V]
       had a fair son and a young apparent heir, yet was
       this orphan such a one . . . that God threatened to send
       for a punishment to his unruly and ungracious people,
       saying by his prophet Isaiah: "I shall give you children
       to be your princes, and infants without wisdom shall
       have the governance of you". . . . The crown and
       glory of this realm is by the negligence of this silly
       man and his unwise counsel minished, defaced,
       and dishonoured' (Hall, page 247).

112   *nine months old.* This was Henry's age when he was
       proclaimed king on 30 August 1422; he was actually
       crowned king in Paris in November 1431. See
       Part One, IV.1.

113   *yet* still, even now
       methinks it appears to me

117   *stand* waste time

118   *Sound* let us but sound

125   *my grandsire and my father* (Henry IV and Henry V)

129   *winding-sheet* burial clothes

faint you do you lose your courage

132–50   *Henry the Fourth ... lawful king.* This is a shortened version of the dynastic claims (set out in detail in *Part One*, II.4 and 5, and *Part Two*, II. 2.9–52) used by York as a justification for his claim to the throne in the parliament of 1460 (Hall, pages 245–8).

132–4   *Henry the Fourth ... title's weak.* York notes, during his oration to parliament in 1460: 'if my claim be good, why have I not justice; for surely learned men of great science and literature say and affirm that lineal descent nor usurped possession can nothing prevail, if continual claim be lawfully made' (Hall, page 246).

133   *his king* (Richard II)

137   *An if* if

138–9   *Richard .... Resigned the crown to Henry the Fourth.* Compare Hall: 'The nobles and commons were well pleased that King Richard should frankly and freely of his own mere motion ... (lest it should be ... reported that he thereunto were ... constrained) resign his crown' (page 12). But contrast Shakespeare's treatment of the event in *Richard II*, IV.1.

139   *Henry.* Here and at other points in the play the name seems to have been pronounced trisyllabically for metrical reasons.

141   *him, being* Richard, who was

142   *his crown perforce* his claim to the crown by force of arms

144   *'twere prejudicial to his crown* it would tend to invalidate his title to the throne
         his (Richard II's)

150   *conscience* knowledge, understanding

154, 158 *despite* spite

155   *deceived* mistaken
         southern. Northumberland speaks as a *northern earl* of the men of Essex, Norfolk, Suffolk, and Kent.
         power armies

161   *ground gape.* Compare Numbers 16.30–32; Psalm
         106.17.

166   *Do right* give justice

169   *usurping blood* (the blood of a usurper)

171–88 *Let me for this my lifetime ... and despised.* This is
         based on Hall's account of the decision taken in the
         parliament of 1460, 'for so much as King Henry had
         been taken as king by the space of thirty-eight years
         and more, that he should enjoy the name and title
         of King and have possession of the realm during his
         life natural. And if he either died or resigned or
         forfeited the same, for infringing any point of this
         concord, then the said crown and authority royal
         should immediately be devoluted to the Duke of York,
         if he then lived, or else to the next heir of his line or
         lineage' (page 249).

173   *reign in quiet.* This is one of Hall's phrases (page 432).
         while as long as

176   *the Prince your son.* Edward, Prince of Wales, was
         born in 1453. He was present at the second Battle of
         Saint Albans (1461), after which he was knighted.
         He was killed by the Yorkists at the Battle of Tewkes-
         bury in 1471.

180   *these articles* the terms of this agreement. Compare
         Hall: 'These articles, with many other, were not
         only written, sealed, and sworn to by the two parties,
         but also were enacted in the high court of parliament'
         (page 249).

182   *these news.* 'News' was often treated as plural in
         sixteenth-century English.

184   *cold* passionless (and hence 'cowardly')

186   *bands* confinement

190   *They seek revenge.* See the note to lines 54–5.

193   *unnaturally* contrary to the law of nature

194   *entail* deliver as an inalienable possession

196–201 *Conditionally that here ... will perform.* Hall does not
         give the details of York's oath, which is found com-

plete in Holinshed: 'I, Richard Duke of York, promise and swear by the faith and truth that I owe to Almighty God that I shall never consent, procure, or stir directly or indirectly, in privy or apert, neither (as much as in me is) shall suffer to be done, consented, procured, or stirred anything that may sound to the abridgement of the natural life of King Henry VI, or to the hurt or diminishing of his reign or dignity royal by violence or any other way against his freedom or liberty' (III.266).

196   *Conditionally* providing

       oath. Compare Holinshed: 'Item, the said Richard Duke of York shall promise and bind himself by his solemn oath, in manner and form as followeth' (III. 266).

203   *forward* promising

205   (stage direction) *Sennet* (a flourish of trumpets signalling a ceremonial entrance or exit)

207   *keep* stay in

209   *I unto the sea from whence I came.* There is no reason in the play or in the chronicles to associate Montague with the sea. In the light of line 239 and the confusion about Montague's relationship to York (see the first note to line 14), it would appear that at some time during the composition of the play Montague and Falconbridge were possible alternatives for this role. See the Account of the Text, pages 283–4.

210   (stage direction) *Enter the Queen.* This confrontation in the parliament of 1460 is Shakespeare's invention. In Hall, 'The Duke of York, well knowing that the Queen would spurn and impugn the conclusions agreed and taken in this parliament, caused her and her son to be sent for by the King; but she, being a manly woman, using to rule and not to be ruled, and thereto counselled by the Dukes of Exeter and Somerset, not only denied to come but also assembled together a great army, intending to take the King

by fine force out of the lords' hands and to set them to a new school' (pages 249–50).

210   *the Queen.* Margaret (1430–82) was the daughter of René, Duke of Anjou and Count of Maine and titular King of Naples, Sicily, and Jerusalem. She married Henry VI in 1445, and identified herself with the Beaufort–Suffolk party at the English court. After Suffolk's death she virtually ruled the country in the King's name.

211   *whose looks bewray her anger.* This is based upon Hall's characterization: 'the fear that they had of the Queen, whose countenance was so fearful and whose look was so terrible that, to all men against whom she took a small displeasure, her frowning was their undoing and her indignation was their death' (page 241).

bewray display

215   *patient* (pronounced trisyllabically)

218   *unnatural.* See the note to line 193.

221   *that pain* (of childbirth)

224   *savage* ferocious

231   *shame* am ashamed

232   *undone* ruined

233   *head* free scope (a metaphor from horse-riding)

234   *As* that

sufferance permission

238   *Warwick is Chancellor and the Lord of Calais.* In Hall, in the parliament of 1455 'the Earl of Salisbury was appointed to be Chancellor and had the Great Seal to him delivered; and the Earl of Warwick was elected to the office of the Captain of Calais' (page 233).

239   *Stern Falconbridge commands the narrow seas.* It is not clear why Falconbridge is mentioned here. In Holinshed (III.260), there is a long account of naval engagements immediately before the description of William Nevil, Lord Falconbridge, leading the

rearguard of Warwick's army at the Battle of Northampton. In Hall (page 301), after the Battle of
Tewkesbury in 1471 William's bastard son, Thomas,
was 'appointed by the Earl of Warwick to be vice-
admiral of the sea and had in charge so to keep the
passage between Dover and Calais, that none which
either favoured King Edward or his friends should
escape untaken or undrowned'. See the note to line 209.

Stern harsh, fierce

the narrow seas (the English Channel)

240   *The Duke is made Protector of the realm.* At the same
parliament of 1455 at which Warwick was made
Captain of Calais, York was made Protector (Hall,
page 233), as he was again in the parliament of 1460,
when he was 'solemnly proclaimed heir apparent to
the crown of England and Protector of the realm'
(page 249).

242   *environèd* encircled

243   *silly* helpless

244   *tossed me on* impaled me aloft on the points of

245   *granted* submitted, yielded

247–8   *I here divorce myself | Both from thy table ... and thy
bed* (the legal formula used in the pronouncement of
divorce)

251   *The northern lords.* Contrast the *southern power* of the
Yorkists at lines 155–6. Compare Hall's 'all the
lords of the north part' (page 250).

       forsworn deserted, abjured allegiance to

256   *Our army is ready.* See the quotation from Hall in the
note to line 210.

265   *terms* words

267   *wingèd with* impelled by

268   *cost* rob me of (or possibly 'cost me')

       empty famished

269   *Tire* feed hungrily

270   *those three lords* (Northumberland, Westmorland,
Clifford)

271   *entreat them fair* treat them courteously

273   (stage direction) *Flourish.* In F this is printed inappropriately with the entry for I.2.

I.2   The scene is located at Sandal Castle near Wakefield in Yorkshire. After being proclaimed Henry's heir in the parliament of 1460, York went home specifically to raise an army to fight the Queen's northern forces: 'The Protector, lying in London, having perfect knowledge of all these doings, assigned the Duke of Norfolk and the Earl of Warwick, his trusty friends, to be about the King; and he with the Earls of Salisbury and Rutland, with a convenient company, departed out of London the second day of December northward; and sent to the Earl of March, his eldest son, to follow him with all his power. The Duke, by small journeys, came to his castle of Sandal beside Wakefield on Christmas eve, and there began to assemble his tenants and friends' (Hall, page 250). There is no warrant in the chronicles for York's decision to break his oath at the behest of his sons before hearing of the Queen's advance on his castle; Holinshed (III.269) hints that his death was 'a due punishment for breaking his oath of allegiance unto his sovereign lord King Henry', but also records that many men 'held him discharged thereof because he obtained a dispensation from the pope'.

    (stage direction) *Edward.* Although ordered by his father to follow him north, Edward never reached Sandal Castle and did not fight at the Battle of Wakefield. He was at Gloucester when he heard of the deaths of his father and brother (Hall, pages 250–51).

1   *give me leave* let me speak

    brother. See the first note to I.1.14.

6   *contention* (dispute about the crown). The word echoes the title of *Part Two* (Q1), *The First Part of the Contention betwixt the Two Famous Houses of York and Lancaster.*

11   *right* just claim, title

13   *breathe* rest, catch its breath

14   *outrun* escape from

15   *quietly reign* rule in peace. See the note to I.1.196–201.

16   *for a kingdom any oath may be broken* (proverbial: 'For a kingdom any law may be broken')

18   *be forsworn* commit perjury

22–7   *An oath is of no moment ... frivolous.* Compare Pandulph's sophistry on the same subject in *King John*, III.1.263–92.

22   *moment* force

26   *depose* take an oath, swear

27   *vain and frivolous* worthless and without legal weight

29–31   *How sweet a thing ... joy.* This is an echo of Christopher Marlowe's *Tamburlaine, Part 1*, II.5.57–61:

> A god is not so glorious as a king.
> I think the pleasure they enjoy in heaven
> Cannot compare with kingly joys in earth:
> To wear a crown enchased with pearl and gold,
> Whose virtues carry with it life and death ...

and II.7.27–9:

> the ripest fruit of all,
> That perfect bliss and sole felicity,
> The sweet fruition of an earthly crown.

30   *circuit* circumference

       Elysium (in Virgil, the region of Hades which housed the souls of the blessed after death; in Greek mythology, an island in the western ocean where the souls of the virtuous lived in perfect happiness)

31   *feign* depict imaginatively

34   *lukewarm*. Compare Westmorland's disgust at Henry's *cold blood* (I.1.184).

36   *presently* at once

37   *whet on* incite

39   *privily* confidentially, secretly

40   *Lord Cobham*. Sir Edward Brook, Lord Cobham, was Member of Parliament for Kent in 1445–60. He was an ardent Yorkist who fought at Saint Albans in 1455 and at Northampton in 1460. Cobham is mentioned in Hall, along with Warwick and Salisbury, as York's 'especial friends' (page 232).

41–3 *With whom the Kentishmen . . . spirit.* In describing the Yorkists' invasion preceding the Battle of Northampton (1460), Hall states that they left Calais and 'passed the sea and landed at Sandwich. And so passing through Kent, there came to them the Lord Cobham . . . and many other gentlemen' (page 243). Holinshed reports that Lord Falconbridge informed the Yorkists that the people of Kent 'were altogether bent in their favour and . . . addicted to do them service both with body and goods' (III.259). Compare Lord Say's praise of Kentishmen in *Part Two*, IV.7.55–9.

43   *Witty* intelligent
     liberal gentlemanly

44   *what resteth more* what else remains to be done

45   *occasion* opportunity

46   *not privy to my drift* not be informed of my intentions

47   (stage direction) *a Messenger*. F's reading, '*Gabriel*' (which is also the speech prefix), may be the name of the contemporary actor who originally played the role. There was a Gabriel Spencer who was once a member of the Admiral's Men company and who was killed in a duel with Ben Jonson on 22 September 1598.

48   *stay* wait

post haste

49–51   *The Queen ... thousand men.* Compare Hall: 'The Queen, being thereof ascertained, determined to couple with him while his power was small and his aid not come; and so having in her company the Prince her son, the Dukes of Exeter and Somerset, the Earl of Devonshire, the Lord Clifford, the Lord Ross, and in effect all the lords of the north part, with eighteen thousand men, or, as some write, twenty and two thousand, marched from York to Wakefield and bade base to the Duke even before his castle' (page 250).

51   *hard* very close

52   *hold* castle, stronghold

55   *post* hasten

56–7   *noble Warwick ... King.* See the quotation from Hall in the headnote to this scene.

58   *policy* political cunning

59   *simple* foolish

60   *fear* doubt

61   (stage direction) *Sir John Mortimer and Sir Hugh Mortimer.* Hall lists these among the slain at the Battle of Wakefield (1460) as York's 'two bastard uncles' (page 250), presumably half-brothers of York's mother, Anne Mortimer.

63   *in a happy hour* opportunely

67–75   *Ay, with five hundred ... success.* This is based on Hall's fuller description of York's attitude: 'he, having with him not fully five thousand persons, determined incontinent to issue out and to fight with his enemies; and although Sir Davy Hall, his old servant and chief counsellor, advised him to keep his castle and to defend the same with his small number till his son, the Earl of March, were come with his power of Marchmen and Welsh soldiers, yet he would not be counselled, but in a great fury said "Ah, Davy, Davy, hast thou loved me so long

and now wouldst have me dishonoured? Thou
never sawest me keep fortress when I was Regent in
Normandy, when the Dauphin himself with his
puissance came to besiege me, but like a man, and
not like a bird included in a cage, I issued and fought
with mine enemies, to their loss ever, I thank God,
and to my honour. If I have not kept myself within
walls for fear of a great and strong prince, nor hid
my face from any man living, wouldst thou that I for
dread of a scolding woman, whose weapon is only her
tongue and her nails, should incarcerate myself and
shut my·gates, then all men might of me wonder and
all creatures may of me report dishonour that a woman
hath made me a dastard"' (page 250).

67   *for a need* if need be
68   (stage direction) *A march* (the sound of drums
      accompanying marching men)
70   *straight* immediately
71   *Five men to twenty*. The same stress on the odds is
      laid in the portrait of the Duke of York in *A Mirror
      for Magistrates* (1559): 'With scant five thousand
      soldiers, to assail | Four times so many' (lines 132-3).
74   *When as* when
75   *the like* a similar

I.3   The location of the scene is somewhere between
       Sandal Castle and the site of the Battle of Wakefield
       (1460). It is based on Hall: 'While this battle was in
       fighting, a priest called Sir Robert Aspall, chaplain
       and schoolmaster to the young Earl of Rutland,
       second son to the above named Duke of York, scarce
       of the age of twelve years, a fair gentleman and a
       maiden-like person, perceiving that flight was more
       safeguard than tarrying, both for him and his master,
       secretly conveyed the Earl out of the field by the
       Lord Clifford's band toward the town; but ere he

could enter into a house, he was by the said Lord
Clifford espied, followed, and taken, and, by reason
of his apparel, demanded what he was. The young
gentleman, dismayed, had not a word to speak,
but kneeled on his knees imploring mercy and desiring
grace, both with holding up his hands and making
dolorous countenance, for his speech was gone for
fear. "Save him," said his chaplain, "for he is a
prince's son and peradventure may do you good
hereafter." With that word the Lord Clifford marked
him and said "By God's blood, thy father slew mine,
and so will I do thee and all thy kin", and with that
word stuck the Earl to the heart with his dagger,
and bade his chaplain bear the Earl's mother and
brother word what he had done and said. In this
act the Lord Clifford was accounted a tyrant and
no gentleman; for the property of the lion, which is a
furious and an unreasonable beast, is to be cruel to
them that withstand him and gentle to such as
prostrate or humiliate themselves before him'
(pages 250–51).

(stage direction) *Alarum* (the sound of the battle being
carried on off stage. In F this direction appears inappropriately before the exit at the end of I.2.)

Rutland. Edmund Earl of Rutland (1443–60) was only
a year younger than Edward, six years older than
George, and nine years older than Richard; but
he is treated as the baby of the family in the play.
At the time of his death he was seventeen.

4   *brat* (not always used contemptuously) child
5   *Whose father slew my father.* See the note to I.1.7–9.
    Whose. The antecedent is *brat*, not *duke*.
9   *hated both of God and man.* This is perhaps an echo
    of Edmund Spenser's *The Faerie Queene*, where
    the phrase is used twice (I.1.13, I.5.48).
    of by
12–13   *So looks the pent-up lion ... paws.* The simile was

185

clearly prompted by Hall's comparison between Clifford and a lion, for which see the quotation in the headnote to this scene.

12   *pent-up* (ravenous with hunger)

14   *insulting* triumphing contemptuously

16   *gentle* noble

19   *mean* unworthy, insignificant

24   *cope with* match yourself against

29   *slake* abate

31   *as a fury to torment my soul*. The reference is probably to the Furies in Greek mythology, who made the guilty mad.

39   *'twas ere I was born*. In *Part Two*, York is depicted as killing Old Clifford at the first Battle of Saint Albans, which dramatically is a few weeks before the present battle. Historically, Rutland was twelve at the time of Saint Albans and seventeen at the Battle of Wakefield.

40   *Thou hast one son* (Henry de Clifford, subsequently the fourteenth Baron, 1455 ?–1523)

41   *sith* since

44   *occasion of* cause for

48   *Di faciant laudis summa sit ista tuae*. This is from Ovid's *Heroides*, II.66: 'May the gods cause this action to be that which makes you most well-known.' It was, of course, this deed which helped to give Clifford the nickname 'The Butcher'.

49   *Plantagenet* (the Duke of York)

50   *cleaving* sticking

52   *Congealed* coagulated

I.4   The scene is located at the Battle of Wakefield (1460). Shakespeare appears to have used both Hall's and Holinshed's accounts of York's death, as the scene contains details which they do not have in common. Hall, page 251: 'Yet this cruel Clifford and deadly bloodsupper, not content with this homicide or

child-killing, came to the place where the dead corpse
of the Duke of York lay and caused his head to be
stricken off and set on it a crown of paper, and so
fixed it on a pole and presented it to the Queen, not
lying far from the field, in great despite and much
derision, saying "Madam, your war is done. Here is
your King's ransom", at which present was much joy
and great rejoicing; but many laughed then that sore
lamented after.' Holinshed, III.269: 'But when [York]
was in the plain field between his castle and the town
of Wakefield, he was environed on every side like fish
in a net; so that though he fought manfully, yet was
he within half an hour slain and dead and his whole
army discomfited. . . . But the same Lord Clifford,
not satisfied herewith, came to the place where the
dead corpse of the Duke of York lay, caused his head
to be stricken off, and set on it a crown of paper,
fixed it to a pole, and presented it to the Queen, not
lying far from the field, in great despite, at which
great rejoicing was showed; but they laughed then
that shortly after lamented. . . . Some write that
the Duke was taken alive and in derision caused to
stand upon a molehill, on whose head they put a
garland instead of a crown, which they had fashioned
and made of sedges or bullrushes. And having so
crowned him with that garland, they kneeled down
afore him (as the Jews did unto Christ) in scorn,
saying to him "Hail, king without rule! Hail, king
without heritage! Hail, duke and prince without
people or possessions!" And at length having thus
scorned him with these and divers other the like
despiteful words, they struck off his head, which (as
ye have heard) they presented to the Queen.'

1   *got the field* won the battle
2   *uncles* (Sir John and Sir Hugh Mortimer; see the note
       to I.2.61)
3   *eager* impetuous

4   *Turn back* turn round, retreat

6   *My sons.* According to the chronicles, only Rutland was present at the Battle of Wakefield; Edward was at Gloucester with his army; George was eleven and Richard eight at the time.

    bechancèd befallen

7   *demeaned* behaved

9   *make a lane* cut a way through the enemy soldiers

12   *purple* bloodied

    falchion (a sword with a single cutting edge)

    painted bedaubed

14   *retire* fall back

18   *out, alas* (a common exclamation of disgust and regret)

19   *budged* gave way

20   *bootless* useless

21   *spend* consume

    with in opposition to

    overmatching (of superior strength)

22   *fatal* (boding death)

    followers pursuing enemies

23   *faint* weak, overcome with fatigue

25   *sands* (of the hour-glass)

    makes. The singular verb form with a plural subject was common in Elizabethan English.

26   *stay* wait, remain

27   *rough* cruel, violent

29   *butt* (target for archery practice)

32   *downright payment.* The quibble is on (1) a vertically administered blow; (2) a down payment of violence.

33   *Phaethon* (three syllables) tried to drive the chariot of the sun, which could only be controlled by his father, Phoebus Apollo, and was killed by a thunderbolt from Jove when he endangered the earth by flying too close to it. He was a common symbol of overweening pride and ambition, but is particularly appropriate here as the sun was one of the devices of the house of York; see the second note to II.1.25.

34   *the noontide prick* (the mark on the sundial on which the midday shadow of the gnomon falls)

35   *the phoenix* (the fabulous bird of Arabia and the classical symbol of immortality, which was born from its own ashes every five hundred years)

36   *A bird* (Edward, who became king in 1461)
       revenge take revenge

39   *Multitudes, and fear* so many of you, and yet afraid

40   *So cowards fight when they can fly no further* (proverbial: 'Despair makes cowards courageous')

43   *Breathe out* utter

44   *but bethink thee* only remember

45   *o'errun my former time* review my past life

46   *for* despite your

47   *bite* hold

48   *faint* grow weak with fear

49   *bandy . . . word for word* exchange words

50   *buckler . . . blows* exchange blows

51, 54   *Hold* stop

56   *grin* bare its teeth, snarl

58   *spurn* kick aside

59   *prize* privilege
       vantages opportunities

60   *impeach of* reproach to, detraction from

61   *woodcock* (proverbial for the ease with which it was snared)
       gin snare

62   *cony* rabbit (but also a slang term for someone who is easily duped)

63   *triumph* gloat, exult
       their conquered booty the objects they have stolen

64   *true* honest
       o'ermatched outnumbered

66   *Brave* fine

68   *raught at* reached out for

69   *parted but* merely divided

71   *revelled* rioted

72   *preachment of* sermon about. The allusion is to I.1.77–
        169 and York's long address to the parliament of
        1460 in the chronicles, which lies behind that scene.
        high descent royal lineage

73   *mess* group of four. (The word was used to describe
        four people eating from the same dish at a feast.)
        back support

74   *wanton* lascivious. This aspect of Edward's character
        is touched upon at II.1.42 and developed at length in
        III.2 and in *Richard III*.
        George. The third son of the Duke of York, he was
        born in 1449. He was created Duke of Clarence in
        1461 and eight years later married Isabella, the
        daughter of Warwick, which alliance caused him to
        give his support to the Lancastrian cause. Changing
        sides, he fought for Edward at Tewkesbury; he was
        murdered while a prisoner in the Tower in 1478.

75–7   *And where's that valiant . . . mutinies.* See V.6.44–56
        and 68–83 and the quotation from Hall (pages 342–3)
        in the headnote to V.6.

75   *prodigy* ominous monstrosity

76   *grumbling* querulous

77   *cheer* urge on
        mutinies rebellions

79   *napkin* handkerchief

83   *withal* with

84   *But* except for the fact

87   *parched* dried up
        entrails. These were considered the seat of the
        emotions.

89   *mad* angry

92   *fee'd* paid (for performing)

96   *marry* (a mild oath, originally meaning 'by the
        Virgin Mary')

97   *chair* throne

100   *his solemn oath.* See the quotation in the headnote to
        I.2.

101   *bethink me* remember
103   *pale* encircle (with the crown)
105   *in his life* while he is still alive
106   *fault* crime
108   *breathe* take a rest
       time to do him dead the opportunity to kill him
109   *office* duty
110   *stay* stop
       orisons prayers
113   *ill-beseeming* inappropriate, unbecoming
114   *triumph* exult
       an Amazonian trull a warlike prostitute. The allusion
       is to the classical female warriors.
115   *captivates* captures
116   *vizard-like* expressionless (like a mask)
117   *with use* by constant practice
118   *assay* attempt
119   *derived* descended
121–2 *Thy father bears ... Jerusalem.* Margaret's father
       was René I (Reignier), Duke of Anjou and Count
       of Maine, King of Naples, Sicily, and Jerusalem.
121   *type* title. Reignier was only a titular monarch.
122   *the Sicils* (Naples and Sicily)
123   *not so wealthy.* Reignier's poverty is one of the crucial
       points in Gloucester's and York's opposition to
       Henry's marriage to Margaret in *Parts One* and *Two*.
       Compare Hall, page 205: 'King Reignier, her father,
       for all his long style had too short a purse'.
       yeoman (land-holding farmer)
124   *insult* triumph in a scornful manner
125–7 *It needs not ... horse to death* (proverbial: 'Set a
       beggar on horseback and he will ride a gallop')
125   *needs not* is unnecessary
       it boots thee not it is useless for you
126   *adage* proverb
       verified proved correct
130   *admired* wondered at

132   *government* self-control leading to right conduct

133   *want* lack

135   *the Antipodes* (the opposite side of the globe)

136   *Septentrion* north (the 'septentrion' being the seven stars making up the constellation Ursa Major)

137   *O tiger's heart wrapped in a woman's hide.* This is the line Robert Greene parodied in his *Groatsworth of Wit* (1592); see the Account of the Text, page 285.

141   *pitiful* full of compassion
        flexible easily moved emotionally

142   *rough* cruel

145–6   *raging wind blows up incessant showers,* | *And when the rage allays, the rain begins* (proverbial: 'Small rain allays great winds' and 'After wind comes rain')

146   *allays* is quieted

147   *obsequies* funeral rites

149   *fell* savage

150   *Beshrew* curse
        passions displays of emotion
        moves. See the second note to line 25.

151   *check* restrain

154   *inexorable* (accented on the third syllable) merciless

155   *Hyrcania* (a region near the Caspian Sea, associated in Latin literature with tigers)

160   *heavy* sorrowful

169   *slaughter-man* killer

171   *inly* internal
        gripes grieves, takes hold of

172   *weeping-ripe* on the point of tears

174   *melting* soft-hearted

176   *gentle* noble

179–80   *Off with his head ... York.* Compare Hall: 'After this victory by the Queen and her part obtained, she caused the Earl of Salisbury, with all the other prisoners, to be sent to Pomfret, and there to be beheaded; and sent all their heads and the Duke's head of York to be set upon poles over the gate of the city of York in despite of them and their lineage' (page 251).

II.1   The scene is located near Mortimer's Cross in Herefordshire. In the chronicles, following the Battle of Wakefield there occurred a series of battles in February 1460, which are reported during the scene. (stage direction) *Edward*. Historically Edward was at Gloucester at this time.

    Richard. Historically Richard was eight years old at this time and had been sent by his mother with his brother George to stay with the Duke of Burgundy in Utrecht; see the note to line 142.

    power army

3   *Clifford's and Northumberland's pursuit*. Historically Clifford and Northumberland were together only at the Battle of Towton (1461), where they commanded the Lancastrian forces with the Duke of Somerset (Hall, page 254).

4   *ta'en* captured

9   *joy* be happy

     resolved informed

10   *is become* is to be found

12   *singled . . . forth* separated from the other soldiers

13   *Methought* it appeared to me

     bore him conducted himself

14   *neat* cattle

15   *a bear encompassed round with dogs* (as in the sport of bear-baiting)

16   *pinched* bitten

17   *aloof* at a distance

19   *fled his enemies* his enemies fled from

20   *prize* privilege

24   *Trimmed* finely dressed

     younker fashionable young man

25   *Dazzle mine eyes* have my eyes grown dim

     three suns. According to Hall, after Edward had collected a force in the West of England to avenge his father's death, he encountered on 2 February 1461 a Welsh Lancastrian power at Mortimer's Cross, when 'the sun (as some write) appeared to the Earl of

193

March like three suns and suddenly joined all to-gether in one; and . . . upon the sight thereof, he took such courage that he fiercely set on his enemies and them shortly discomfited; for which cause, men imagined that he gave the sun in his full brightness for his cognizance or badge' (page 251).

27   *with* by

    racking (passing like smoke)

32   *figures* foretells

34   *cites* urges, summons

36   *by our meeds* because of our worth

38   *over-shine* illuminate

    this (this strange sun)

40   *target* (a lightweight shield)

41   *daughters.* Richard is punning on *suns*/'sons'.

42   *You love the breeder better than the male.* See the first note to I.4.74 and compare Hall: 'Edward, which loved well both to look and to feel fair damsels' (page 265).

    breeder child-bearer (hence the female)

    (stage direction) *blowing a horn.* This denoted an express rider.

43   *heavy* sorrowful

46   *When as* when

50   *Environèd* surrounded. The word is from Hall's account; see the headnote to I.4.

51   *the hope of Troy* (Hector; see the note to IV.8.25)

53   *Hercules himself must yield to odds* (proverbial: 'Hercules himself cannot deal with two')

54–5   *many strokes ... oak* (proverbial: 'Many strokes fell great oaks')

57   *ireful* angry

59   *in high despite* with supreme scorn

62   *harmless* innocent

63   *rough* cruel

65–6   *They took his head ... the same.* See the note to I.4.179–80.

68-9   *Sweet Duke of York, our prop to lean upon, | Now*
        thou art gone, we have no staff, no stay. Compare
        Marlowe's *The Massacre at Paris*, 22.4–5: 'Sweet
        Duke of Guise, our prop to lean upon, | Now thou
        art dead, here is no stay for us.'

69   *stay* support

70   *boisterous* savage

71   *The flower of Europe for his chivalry.* This is a phrase
        used by Hall to describe several warriors, including
        Edward IV and the Black Prince.
        chivalry knightly prowess

72   *treacherously* in a cowardly fashion

74   *soul's palace* (the body)

75   *she* (my soul)
        that so that

78   *more joy* happiness again

80   *furnace-burning heart.* The Elizabethans believed that
        anger turned the heart to fire, so that the blood
        boiled.

82   *wind* breath
        speak withal employ in speech

83   *kindling* (acting as a bellows on)

87   *venge* avenge

88   *renownèd* made famous

90, 93 *chair* ducal seat

90   *with me is left* (as York's heir)

91-2   *if thou be ... sun.* Compare the proverb 'Only the
        eagle can gaze at the sun', which was based on the
        belief that the eagle trained its young to stare at the
        sun as a means of selecting those worthy of survival.

91   *princely eagle.* In the Great Chain of Being (the
        system by which all parts of the universe were
        arranged in an ordered pattern), the eagle was the
        highest in the hierarchy of birds.
        bird fledgling

94   (stage direction) *March* (the sound of instruments
        accompanying marching men)

95   *What fare* what's happening (to our cause)
       abroad about in the world

96   *recompt* narrate

97   *baleful* deadly
       each word's deliverance the utterance of every word

98   *poniards* daggers

102   *held* prized, valued
       dearly as dearly

103   *stern* fierce

105   *measure* quantity

106   *sith* since

108   *latest* last

109   *posts* fast-moving messengers

110   *depart* death

111–40   *I, then in London ... fight again.* Warwick here
describes the second Battle of Saint Albans, which
took place on 17 February 1461, fifteen days after
Mortimer's Cross: 'The Queen still came forward
with her northern people, intending to subvert and
defeat all conclusions and agreements enacted
and assented to in the last parliament. And so after
her long journey, she came to the town of Saint
Albans, whereof the Duke of Norfolk, the Earl of
Warwick, and other, whom the Duke of York had
left to govern the King in his absence, being advertised, by the assent of the King gathered together a
great host and set forward toward Saint Albans,
having the King in their company as the head and
chieftain of the war; and so, not minding to defer
the time any further, upon Shrove Tuesday, early in
the morning, set upon their enemies. Fortune that
day so favoured the Queen that her part prevailed and
the Duke and the Earl were discomfited and fled'
(Hall, page 252).

111   *keeper* gaoler

112   *Mustered ... friends.* After this line many modern
editors insert a line based on Q1: 'And very well

appointed, as I thought.' However, no such insertion is necessary to make sense of the passage as it stands in F.

114   *in my behalf* for my own advantage

115   *advertisèd* informed

116–18 *she was coming . . . your succession.* See the quotation from Hall in the note to lines 111–40.

117   *dash* rescind, overturn
      late recent

118   *Touching* concerning

120   *Our battles joined* the main bodies of our armies encountered each other

121   *coldness* passionless quality

123   *heated spleen* aroused courage

125   *rigour* ferocity

128   *like to lightning came and went* (a proverbial phrase)

130   *flail* (a threshing implement comprising two laths hinged by a strip of leather)

137–40 *myself . . . fight again.* In Hall, after the second Battle of Saint Albans 'the Earl of Warwick, in whom rested the chief trust of that faction, after the last conflict had at Saint Albans, had met with the said Earl of March at Chipping Norton by Cotswold; and . . . they with both their powers were coming toward London' (page 253).

138   *post-haste* riding at full speed

139   *the Marches* (the Welsh borderlands, where according to Hall (page 251) the people 'above measure favoured the lineage of the Lord Mortimer, [and] more gladly offered . . . their aid and assistance' to Edward)

140   *Making another head* gathering more armed men

141   *gentle* noble

142   *when came George from Burgundy to England.* Compare Hall: 'The Duchess of York, seeing her husband and son slain and not knowing what should succeed of her eldest son's chance, sent her two younger sons,

George and Richard, over the sea to the city of Utrecht in Almain, where they were of Philip Duke of Burgundy well received and feasted; and so there they remained till their brother Edward had obtained the realm and gotten the regiment' (page 253).

144   *for* as for

145   *your kind aunt, Duchess of Burgundy.* The Duchess at this time was Isabel, the daughter of John I of Portugal and his wife, John of Gaunt's daughter, Philippa of Lancaster. She was, therefore, the third cousin of Edward. There is no reference to her in the chronicles' account of the events at this time.

147   *'Twas odds, belike* it was presumably because his troops were outnumbered

149   *scandal of retire* disgraceful reputation for retreating

152   *diadem* crown
        faint timorous

153   *awful* awe-inspiring

161   *Numbering our Ave-Maries with our beads.* The line is almost identical to *Part Two*, I.3.54.
        beads (rosary beads)

163   *Tell* count (by means of blows rather than beads of the rosary)

165, 166 *therefore* for that reason

167   *Attend* listen to

167–75 *The proud insulting . . . house of Lancaster.* See the quotation from Hall in the note to lines 111–40.

167   *insulting* contemptuously exulting

168   *haught* haughty

169   *of their feather many moe proud birds* (proverbial: 'Birds of a feather flock together')
        moe (an archaic form of 'more')

170   *wrought the easy-melting King like wax* (proverbial: 'As pliable as wax')
        wrought worked, manipulated
        easy-melting easily persuaded

172   *enrollèd* recorded (by being written in the official rolls)

174   *frustrate* render null and void

       what beside anything else

175   *make* prove effective

176   *thirty thousand.* Hall says the Lancastrian force 'accounted sixty thousand men' (page 255); the figure in Q1 is fifty thousand.

178   *Earl of March* (Edward. Compare Hall: 'The Earl of March, so commonly called, but after the death of his father in deed and in right very Duke of York' (page 251).)

179   *the loving Welshmen.* See the note to line 139.

       loving friendly, loyal

180   *five and twenty thousand.* Hall's number of Yorkists is 'forty-eight thousand, six hundred, and sixty persons' (page 255); Q1's figure is forty-eight thousand.

181   *Why, via! To London.* Compare Hall: 'The Earls of March and Warwick, having perfect knowledge that the King and Queen with their adherents were departed from Saint Albans, determined first to ride to London as the chief key and common spectacle to the whole realm, thinking there to assure themselves of the east and west part of the kingdom' (page 253).

       via forward, onward

       amain at full speed

184   *turn back* turn our backs in retreat

187   *stay* stand firm

190   *forfend* forbid

192   *degree* step (on the ladder of rank)

193-4   *King of England ... along.* Compare Hall: 'What should I declare how the Kentishmen resorted, how the people of Essex swarmed, and how the counties adjoining to London daily repaired to see, aid, and comfort this lusty prince' (page 253); '[Edward] was conveyed to Westminster and there sat in the hall with the sceptre royal in his hand, where, to all

the people which there in a great number were
assembled, his title and claim to the crown of England
was declared. ... It was again demanded of the
commons if they would admit and take the said
earl as their prince and sovereign lord, which all with
one voice cried "Yea, yea!"' (page 254).

196   *fault* offence, default
198   *Stay we* let us remain here
200   *as hard as steel* (proverbial phrase)
203   *Saint George* (patron saint of England, and thus the
      appropriate battle-cry for Edward, who considers
      himself the rightful king)
206   *puissant host* powerful army
208   *it sorts* things are working out

II.2   The scene is located in York. There is no comparable
       episode in the chronicles; Shakespeare designs a
       confrontation scene, fashioned from historical inci-
       dents which happened at various times during the
       reign of Henry VI.
       (stage direction) *drum and trumpets* (drummer and
       trumpeters)
1   *brave* splendid
2   *that arch-enemy* (Richard Duke of York; see I.4.179-
       80)
4   *object* sight
5   *wrack* shipwreck
8   *wittingly* knowingly, intentionally
       infringed my vow. The reference is to I.1.194-200.
9   *lenity* gentleness
13   *forest* wild, untamed
14   *spoils* seizes as prey
15   *sting.* The Elizabethans believed that snakes had a
       sting located in their tail.
17   *The smallest worm will turn, being trodden on* (proverb-
       ial: 'Tread on a worm and it will turn')

18   *in safeguard of* in order to defend

19   *level* aim

22   *raise his issue* elevate his son in rank

25   *argued* proved

26   *Unreasonable* (having no ability to think rationally)

27   *fearful* fear-inducing

28   *tender* (1) young; (2) precious

30   *sometime* on other occasions

       fearful terrified

37   *great-grandfather and grandsire* (Henry IV and Henry V)

38   *fondly* foolishly

41   *melting* (softened by gentle feelings)

44   *Inferring* adducing

46   *things ill got had ever bad success* (proverbial: 'Ill-gotten goods never prove well')

       success outcome

47–8   *happy always was it for that son | Whose father for his hoarding went to hell* (proverbial: 'Happy is the child whose father goes to the devil')

47   *happy* fortunate

48   *for* because of

51   *at such a rate* at such great cost

57   *soft courage* faint-heartedness

       faint lose heart

58–61 *You promised knighthood . . . a knight.* This is based on Hall's account of the knighting of the Prince the day after the second Battle of Saint Albans: 'When Queen Margaret had thus well sped, first she caused the King to dub Prince Edward his son knight' (page 252).

58   *forward* promising

59   *presently* immediately

62   *right* justice

64   *apparent* (heir apparent)

65   *that quarrel* (the defence of the crown)

66   *toward* (accented on the first syllable) promising

67–9   *Royal commanders ... Duke of York.* Compare Hall: 'for all these devices were shortly transmuted ... to the Queen that the Earl of March ... and ... the Earl of Warwick ... with both their powers were coming toward London' (pages 252–3).

69   *backing* in support
      the Duke of York (Edward)

70–71   *in the towns ... him.* See the note to II.1.193–4.

72   *Darraign your battle* set your forces in battle formation

73–4   *I would your highness ... absent.* This is based on Hall's comment on the battles of Wakefield and Saint Albans: 'Happy was the Queen in her two battles, but unfortunate was the King in all his enterprises; for where his person was present, there victory fled ever from him to the other part and he commonly was subdued and vanquished' (page 252).

74   *success* results

78   *cheer* encourage

80   *Saint George.* See the note to II.1.203.

81   *perjured* (because he has broken his oath concerning the Yorkist succession)
      grace mercy, pardon

82   *diadem* crown

83   *bide* await
      mortal fortune deadly outcome

84   *rate* scold
      minions royal favourites

85   *terms* language

89–92   *Since when ... son in.* See the note to II.1.111–40. Both F1 and Q1 give these lines to George.

90   *You* (the Queen)

92   *blot out me* cross out my name (from the official records)

93   *reason* rightly

95   *butcher.* See the third note to the stage direction at I.1.49.

97 *any he* any other man
   sort gang
99 *yet* even so I am
103 *Saint Albans* (the second battle there, on 17 February 1461)
109 *hold* regard
   reverently with respect
110 *refrain* hold back
111 *execution of* action proceeding from
    big-swollen (with anger)
112 *child-killer*. The phrase is Hall's; see the headnote to I.4. The historical Richard was, of course, nine years younger than Rutland.
114 *dastard* traitor
115 *tender*. See the note to line 28.
119 *give no limits to* set no restrictions on
122 *still* silent
123 *executioner*. Richard refuses to regard Clifford's killing of his father and brother as the actions of a soldier.
124 *resolved* convinced
125 *lies upon his tongue* consists merely of the words he speaks
127 *broke their fasts* had breakfast
128 *ne'er shall dine* will be dead by dinner-time
129 *deny* refuse
    upon be upon
133 *Whoever got thee*. The doubt about Edward's parentage is a dramatic echo of Suffolk's affair with the Queen in *Part Two*, and is based on Hall's description of the birth of the Prince: 'on the thirteenth day of October was the Queen delivered at Westminster of a fair son, which was christened and named Edward and after grew to a goodly and perfect man ... whose mother sustained not a little slander and obloquy of the common people, saying that the King was not able to get a child and that this was not his son,

203

with many slanderous words to the Queen's dishonour'
(page 230).

133 *got* begot

134 *wot* know

135 *sire nor dam* father nor mother

136 *stigmatic* one stamped with deformity

137 *Marked* branded

138 *venom toads* (proverbial: 'Full as a toad of poison')
lizards' dreadful stings. Lizards, like snakes, were
believed to have a sting in their tail.

140 *the title of a king.* See the notes to I.4.121–2.

141 *channel* open drain

142 *extraught* descended

143 *detect* reveal, betray

144–5 *A wisp of straw ... herself.* The allusion is to the
practice of making shrewish women wear a crown of
straw.

145 *callet* harlot

146 *Helen of Greece* (the wife of Menelaus, the most
beautiful woman of the ancient world, whose abduction by the Trojan Paris led to the siege and
sack of Troy)

147 *thy husband may be Menelaus* (Henry can be considered
a cuckold; see the first note to line 133)

148 *Agamemnon* (the brother of Menelaus and the leader
of the Greek army which destroyed Troy in revenge
for Helen's abduction)

150 *His father* (Henry V)
revelled made merry, did his pleasure

152 *he* (Henry VI)
matched married
state royal position

154 *a beggar.* The allusion is to Margaret's father's poverty.

155 *graced thy poor sire with his bridal day.* The allusion is
to the over-generous marriage arrangements negoti-
ated by Suffolk and the fact that Henry paid for all
the wedding expenses; see *Part Two*, I.1.40 ff.

thy poor sire (Reignier, Margaret's father)

his (Henry VI's)

157   *forth of* out of

159   *broached* opened up, started

160   *title* legal claim to the crown

        still had slept would have remained unpressed

162   *Had slipped* would have left unasserted

164   *increase* harvest

165   *usurping* (because she is the wife of a usurping king)

166   *something* to some extent

168   *leave* leave off

169   *bathed thy growing* watered your growth

171   *conference* discussion

172   *deniest* forbid

176   *wrangling* quarrelsome

177   *words* angry exchanges

II.3   The scene is located on the battlefield between Towton and Saxton in Yorkshire. It is based upon Hall's account of the skirmish at Ferrybridge, which occurred prior to the main battle at Towton and in which a small Yorkist force was wiped out by the Lancastrians under Clifford: 'The Lord Clifford determined with his light horsemen to make an assay to such as kept the passage of Ferrybridge, and so departed from the great army on the Saturday before Palm Sunday; and early, ere his enemies were ware, got the bridge and slew the keepers of the same and all such as would withstand him. The Lord Fitzwater, hearing the noise, suddenly rose out of his bed and, unarmed, with a poleaxe in his hand, thinking that it had been a fray amongst his men, came down to appease the same; but ere he either began his tale, or knew what the matter meant, he was slain, and with him the Bastard of Salisbury, brother to the Earl of Warwick, a valiant young gentleman and of great audacity. When the Earl of Warwick was informed of this feat, he, like a man desperate, mounted on his hackney and came blowing to King Edward, saying "Sir, I pray God have mercy of their souls which in the beginning of your enterprise hath lost their lives; and, because I see no succours of the world, I remit the vengeance and punishment to God our creator and redeemer"; and, with that, lighted down and slew his horse with his sword, saying "Let him fly that will, for surely I will tarry with him that will tarry with me", and kissed the cross of his sword.

'The lusty King Edward, perceiving the courage of his trusty friend the Earl of Warwick, made proclamation that all men which were afraid to fight should incontinent depart; and to all men that tarried the battle he promised great rewards, with this addition, that if any soldier, which voluntarily would abide and in or before the conflict fly or turn his back, that then he that could kill him should have a great remuneration and double wages' (page 255).

(stage direction) *Excursions* (military sorties)

1	*Forspent* exhausted
2	*breathe* take a rest
5	*spite of spite* whatever happens
	needs must I I must
6	*ungentle* ignoble
7	*sun.* The reference is to Edward's badge; see the second note to II.1.25.
8	*hap* fortune
9	*hap . . . hope.* The two words were pronounced sufficiently alike to make a quibble possible.
12	*Bootless* useless
15–19	*Thy brother's blood . . . my death.* Compare Genesis 4.10: 'The voice of thy brother's blood crieth unto me out of the ground.'
15	*Thy brother.* This is not Sir Thomas Nevil, who

was killed at the Battle of Wakefield, but the Bastard of
Salisbury (see the quotation from Hall in the headnote to this scene).

16   *Broached with* set flowing by
18   *dismal* (boding evil)
21   *fetlocks* hooves
       smoking steaming hot
23   *let the earth be drunken with our blood.* Compare the
Geneva version of Judith 6.4: 'their mountains shall
be drunken with their blood'.
24   *I'll kill my horse, because I will not fly.* See the quotation from Hall in the headnote to this scene.
25   *stand* delay
26   *Wailing* bemoaning
       whiles while
27   *look upon* act like a spectator (at a tragic play)
28   *counterfeiting* pretending, role-playing
32   *measure* full quantity
36   *I throw . . . my heart to Thee.* Compare Psalm 25.1.
37   *Thou setter-up and plucker-down of kings.* Compare
Daniel 2.21: 'he taketh away kings, he setteth up
kings'. Warwick is described in the same terms at
III.3.157 and V.1.26.
38   *stands* agrees, accords
40   *brazen* everlasting (because strongly built)
44   *gentle* noble
47   *winter* (as a symbol of death)
51   *stand to* support
52–3   *such rewards | As victors wear at the Olympian games.*
Contrast the more mercenary rewards that Edward
actually offered his troops after Ferrybridge in the
passage from Hall quoted in the headnote to this
scene.
54   *quailing* faltering
56   *Forslow* delay
       amain at full speed

II.4   The scene is located in a part of the battlefield at Towton (29 March 1461). It was suggested by Hall's account of Warwick's anger at the death of his illegitimate brother at Ferrybridge; see the headnote to II.3

         singled singled out

3   *bound* obliged by duty

4   *environed* surrounded

         brazen impenetrable

8   *triumphs* glories

9   *cheers* urges on

11   *have at thee* here I come fighting

12   *chase* animal to hunt, quarry

II.5   The scene is located at the Battle of Towton. It is not based on any event recorded in the chronicles; but it does utilize some comments made by Hall in connexion with this battle and follows his account of the Lancastrian flight from the field.

3   *What time* at the moment when

         blowing of his nails (to warm his hands)

5–10   *Now sways it ... another best.* This was obviously suggested by Hall: 'This deadly battle and bloody conflict continued ten hours in doubtful victory. The one part sometime flowing and sometime ebbing' (page 256).

6   *with* against

13   *equal poise* evenly balanced weights

         fell cruel

14   *Here on this molehill will I sit me down.* This action (and the verbal reminder) constitutes visual irony, as it would probably be the same stage molehill on which York was murdered in I.4.

16–18   *Margaret my Queen ... I am thence.* See the note to II.2.73–4.

17   *chid* brusquely commanded

22   *homely* simple
        swain shepherd
24   *dials* sundials
        quaintly with skill, elaborately
27   *brings about* brings the end of
33   *contemplate* pray
34   *sport* amuse, entertain
36   *poor fools* innocent creatures
        ean bear lambs
39   *the end* the purpose for which
40   *bring white hairs unto a quiet grave.* The phrase is
        from Genesis 42.38.
43   *silly* helpless, innocent
44   *canopy.* This could be a reference either to the cere-
        monial covering carried over a monarch in procession
        or to the canopy over a four-poster bed. In view of
        lines 49 and 53, the latter seems more likely.
47   *curds* milk-dish
48   *leather bottle* (used in rural districts)
49   *wonted* customary
50   *secure* free from worries
51   *delicates* delicacies
53   *curious* elaborately decorated
54   *waits on* attend
        (stage direction) *Enter a Son . . . his arms.* The idea for
        this representation at the personal level of the nature
        of civil war comes from Hall: 'This conflict was in
        manner unnatural, for in it the son fought against the
        father, the brother against the brother, the nephew
        against the uncle, and the tenant against his lord,
        which slaughter did not only sore debilitate and much
        weaken the puissance of this realm, considering
        that these dead men when they were living had force
        enough to resist the greatest prince's power of all
        Europe' (page 256). The actual form of the device
        may have been influenced by Norton and Sackville's
        Gorboduc (1562), V.2.212–14: 'One kinsman shall

bereave another's life, | The father shall unwitting slay the son, | The son shall slay the sire and know it not.'

55   *Ill blows the wind that profits nobody* (proverbial: 'It is an ill wind that blows no man good')

57   *possessèd with* in possession of
       store of crowns quantity of gold coins

58   *haply* by chance

63   *heavy* sorrowful

64, 66   *pressed* forcibly enlisted in the army

65   *man* servant

66   *part of York* Yorkist side

68   *bereavèd* deprived

69   *Pardon me, God, I knew not what I did.* This is an echo of Christ's words on the Cross (Luke 23.34).

70   *knew* recognized

75   *abide* endure

78   *blind* blinded
       o'ercharged overloaded
       (stage direction) *Enter a Father . . . in his arms.* See the note to the stage direction at line 54.

79   *stoutly* valiantly

81   *bought* procured

85-6   *what showers arise, | Blown with the windy tempest of my heart* (proverbial: 'After wind comes rain')

89   *stratagems* deeds of violence
       fell cruel

90   *Erroneous* criminal

91   *beget* produce

93   *bereft* deprived
       late recently

94   *above* piled on

95   *stay* put a stop to
       ruthful pitiable

98   *fatal* doom-laden

99   *one* (the red rose of Lancaster)
       purple red

100   *other* (the white rose of York)
          presenteth symbolizes

102   *If you contend, a thousand lives must wither.* Compare
          Part One, II.4.124–7:

>   this brawl today,
> Grown to this faction in the Temple garden,
> Shall send between the red rose and the white
> A thousand souls to death and deadly night.

          contend make war

104   *Take on with me* scream at me
104, 106,

108   *satisfied* comforted
107   *chances* events
108   *Misthink* think ill of
114–15   *These arms of mine shall be thy winding-sheet;* | *My*
          heart, sweet boy, shall be thy sepulchre. Compare
          Marlowe's *The Jew of Malta*, III.2.11: 'These arms
          of mine shall be thy sepulchre.'
114   *winding-sheet* burial clothes
118   *obsequious* punctilious in performing mourning rites
120   *Priam* (the King of Troy, father of fifty sons, who
          according to Homer mourned only his eldest son,
          Hector)
123   *overgone* worn out
126   *chafèd* enraged
128–33   *Mount you ... hence amain.* This is based on Hall:
          'After this great victory, King Edward ... sent out
          men on light horses to espy in what part King Henry
          lurked, which, hearing of the irrecuperable loss of his
          friends, departed incontinent with his wife and son to
          the town of Berwick' (page 256).
128   *post amain* ride immediately at full speed
129   *brace* pair
131   *for very wrath* in total anger
132   *steel* swords
134–6   *Away! For vengeance ... away before.* Compare Hall:

'The Dukes of Somerset and Exeter fled from the field and saved themselves' (page 256).

135   *expostulate* talk about it

139   *Whither the Queen intends* wherever the Queen is planning to go

II.6   The scene is located on the battlefield at Towton. It is built up from details given in the chronicles of the events following the battle: the end of the skirmish at Ferrybridge, Edward's march to York, the parliament of 1461, and Warwick's visit to France in 1464.

(stage direction) *Enter Clifford, wounded.* Historically Clifford's death occurred during the second skirmish at Ferrybridge rather than during the main battle at Towton: 'Lord Falconbridge, Sir Walter Blount, Robert Horne, with the forward, passed the river at Castleford, three miles from Ferrybridge, intending to have environed and enclosed the Lord Clifford and his company; but they, being thereof advertised, departed in great haste toward King Henry's army, but they met with some that they looked not for and were attrapped ere they were ware. For the Lord Clifford, either for heat or pain putting off his gorget, suddenly with an arrow (as some say) without an head was stricken into the throat and incontinent rendered his spirit. ... this end had he which slew the young Earl of Rutland, kneeling on his knees' (Hall, page 255). The stage direction in Q1 is closer to Hall and may record how the scene was acted in the Elizabethan theatre: 'Enter *Clifford* wounded, with an arrow in his necke.'

1   *Here burns my candle out; ay, here it dies* (proverbial: 'His candle burns within the socket')

3   *Lancaster* (the house of Lancaster)

5   *My love and fear* the affection for me and my formidable qualities

	glued attached
6	*now* now that
	commixture compound
7	*Impairing* weakening
	misproud falsely proud
8	*The common people swarm like summer flies.* This line from Q1 seems necessary as both lines 9 and 17 appear to demand an earlier statement of the idea.
9	*the sun* (another allusion to Edward's badge)
11–13	*O Phoebus, hadst thou ... the earth.* See the note to I.4.33.
12	*check* drive, control
14	*swayed* ruled
15	*thy father and his father* (Henry V and Henry IV)
17	*sprung* multiplied
19	*mourning widows* widows mourning
20	*kept thy chair* retained your throne
21	*cherish* nourish, cause to grow
22	*lenity* lenience
23	*plaints* lamentations
	cureless incurable
24	*hold out* sustain
27	*The air hath got into my deadly wounds* (proverbial: 'Fresh air is ill for the diseased or wounded man')
28	*much effuse* great effusion
	faint weak
30	(stage direction) *retreat* (drum and trumpet signal to retire)
31	*breathe we* let us rest
33	*bloody-minded* bloodthirsty
34	*led* dominated
35	*fretting gust.* The pun is on (1) an intermittently gusty wind; (2) a woman's nagging.
36	*Command* force
	argosy (large merchant ship)
	stem cut through with its prow
39	*his* (Richard's)

40   *marked* (1) destined; (2) stabbed

42   *heavy* sorrowful

43   *departing* separation

45   *If* whether

       gently used treated with honour

46   *doom* judgement, decision

48   *when his leaves put forth* (in his early youth)

50   *spray* shoot, sprouting twig

52–3   *From off the gates . . . there.* See I.4.179–80, and compare Hall, who makes no mention of Clifford: 'After this great victory, King Edward rode to York, where he was with all solemnity received; and first he caused the heads of his father, the Earl of Salisbury, and other his friends to be taken from the gates and to be buried with their bodies. And there he caused the Earl of Devonshire and three other to be beheaded, and set their heads in the same place' (page 256).

54   *this* (Clifford's head)

       supply the room take the place

55   *Measure for measure must be answerèd* (proverbial and based upon Mark 4.24: 'With what measure ye mete, with the same shall it be measured to you again')

       answerèd given in return

56   *fatal screech-owl to our house* bird of ill omen whose cry prophesied the coming of death to our family

58   *dismal* sinister

59   *ill-boding* (prophesying evil)

60   *is bereft* has been taken from him

63   *nor . . . nor* neither . . . nor

65   *policy* cunning strategy

       counterfeit pretend (to be dead)

68   *vex* torment

       eager sharp, biting

70   *bootless* fruitless

71, 72   *faults* crimes

75   *Captain Margaret.* Compare Hall: 'take upon her the name of captain' (page 298).

76   *fence* protect

       wont accustomed to

80   *If this right hand would buy two hours' life* if only the loss of my right hand could purchase two more hours of life for Clifford

81   *despite* contempt

82   *This hand* (his left hand)

83   *unstanchèd* unquenchable

86   *rear* raise

89–93   *From whence shall Warwick . . . rise again.* Warwick's visit to France to arrange a marriage for Edward took place in 1464, three years after Towton: 'Sure it is that the same year [Warwick] came to King Louis XI, then being French king, lying at Tours, and with great honour was there received and honourably entertained; of whom, for King Edward his master, he demanded to have in marriage the Lady Bona, daughter to Louis Duke of Savoy, and sister to the Lady Charlotte, then French queen, being then in the French court . . . trusting that by this marriage, Queen Margaret . . . should have no aid, succour, nor any comfort of the French King nor of none of his friends nor allies' (Hall, page 263).

90   *Lady Bona.* Daughter of Louis, first Duke of Savoy, and sister of Charlotte, wife of Louis XI, she ultimately married the Duke of Milan in 1468 and died in 1485.

91   *sinew* join, knit

92   *France* (the King of France)

93   *scattered* defeated, cast down

95   *look to have them* be prepared for them to

       buzz spread false reports

100   *in* on

       seat throne

103–4   *Richard, I will . . . Clarence.* After his coronation on 29 June 1461 and at his first parliament, Edward created 'his two younger brethren dukes, that is to say: Lord George, Duke of Clarence; Lord Richard, Duke of Gloucester' (Hall, page 258).

104–5   *as ourself,* | *Shall do and undo as him pleaseth best* shall have power to act with the same freedom as the King. Warwick in effect ruled England during the early years of Edward's reign.

107   *Gloucester's dukedom is too ominous.* This is a reference to Hall's comments on the title when he reports the murder of Humphrey Duke of Gloucester: 'It seemeth to many men that the name and title of Gloucester hath been unfortunate and unlucky to divers which for their honour have been erected by creation of princes to that style and dignity, as Hugh Spencer, Thomas of Woodstock, son to King Edward III, and this Duke Humphrey, which three persons by miserable death finished their days; and after them King Richard III, also Duke of Gloucester, in civil war was slain and confounded; so that this name of Gloucester is taken for an unhappy and unfortunate style' (pages 209–10).

110   *in possession* awarded

III.1   The location is some open hunting land in the north of England. Historically, after Towton, Henry went from Berwick into Scotland, while Margaret and Prince Edward went to France. After the Battle of Hexham (1464), Hall records that 'when King Henry was somewhat settled in the realm of Scotland, he sent his wife and his son into France to King Reignier, her father, trusting by his aid and succour to assemble a great army and once again to possess his realm and dignity; and he in the mean season determined to make his abode in Scotland to see and espy what way his friends in England would study or invent for his restitution and advancement. . . . But whatsoever

jeopardy or peril might be construed or deemed to
have ensued by the means of King Henry, all such
doubts were now shortly resolved and determined
and all fear of his doings were clearly put under and
extinct. For he himself, whether he were past all
fear or was not well stablished in his perfect mind or
could not long keep himself secret, in a disguised
apparel boldly entered into England. He was no
sooner entered but he was known and taken of one
Cantlow and brought toward the King, whom the
Earl of Warwick met on the way, by the King's
commandment, and brought him through London to
the Tower, and there he was laid in sure hold' (pages
257, 261).

(stage direction) *Keepers* gamekeepers. In F the
names of the two actors who originally played these
roles, '*Sinklo*' and '*Humfrey*', are used in this
entry and as speech prefixes throughout the scene.
John Sincklo appeared in other Shakespeare plays,
and Humphrey Jeffes is known to have been a member
of the Earl of Pembroke's Company in 1597.

cross-bows (a weapon which fired a bolt from a small
bow mounted on a rifle-like stock)

1   *Under this thick-grown brake.* The actual locale may
have been suggested by Robert Fabyan's 'this
year was King Henry taken in a wood in the north
country' (*The New Chronicles of England and France*
(1516), page 654 (1811 reprint)).

    brake thicket

    shroud hide

2   *laund* glade

    anon soon

3   *stand* blind, cover (from which to shoot)

4   *Culling* selecting

6   *noise.* The cross-bow discharged far more noisily than
the hand bow.

7   *shoot* shot

7	*lost* prevented
8	*at the best* as well as we can
9	*for* so that
11	*self* exact
12	*stay* wait
	(stage direction) *disguised*. See the quotation in the headnote to this scene.
13	*even of* precisely because of
14	*wishful* longing
17	*anointed* (at his coronation)
18	*Caesar* (the prototype emperor)
19	*press* push towards you (the allusion being to the conspirators)
	speak for right ask for justice
20	*of* from
22	*fee*. The horns and skin of a hunted deer were awarded to the gamekeeper.
23	*quondam* former
24–5	*Let me embrace thee, sour adversity,* | *For wise men say it is the wisest course* (proverbial: 'Adversity makes men wise')
24	*embrace* welcome
27	*Forbear* hold back
29–31	*the great commanding ... for Edward.* See the note to II.6.89–93.
31	*To* as a
33	*Warwick is a subtle orator.* Warwick's oratorical powers are not stressed either in the play or in the chronicles; but *A Mirror for Magistrates* speaks of his 'crafty-filed tongue'.
37	*battery in* assault upon
38	*Her tears will pierce into a marble heart* (proverbial: 'Constant dropping will wear the stone')
40	*Nero* (Roman emperor who was a common representative of extreme cruelty)
	tainted with remorse touched with pity (which would be contrary to his nature)

41	*plaints* lamentations
	brinish (filled with salt)
47	*That* the result being that
	for on account of her
48	*tells his title* demonstrates Edward's right to the throne
	smooths glosses over
49	*Inferreth* adduces
51	*what else* other things also
52	*place* position as king
55	*what* who
63	*decked* ornamented
	Indian stones gems
64-5	*my crown is called content;	A crown it is that seldom kings enjoy* (proverbial: 'A mind content is a crown')
71	*apprehend* arrest
75	*country* region, area
76	*anointed king at nine months old.* See the note to I.1.112.
80	*but* only
82	*simple* foolish
85	*with* in accordance to the dictates of
	wind breath
87	*Commanded . . . by* in the control of
88	*lightness* fickleness

III.2   The location of the scene is the royal palace in London. Hall gives two accounts of Edward's courtship of Lady Grey. The first (page 264) claims that the meeting took place accidentally while Edward was hunting, and some of the details and wording of the passage were clearly in Shakespeare's mind when he was writing the scene. But it was obviously the second account (pages 365-6) that formed the main source for the scene: 'Now happeneth it in the mean season there came to make a suit to the King by petition Dame Elizabeth Grey

(which after was his queen), then a widow, born of
noble blood, specially by her mother, which was
Duchess of Bedford. . . . this poor lady made suit to
the King to be restored to such small lands as her
husband had given her in jointure; whom when the
King beheld and heard her speak, as she was both
fair and of good favour, moderate of stature, well
made and very wise, he not alonely pitied her but
also waxed enamoured on her, and, taking her
secretly aside, began to enter into talking more
familiarly, whose appetite, when she perceived, she
virtuously denied him; but that she did so wisely,
and that with so good manner and words so well
set, that she rather kindled his desire than quenched
it. And finally, after many a meeting and much wooing
and many great promises, she well espied the King
his affection toward her so greatly increased that she
durst somewhat the more boldly say her mind, as to
him whose heart she perceived more fervently set
than to fall off for a word. And in conclusion she
showed him plain that as she wist herself too simple
to be his wife, so thought she herself too good to be
his concubine. The King, much marvelling of her
constancy, as he that had not been wont elsewhere
so stiffly said nay, so much esteemed her continency
and chastity that he set her virtue instead of possession
and riches; and thus taking counsel of his own desire
determined in haste to marry her.'

(stage direction) *Lady Grey*. Lady Elizabeth Grey
(1431–92) was the daughter of Sir Richard Woodville,
Earl Rivers, and the wife of Sir John Grey, the son of
Lord Ferrers. After her husband's death at the second
Battle of Saint Albans, she secretly married Edward
IV in 1464 and was crowned queen at Westminster in
1465.

2 *Sir Richard Grey*. This was actually Sir John Grey
(1432–61), the eighth Lord Ferrers of Groby and the

older son of Edward Grey. He is mentioned by Hall as having been knighted by Henry VI on the same day as he died at Saint Albans.

3-7   *His lands then seized ... his life.* Shakespeare either misunderstood Hall or deliberately changed his source; for it is clear that Grey fought and died for the Lancastrian rather than the Yorkist cause.

4   *repossess* regain possession of

5, 9   *deny* refuse

12   *hath a thing to grant* will be obliged to grant sexual favours to Edward

14   *He knows the game.* Compare Hall's description of Edward: 'He was in youth greatly given to fleshly wantonness' (page 345).
        game (1) quarry; (2) procedures for seduction
        keeps the wind keeps downwind (like a hunting dog tracking its quarry)

18   *brook* endure

19   *resolve me* give me an answer

20   *pleasure* wish

21   *warrant* guarantee. Richard quibbles on *pleasure* (sexual desire) and *satisfy* (give sexual satisfaction to).

22   *An if* if
        pleasure you give you pleasure (in the sexual sense)

23   *Fight closer ... catch a blow* (1) move nearer your opponent or he will be able to stab you (fencing terms); (2) leave no opening in your defence or Edward will assault you sexually

24   *fear her not* am not worried about her
        fall (1) slip (and thus be at her opponent's mercy); (2) lie down for the sexual act

25   *take vantages* seize his opportunity (1) to win the fencing bout; (2) to seduce her

27   *beg a child of her* (1) ask for the legal custody of her child; (2) ask her to conceive a child by him

28   *whip me* (an oath: 'treat me as a criminal')

30   *have four* have a fourth child (by Edward)

30   *be ruled by him* (1) be his subject; (2) submit to him
      sexually

32   *pitiful* compassionate. Compare Hall's first account
      (page 264): 'requiring him of pity'.

33   *give us leave* allow us to speak alone (by moving out of
      earshot)
      try test
      wit intelligence

34   *good leave have you* we are glad to leave you together
      you will have leave (1) you will talk alone; (2) you will
      take sexual liberties

35   *youth take leave* your youth passes
      leave you to the crutch (1) leave you in old age (walking
      with a crutch); (2) leave you to your concern with her
      loins

38, 40   *do them good* cause them to prosper

41   *Therefore* for that reason

43   *bind me to your highness' service* (1) oblige me to act as
      your dutiful subject; (2) cause me to satisfy your
      sexual demands

44   *service* (1) duty; (2) sexual act

45   *rests in me* lies in my power

46   *take exceptions to* object to
      my boon the favour I am about to ask

47   *except* unless

48   *do* (1) perform; (2) copulate

50   *plies* presses, urges
      much rain wears the marble. See the note to III.1.38.

51   *As red as fire! Nay, then her wax must melt* (proverbial;
      compare Hall's earlier account (page 264): 'where
      he was a little before heated with the dart of Cupido,
      he was now set all on a hot burning fire')

57   *seals* ratifies

58   *stay thee* do not go
      fruits of love sexual favours

59   *fruits of love* feelings of a loyal subject

64   *troth* faith

66 *perceive my mind* (1) grasp my meaning; (2) see my desire

67-8 *what I perceive | Your highness aims at* (1) what I see you are asking for; (2) the sexual act I realize you have in view

68 *aim aright* guess correctly

69 *plain* honestly
  lie with go to bed with (with a quibble on 'dishonestly')

70 *plain . . . lie.* Lady Grey continues the quibble on the meanings of these words in line 69.

72-3 *mine honesty . . . purchase them.* This seems to be based on Hall's first account (page 264): 'so for her own poor honesty she was too good to be either his concubine or sovereign lady.'

72 *honesty* chastity

73 *that loss* loss of that
  purchase buy (what actually are mine by right)

76 *merry inclination* disposition to joke with me

77 *sadness* serious nature

83 *bluntest* crudest, most outspoken

84-8 *Her looks doth argue . . . else my queen.* These lines seem to derive from Hall's first account (page 264): 'for she was a woman more of formal countenance than of excellent beauty, but yet of such beauty and favour that with her sober demeanour, lovely looking, and feminine smiling (neither too wanton nor too humble) beside her tongue so eloquent and her wit so pregnant'.

84 *replete with* full of

85 *wit* quickness of mind

86 *challenge* lay claim to

88 *love* mistress

90 *'Tis better said than done* (proverbial: 'Easier said than done')

91 *subject* (1) topic; (2) citizen of your realm
  withal with

93   *state* royal position, kingship

97-8   *I know I am ... concubine.* Compare Hall's earlier
        account (page 264): 'as she was for his honour far
        unable to be his spouse and bedfellow, so ... she was
        too good to be ... his concubine'.

97   *too mean* of too low a social rank

99   *cavil* raise pointless objections

100   *my sons.* By Sir John Grey, Elizabeth had two sons:
        Thomas, later Marquess of Dorset (d. 1501); and
        Sir Richard (d. 1483).

102-5   *Thou art a widow ... many sons.* In Hall, Edward
        replies to his mother's criticism of his marrying a
        commoner: 'she is a widow and hath already children.
        By God his Blessed Lady, I am a bachelor and have
        some too; and so each of us hath a proof that neither
        of us is like to be barren. And therefore, madam, I
        pray you be content; I trust to God she shall bring
        forth a young prince' (page 367).

104   *other some* some others
        happy fortunate

107-8   *The ghostly father ... for shift.* This exchange is
        based on the bawdy jest 'to shrive a woman to her
        shift'; compare *Part One*, I.2.119.

107   *ghostly father* priest, spiritual man (with a quibble on
        Edward's *father* in line 105)
        done his shrift (1) heard confession and given absolu-
        tion; (2) performed the rites of seduction

108   *shriver* (1) father confessor; (2) lover
        for shift (1) as a trick; (2) for a woman's chemise

109   *muse* wonder

110   *sad* downcast

112   *To who.* George believes that Edward will marry
        Elizabeth to one of his subjects and keep her as a mis-
        tress.

113   *That would be ten days' wonder at the least.* Richard
        modifies the proverb 'A wonder lasts but nine days'
        in order to express his surprise at the proposal.

115   *in extremes* of the largest kind

116–17   *jest on, brothers . . . lands.* In Hall, Edward 'asked . . . counsel of his secret friends, and that in such manner that they might easily perceive it booted not to say nay' (page 366).

118–20   *My gracious lord . . . unto the Tower.* See the head-note to III.1.

122   *of his apprehension* about his arrest

125   *wasted* stricken with disease. Richard clearly refers to syphilis, which was believed to attack the bones.

127   *cross me from* stand between me and
       golden time kingship

129   *burièd* suppressed, eliminated

131   *unlooked-for* (1) unanticipated; (2) undesirable
       issue children

132   *take their rooms* assume their positions in line to the throne
       place. Richard quibbles on the meaning of *room.*

133   *cold premeditation* comfortless forecast

137   *were equal with his eye* was on the place his eye can see

138   *sunders* separates

139   *lade* drain (by bailing)

141   *means* obstacles

142   *cut the causes off* murder the people (who stand between me and the throne)

143   *Flattering me with* deceiving myself with what I know to be

144   *quick* alive to possibilities, impatient
       o'erweens is overpresumptuous

148   *make my heaven in a lady's lap* find my greatest delight in lovemaking

149   *deck* adorn

150   *'witch* entice, bewitch

152   *accomplish* get possession of

153   *forswore* rejected
       in while I was still in

154   *for* in order that

157   *make an envious mountain* maliciously place a hump

161   *chaos* piece of shapeless matter

       unlicked bear-whelp. It was believed that bear cubs were born without form and licked into proper shape by their mother; hence the proverbial saying 'to lick into shape'.

162   *carries no impression like the dam* does not resemble in appearance the shape of the mother

164   *monstrous fault* unnatural error

166   *check* rebuke

       o'erbear dominate

167   *better person* more handsome physical appearance

171   *impalèd* encircled

173   *many lives* (specifically at this time: Edward, George (Clarence), Henry, Prince Edward)

       home my goal

175   *rents* tears

176   *way* path

178   *find it out* discover it

182   *I can smile, and murder whiles I smile* (proverbial: 'To smile in one's face and cut one's throat')

184   *artificial* hypocritical

185   *frame my face to* assume an expression appropriate for

186–93 *I'll drown more ... to school.* Richard selects outstanding representatives of the qualities he sees in himself which are necessary to get the crown: deception (the mermaid), effortless murder (the basilisk), persuasion (Nestor), cunning (Ulysses), treachery (Sinon), a mercurial nature (the chameleon), changeability (Proteus), ruthless political manoeuvring (Machiavelli).

186   *the mermaid*. It was believed that sirens lured sailors on to the rocks with their singing.

187   *the basilisk* (a mythological serpent which could kill with a look; compare the proverb 'The basilisk's eye is fatal')

188   *Nestor* (King of Pylos, the oldest and wisest of the Greek leaders at the siege of Troy)

189   *Ulysses* (King of Ithaca, hero of Homer's *Odyssey*, famous for his cunning)

190   *Sinon* (son of Sisyphus, he was the Greek in Virgil's *Aeneid* who persuaded the Trojans to admit the wooden horse into the city)

191   *the chameleon* (a type of lizard, proverbial for being able to change colour in order to merge with whatever background it found itself against)

192   *Proteus* (the shepherd of the flock of Poseidon, proverbial for his ability to transform himself into anything he wished)
    for advantages to serve my purpose

193   *Machiavel* (Niccolò Machiavelli (1469–1527), the Florentine political philosopher and author of *The Prince* (1513). On the Elizabethan stage he was the type of ruthless, atheistic power-seeker for political or personal ends.)

III.3   The location of the scene is the French royal palace. Historically Warwick made two visits to France, the first in 1464 to ask for Lady Bona's hand for Edward, the second in 1470 when he fled with Clarence after an abortive uprising against Edward. Shakespeare uses materials for this scene from Hall's accounts of both visits, to which he adds descriptions of characters from other parts of the chronicles.

(stage direction) *Lewis*. Louis XI (1423–83) was the son of Charles VII and Marie of Anjou. In 1436 he married Margaret, daughter of James I of Scotland.

Bourbon. Louis Count of Roussillon was the bastard son of Charles Duke of Bourbon and the husband of the illegitimate daughter of Louis XI.

Earl of Oxford. This was John de Vere (1443–1513), the thirteenth Earl. In 1464 he obtained a reversal of

227

his father's attainder; but he was arrested in 1468 and imprisoned in the Tower on the suspicion of conspiring with the Lancastrians. He was released the following year and fled to France, returning to England with Warwick's forces in 1470. According to Hall, on Margaret's visit to the French court in 1470 he 'came by fortune to this assembly' (page 281).

1–41   *Fair Queen of England ... succour thee.* Shakespeare here conflates two passages from the chronicles: (1) Margaret's visit to her father with the purpose of raising an army, after the defeat at Towton in 1464; (2) her travelling from her father's court to visit the French King in 1470, 'hoping of new comfort', when she had 'heard tell that the Earl of Warwick and the Duke of Clarence had abandoned England and were come to the French court' (Hall, page 281).

2   *state* rank (as Queen)

5   *strike her sail* humble herself (literally 'lower her ship's sail as a mark of deference to a mightier vessel')

7   *Albion* England

8   *mischance* misfortune

10   *like seat unto* a position in keeping with

16   *sit thee* be seated

19   *grief* grievances

20   *France* (the King of France)

25   *of* from being

26   *in Scotland.* Margaret has not been informed of the events of III.1.

    forlorn outcast

34   *Scotland hath will to help.* Compare Hall, who claims that Henry was shown great humanity by the King of Scotland, 'in whom only now consisted the whole hope and especial trust of his aid and succour' (page 256).

37   *heavy* sorrowful

39   *While we bethink* until I devise

break it off bring it to an end

40   *stay* delay

41   *stay* (1) delay; (2) support

42   *waiteth on* attends

43   *breeder* producer

43–108   *Enter Warwick . . . house of York.* There is no warrant in the chronicles for this confrontation between Warwick and Margaret.

44   *What's he* who is he that

48   *this is he that moves both wind and tide.* This was probably suggested by Hall, who says of Warwick: 'the common people . . . judged him able to do all things . . . which way he bowed, that way ran the stream' (page 232).

56   *sister* (sister-in-law; see the note to II.6.90)

58   *go forward* take place

60   *leave and favour* kind permission

62   *passion* passionate longing

63   *fame* report

     late recently

     heedful attentive, receptive

69, 71   *tyrant.* Edward is viewed as a usurper by Margaret.

70   *purchase* obtain

75   *draw not on thy* draw not down upon you

76   *sway the rule* control the country

77   *time suppresseth wrongs* (proverbial: 'Time cures every disease')

78   *Injurious* offensive, insulting

81   *disannuls* renders null and void

82   *Which* who

     did subdue the greatest part of Spain. This was one of the feats generally attributed to John of Gaunt and was the subject of some popular literature of the time.

84   *mirror to* model to be followed by

88   *haps it* does it happen that

89–90   *Henry the Sixth hath lost | All that which Henry the*

Fifth had gotten. This was Warwick's earliest complaint against Henry VI's reign; see *Part Two*, I.1.114-21.

92   *tell* (1) narrate; (2) number

93   *threescore and two years* (the sixty-two years from the accession of Henry IV in 1399 to the establishment of Edward IV's claim in 1461)
silly trifling

94   *make prescription for a kingdom's worth* base a legal claim to the value of a whole realm

96   *thirty and six years.* Oxford exaggerates the extent of Warwick's loyalty to Henry. He was born in 1428, which makes him thirty-six at the time of the events dramatized in this scene. Historically he espoused the Yorkist cause in 1459.

97   *bewray* disclose

98   *fence* protect

99   *buckler* shield

101   *injurious doom* unjust sentence

102-3   *Lord Aubrey Vere ... my father.* John, the twelfth Earl of Oxford, and his son Aubrey were staunch Lancastrians. On the charge that they had arranged a Lancastrian invasion on the east coast they were attainted by Edward IV, imprisoned in the Tower, and executed in 1462.

104   *in the downfall of his mellowed years* towards the very end of his mature life. Compare Hall: 'the Earl of Oxford, far stricken in age' (page 258).

105   *the door of death* (proverbial: 'To be at death's door')

111   *use further conference* have more conversation
(stage direction) *aloof* to one side

112   *Warwick's words bewitch him not.* Compare Henry's similar fear at III.1.33-4.

116   *pawn my credit* stake my reputation

117   *is he gracious in the people's eye.* Hall makes a great point of Edward's popular acclaim: 'Lord Falconbridge ... asked them if they would serve, love,

and obey the Earl of March as their earthly prince
and sovereign lord; to which question they answered
"Yea, yea!", crying "King Edward!", with many
great shouts and clapping of hands' (pages 253–4).
gracious favoured

119–37   *Then further, all ... shall be counterpoised.* Compare
Hall: 'This marriage seemeth politically devised
and of an high imagination to be invented, if you
will well consider the state and condition of King
Edward's affairs, which at this time had King Henry
VI in safe custody ... and the most part of his
adherents ... either profligated or extinct' (page 263).

119   *all dissembling set aside* without any pretence

120   *for truth* truly
       measure extent

122   *beseem* be fitting for

124   *eternal* heavenly, divine

126   *maintained* nourished

127   *envy* malice
       disdain vexation

128   *quit his pain* satisfy his passion

129   *resolve* decision

132   *desert* merits

133   *Mine ear hath tempted judgement to desire* what I have
heard has led me to think longingly

135   *articles* terms of agreement

136   *Touching* regarding
       the jointure (the amount settled on the bride by the
groom)

137   *counterpoised* equally balanced

141   *device* stratagem

146   *good success* successful outcome

150   *estate* condition, rank

151   *at his ease* free from trouble

153   *quondam* former

155   *France* (the King of France)

157   *Proud setter-up and puller-down of kings.* See the

note to II.3.37. In his discussion of Warwick's agreement with Margaret in 1470, Hall notes about Warwick's power: 'each of them looking to be exalted when the Earl on him smiled; and each of them again thinking to be overthrown when the Earl of him lowered' (page 281).

160   *conveyance* trickery

161   *birds of self-same feather* (proverbial: 'Birds of a feather flock together')

          (stage direction) *Post* express messenger

163–4   *My lord ambassador . . . Marquess Montague.* Compare Hall: 'when the Earl of Warwick had perfect knowledge, by the letters of his trusty friends, that King Edward had gotten him a new wife, and that all that he had done with King Louis in his ambassade for the conjoining of this new affinity was both frustrate and vain, he was earnestly moved and sore chafed with the chance' (page 265).

169   *as* as if

172   *unhoped* unexpected

175   *soothe your forgery* gloss over your deceit

176   *persuade me* recommend to me

180   *proveth* demonstrates the extent of

181–5   *King Lewis, I here . . . see his shame.* Compare Hall: 'All men for the most part agree that this marriage was the only cause why the Earl of Warwick bare grudge and made war on King Edward; other affirm that there were other causes.' However, in the chronicles, although Warwick was 'thus moved, inflamed, and set against the King', he sailed to England 'and with reverence saluted the King, as he was wont to do, and declared his ambassade and the exploit of the same, without any spot of grudge to be perceived, as though he were ignorant of the new matrimony' (pages 265–6).

183   *clear from* not guilty of

184–5   *No more . . . shame.* Compare Hall: 'the Earl of

Warwick ... thought it necessary that King Edward should be deposed from his crown and royal dignity as an inconstant prince, not worthy of such a kingly office' (page 265).

186   *by* owing to

187   *My father* (Richard Nevil, first Earl of Salisbury, who was captured with the Duke of York at the Battle of Wakefield (1460) and later beheaded at Pomfret, his head being displayed on the walls of York)
        untimely before the proper time

188–92   *Did I let pass ... is honour.* Compare Hall, who comments on Edward's treatment of Warwick: 'By this a man may see that often it chanceth that friends for one good turn will not render another, nor yet remember a great gratuity and benefit in time of necessity to them showed and exhibited; but for kindness they show unkindness, and for great benefits received with great displeasure they do recompense' (page 265).

188   *let pass* overlook
        th' abuse done to my niece. This is based on one of Hall's reasons for Warwick's enmity: 'it erreth not from the truth that King Edward did attempt a thing once in the Earl's house which was much against the Earl's honesty (whether he would have deflowered his daughter or his niece the certainty was not for both their honours openly known), for surely such a thing was attempted by King Edward, which loved well both to look and to feel fair damsels' (page 265).
        abuse injury, wrong

189   *impale him* encircle his head

190   *native right* right to the throne by reason of his birth

191   *guerdoned* rewarded

192   *my desert* what I deserve

193–8   *to repair ... his former state.* During Warwick's second visit to France 'the Duke and the Earls took a solemn oath that they should never leave the war

233

until such time as King Henry VI or the Prince, his son, were restored to the full possession and diadem of the realm' (Hall, page 281).

193   *repair* restore

194   *I here renounce him and return to Henry.* Hall claims that Edward's marriage in 1464 was the cause of Warwick's animosity; but the Earl actually joined the Lancastrian cause six years later.

196   *true servitor* loyal servant

198   *state* royal position

200   *I forgive and quite forget old faults* (proverbial)
      faults offences

206   *tyrant* usurper
      seat throne

208–9   *as for Clarence ... from him.* According to Hall, Clarence made an alliance with Warwick soon after Edward's marriage: 'The Earl of Warwick, being a man of a great wit, far casting, and many things vigilantly foreseeing, either perceived by other or had perfect knowledge of himself that the Duke of Clarence bore not the best will to King Edward, his brother' (page 271).

209   *fall from* desert

210   *matching* marrying
      for wanton because of unbridled

212–28   *Dear brother, how shall ... for his sake.* Compare Hall: 'The French King and his Queen were not a little discontent (as I cannot blame them) to have their sister first demanded and then granted, and in conclusion rejected and apparently mocked without any cause reasonable' (page 265).

222   *in post* at a great speed

224   *masquers* (performers, usually amateurs, who took part in a masque or allegorical show, often performed to celebrate a wedding)

226   *fear* terrify

228   *I'll wear the willow garland for his sake* (proverbial,

describing the traditional symbol of the deserted
sweetheart)

229 *weeds* clothes

233 *reward* (payment traditionally given to royal messengers)

233–7 *But, Warwick ... a fresh supply.* In Hall, after
Warwick received offers of help for his intended
invasion from his friends in England, he 'fully
determined, with the Duke and the Earls of Oxford
and Pembroke (because Queen Margaret and her son
were not fully yet furnished for such a journey),
to go before with part of the navy and part of the
army, and to attempt the first brunt of fortune
and chance, which if it well succeeded, then should
Queen Margaret and her son with the residue of
the navy and people follow into England' (page 282).

236 *serves* proves opportune

237 *supply* reinforcement (of troops)

240–50 *This shall assure ... hand.* Compare Hall: 'And
first to begin withal, for the more sure foundation
of the new amity, Edward Prince of Wales wedded
Anne, second daughter to the Earl of Warwick,
which lady came with her mother into France'
(page 281). See the notes to IV.1.118.

244 *motion* proposal

251 *stay* delay

251–4 *These soldiers shall ... war's mischance.* Compare Hall:
'When the league was concluded ... the French
King lent them ships, money, and men; and that
they might the surer sail into England, he appointed
the Bastard of Burgoyn, Admiral of France, with
a great navy' (page 281).

253 *waft* transport by sea

254 *long till* am impatient for the time when

255 *For mocking marriage with a dame of France.* See the
quotation from Hall in the note to lines 212–28.
mocking (1) pretending to want; (2) scornfully treating

258   *Matter* the business
       charge commission
259   *demand* request
260   *stale* laughing-stock
262, 263 *chief* main person

IV.1   The scene is located in the royal palace in London.
        The material is based on a conversation between
        Clarence and Warwick shortly after the latter's
        return from his French embassy in 1464, when he
        decided to proceed secretly against Edward in
        revenge for the wrong he had received during the
        marriage negotiations: 'The Earl of Warwick ...
        thinking that if he might by policy or promise allure
        the Duke to his party that King Edward should be
        destitute of one of his best hawks when he had most
        need to make a flight. So at time and place convenient
        the Earl began to complain to the Duke of the in-
        gratitude and doubleness of King Edward, saying
        that he had neither handled him like a friend nor
        kept promise with him according as the estate of a
        prince required. The Earl had not half told his tale
        but the Duke, in a great fury, answered: "Why, my
        lord, think you to have him kind to you that is unkind,
        yea, and unnatural to me, being his own brother?
        Think you that friendship will make him keep promise
        where neither nature nor kindred in any wise can
        provoke or move him to favour his own blood?
        Think you that he will exalt and promote his cousin
        or ally which little careth for the fall or confusion of
        his own line and lineage? This you know well enough:
        that the heir of the Lord Scales he hath married to
        his wife's brother, the heir also of the Lord Bonville
        and Harington he hath given to his wife's son, and
        the heir of the Lord Hungerford he hath granted
        to the Lord Hastings – three marriages more meeter

for his two brethren and kin than for such new found-
lings as he hath bestowed them on. But, by sweet
Saint George I swear, if my brother of Gloucester
would join with me, we would make him know that we
were all three one man's sons, of one mother and one
lineage descended, which should be more preferred
and promoted than strangers of his wife's blood" '
(Hall, page 271).

(stage direction) *Somerset*. For this character Shakespeare blends aspects of two historical Dukes of
Somerset: (1) Henry Beaufort (1436–64), third
Duke, in his transfer of allegiance from Lancastrians
to Yorkists in 1462 and his change back again in
1464, when he was beheaded by the Yorkists after
the Battle of Hexham; (2) Edmund Beaufort (1438–
71), younger brother of Henry and fourth Duke,
who was always a staunch Lancastrian. He led the
vanguard of Margaret's army at the Battle of Tewkesbury in 1471, where he was taken prisoner and
beheaded.

5   *stay* wait
6   *forbear* leave off

(stage direction) *Pembroke*. William Herbert, first
Earl, was the son of Sir William. He was knighted by
Henry VI in 1449 after service in France. He became
an ardent Yorkist and was captured and executed in
1469 when attempting to put down a rebellion
fomented by the Earl of Warwick.

Stafford. Sir Humphrey (b. 1439) was knighted by
Edward IV after the Battle of Towton and created
Lord Stafford in 1464 and Earl of Devon in 1469.
His quarrel with Pembroke and withdrawal of his
troops at Banbury in 1469 led to a Yorkist defeat,
for which Edward had him executed for treason.

Hastings. Sir William (*c*. 1430–1483) was a favourite
of the Duke of York and was ennobled on the accession
of Edward IV. He was instrumental in Edward's

    escape from Warwick's invading troops in 1470 and in persuading Clarence to desert the Lancastrian cause. Ultimately he was beheaded without a trial by Richard III.

8   *mind* have a good mind

10   *malcontent* disturbed

12   *Which* who

13   *abuse* ill-usage, insult

18   *hasty marriage seldom proveth well* (proverbial: 'Marry in haste and repent at leisure')

21–3   *God forbid that I . . . so well together.* Richard typically parodies the marriage service, probably with sexual overtones.

21   *severed* parted

23   *sunder* separate
        yoke are coupled (like oxen)

24   *mislike* displeasure

32   *gave in charge* commissioned him to do

33   *Is now dishonourèd by this new marriage.* Richard rightly sees that it is Warwick's honour that is threatened by Edward's behaviour; see Warwick's reaction at III.3.184.

35   *invention* falsehood

40   *England is safe, if true within itself.* This was a popular patriotic cliché; compare *King John*, V.7.112–14:

    This England never did, nor never shall,
    Lie at the proud foot of a conqueror
    But when it first did help to wound itself.

41   *backed with* supported by

43–4   *with the seas | Which He hath given for fence impregnable.* Compare *Richard II*, II.1.43–9:

    This fortress built by nature for herself
    Against infection and the hand of war. . . .
    This precious stone set in the silver sea,
    Which serves it in the office of a wall,
    Or as a moat defensive to a house
    Against the envy of less happier lands. . . .

44   *fence* surrounding defensive barrier

45   *only* alone

48   *the heir of the Lord Hungerford.* Mary was the only
       daughter of Sir Thomas and his wife, Anne Percy.
       After her father's execution in 1469 for supporting
       Henry VI, she became the ward of Lord Hastings,
       whose son Edward she married in 1480. Shakespeare
       has taken the 'Lord Hastings' of Hall to be the father
       rather than the son; see the headnote to this scene.

52   *the heir and daughter of Lord Scales.* Elizabeth,
       daughter of Thomas, the seventh Baron, was married
       in 1460 to Anthony Woodville, Earl Rivers, older
       brother of Lady Grey.

55   *in your bride you bury brotherhood* in providing for
       your wife's relations you ignore the nearer claims
       of your brothers

56-7 *the heir | Of the Lord Bonville on your new wife's son.*
       Cicely, the daughter of William Lord Harington
       and Bonville, became the second wife of Thomas
       Grey, first Marquess of Dorset and Elizabeth
       Grey's son by her first husband.

58   *go speed* search for success

60   *malcontent* discontented

63   *play the broker* act as marriage go-between
       in on

64   *mind* intend

68   *state* condition in life

70   *not ignoble of descent.* See the quotation from Hall in
       the headnote to III.2.

71   *meaner* people of more lowly birth. Lady Grey was
       the first commoner to be Queen of England.

73   *dislikes* disapproval
       would wish to

75   *forbear to fawn upon* refrain from currying favour
       because of

83   *I hear, yet say not much, but think the more* (proverbial:
       'Though he said little he thought the more')

87   *pardon* permission

239

89   *Go to* very well then

90   *guess* remember

92   *depart* departure

96   *brave* defiantly courageous

99–100 *Tell him ... his sake*. See the note to III.3.228.

101–2 *I blame not her ... wrong*. This seems to echo Hall's wording in his description of the French reception of the news of Edward's marriage; see the note to III.3.212–28.

103   *in place* present

104–5 *Tell him ... armour on*. See the note to III.3.229.

104   *done* finished with, put off

106   *Amazon* (one of a mythical race of female warriors)

107   *injuries* insults

109   *discharged* dismissed

113   *I will arm me, being thus forewarned* (proverbial: 'Forewarned is forearmed')

118   *the elder*. The same error is made at III.3.242; see the note to III.3.240–50.
       Clarence will have the younger. Clarence married Isabella, Warwick's elder daughter, at Calais in 1469 and immediately joined his father-in-law in his invasion of England to dethrone Edward. Compare Hall: 'after that the Duke had sworn on the sacrament to keep his promise and pact inviolate made and concluded with the Earl of Warwick, he married the Lady Isabel, eldest daughter to the said Earl, in Our Lady Church at Calais with great pomp and solemnity' (page 272).

119   *sit you fast* hold on to your throne securely. As Edward's immediately younger brother, Clarence was next in line for the crown.

121   *want* lack

122   *not prove inferior to yourself* do at least as well as you have done

127   *armed against* prepared for
       can that can

129–31   *Pembroke and Stafford ... landed.* Compare Hall:
'When King Edward (to whom all the doings of the
Earl of Warwick and the Duke his brother were
manifest and overt and were come to that point that
he expected and looked for) was by divers letters
sent to him certified that the great army of northern
men were with all speed coming toward London,
therefore in great haste he sent to William Lord
Herbert, whom within two years before he had
created Earl of Pembroke, that he should without
delay encounter with the northern men with the
extremity of all his power. . . . And to assist and
furnish him with archers was appointed Humphrey
Lord Stafford . . . and with him he had eight hundred
archers' (page 273).

130   *prepare* preparation

132   *straight* immediately

134   *Resolve* settle

135   *near to Warwick by blood and by alliance.* Montague
was Warwick's brother; Hastings was married to
Catherine Nevil, Warwick's sister.

138   *hollow* false

139   *mind* intend

141   *in suspect* under suspicion

142   *So God help Montague as he proves true.* In the chronicles, Montague's attitude is much more complex.
After the restoration of Henry VI in 1471, Montague
came to London 'excusing himself that only for fear
of death he declined to King Edward's part, which
excuse was so accepted that he obtained his pardon,
which after was the destruction of him and his
brother; for if he had manfully and apertly taken
King Edward's part, surely he being an open enemy
had much less hurted than being a feigned, false,
and a coloured friend' (Hall, page 286).

143   *And Hastings as he favours Edward's cause.* Compare
Hall: 'the Lord Hastings, his Chamberlain, which

had married the Earl's sister and yet was ever true
to the King, his master' (page 283).

145   *despite* spite
      that who
146   *so* good
148   *power* army

IV.2   The scene is located on open land in Warwickshire.
           Historically the main sequence of events was: (1)
           Warwick made his secret alliance with Clarence
           after returning from the abortive marriage negoti-
           ations; (2) he fomented a rebellion in the north of
           England; (3) the Yorkist forces under Stafford and
           Pembroke were defeated at Banbury on 26 July
           1469; (4) Edward was captured in a night attack
           on his camp; (5) Warwick went to France to request
           help from Louis XI; (6) Clarence followed and was
           married to Warwick's elder daughter, Isabella;
           (7) Warwick and Clarence invaded England with
           French troops. For this scene Shakespeare makes
           Warwick's invasion precede Edward's capture after
           Banbury; but, of course, the events follow dramatically
           Warwick's reconciliation with Margaret depicted
           in III.3. The various parts of the chronicles used to
           create the scene are cited in the relevant notes
           below.

1   *hitherto* thus far

2   *The common people by numbers swarm to us.* After
           Warwick's invasion, Hall notes 'It is almost in-
           credible to think how soon the fame of the Earl's
           landing was blown over and through all the whole
           realm, and how many thousand men of war at the
           very first tidings of his landing were suddenly
           assembled and set forward to welcome him' (page 282).
           by in large

4-12   *Speak suddenly ... be thine.* When Warwick

approached Clarence after his return from his
marriage embassy, 'he had that which he both sore
thrusted and lusted for; and then began boldly to
disclose to the Duke his intent and purpose even at
the full, requiring him to take part with him and
to be one of the attempted confederacy. ... And the
rather to win the Duke's heart, the Earl, beside
divers and many fair promises made to the Duke,
offered him his eldest daughter ... in marriage'
(Hall, page 271).

4   *suddenly* quickly
5   *Fear not* you may be sure of
6   *gentle* noble
8   *rest* remain
9   *pawned* pledged
12 *my daughter shall be thine.* See the second note to
    IV.1.118.
13-25 *now what rests ... surprise him.* After the Yorkist
    defeat at Banbury in July 1469, Hall records 'the
    King, conceiving a certain hope of peace in his
    own imagination, took both less heed to himself and
    also less feared the outward attempts of his enemies,
    thinking and trusting truly that all things were at a
    good point and should be well pacified. All the
    King's doings were by espials declared to the Earl
    of Warwick, which, like a wise and politic captain,
    intending not to lose so great an advantage to him
    given but trusting to bring all his purposes to a
    final end and determination by only obtaining this
    enterprise: in the dead of night, with an elect company
    of men of war, as secretly as was possible set on the
    King's field, killing them that kept the watch, and ere
    the King were ware (for he thought of nothing less
    than of that chance that happened), at a place called
    Wolney, four miles from Warwick, he was taken
    prisoner and brought to the Castle of Warwick' (page
    275).

13   *rests* remains
        coverture protective darkness
14   *carelessly* without the necessary military precautions
15   *lurking* loitering
16   *simple* nothing else but an immediately personal
17   *at our pleasure* whenever we wish
18   *adventure* venturing (into the camp)
19–21   *as Ulysses . . . fatal steeds.* During the siege of Troy
        it was predicted by the gods that should the horses
        of the Thracian prince Rhesus drink at the River
        Xanthus and graze on the Plains of Troy, the city
        would not fall. Ulysses and Diomede, under the
        cover of darkness, stole the horses while they were
        being taken to Troy and killed Rhesus, thus pre-
        venting the prophecy's coming true.
19   *Ulysses.* See the note to III.2.189.
        stout valiant
        Diomede (three syllables). He was the King of Argos
        and, after Achilles, the bravest of the Greek leaders
        at Troy.
20   *sleight* cunning
21   *fatal* (connected with prophecy)
23   *At unawares* unexpectedly
25   *surprise him* capture him unawares
28   *sort* manner

IV.3   The scene is located at Edward's camp near Warwick.
        Historically the event took place at Wolney, four
        miles from Warwick. The capture of Edward drama-
        tized in this scene is based upon the attack on Edward's
        camp after the Battle of Banbury in July 1469 (see the
        headnote to IV.2); but Shakespeare depicts it as
        happening after Warwick's invasion with French
        troops, which actually occurred in 1470.
1   *stand* post
2   *by this is set him down* by this time has settled down

11   *the King's chiefest friend.* See the note to IV.1.143.

13–15   *his chief ... more dangerous.* For the historical reasons for Edward's military carelessness, see the quotation from Hall in the note to IV.2.13–25.

13   *lodge* sleep

       about round about

14   *keeps* remains

15   *'Tis the more honour, because more dangerous* (proverbial: 'The more danger the more honour')

16–17   *give me worship and quietness; | I like it better than a dangerous honour* (proverbial: 'Honour and ease are seldom bedfellows')

16   *worship* comfortable dignity

18   *estate* situation

       he (Edward)

19   *doubted* feared

20   *halberds* (weapons composed of axe-heads fixed to the tops of spear-length poles)

       shut up prevent, bar

       his (Warwick's)

25   *But if you will only*

27   (stage direction) *gown* dressing-gown

32   *the case is altered* (proverbial) the circumstances are different

33   *embassade* embassy

37, 39   *use* treat

40   *study for* think out carefully plans for

41   *shroud* protect

43   *down* fall

44   *despite* spite

45   *complices* accomplices

47   *state* sovereignty

48   *compass* range (represented by the circumference of the wheel of Fortune)

49   *for his mind* in his own imagination

50   *Henry now shall wear the English crown.* At the time of Edward's capture after the Battle of Banbury in

July 1469, Warwick had no intention of deposing him. It was only after his invasion in 1470 that he decided to reinstate Henry VI (see the headnote to IV.2).

53–4   *See that forthwith ... York.* This is based on Hall: 'And to the intent that the King's friends might not know where he was, nor what was chanced of him, he caused him by secret journeys in the night to be conveyed to Middleham Castle in Yorkshire, and there to be kept under the custody of the Archbishop of York, his brother' (page 275).

53   *Duke Edward.* When Warwick invaded England in 1470, he proclaimed that he wished all men 'to prepare themselves to fight against Edward Duke of York, which, contrary to all right, justice, and law, had untruly usurped the crown and imperial dignity of this realm' (Hall, page 282).

54   *Archbishop of York* (Warwick's younger brother, George Nevil (1433?–1476), installed in the archbishopric in 1465. He presided at the marriage of Clarence and Isabella Nevil at Calais.)

55   *When I have fought with Pembroke and his fellows.* This is a detail based upon the chronicles' account of the Battle of Banbury, at which Stafford deserted Pembroke, who was defeated, captured, and beheaded (Hall, page 274). Historically this preceded the capture of Edward in the night attack on his camp.
fellows companions

59   *What fates impose, that men must needs abide* (proverbial: 'Man proposes, God disposes')
abide endure

60   *boots not* is useless

IV.4   The scene is located in the royal palace in London. It is based on the chronicles' account of the behaviour of Edward's supporters after they heard of his flight to the continent when the news of Warwick's invasion in 1470 reached him: 'all King Edward's trusty friends went to divers sanctuaries, daily looking and hourly hearkening to hear of his health and prosperous return, who afterward served him manfully and truly. Amongst other, Queen Elizabeth, his wife, almost desperate of all comfort, took sanctuary at Westminster, and there in great penury, forsaken of all her friends, was delivered of a fair son called Edward' (Hall, page 285).

(stage direction) *Rivers*. Anthony Woodville (1442–83), Elizabeth Grey's older brother, became the second Earl Rivers in 1469. Ultimately he was beheaded on the orders of Richard Duke of Gloucester.

1	*you in this sudden change* this sudden change in you
3	*late* recent
8	*falsehood* treachery
9	*surprised* taken prisoner
	at unawares unexpectedly
10	*have to* am given to
11	*new committed to* recently placed in the custody of
12	*by that* because of that (relationship)
19	*bridle passion* keep myself from giving way to a violent outbreak of grief
21	*draw in* hold back
22	*blood-sucking sighs*. It was believed that every sigh drew a drop of blood from the heart.
23	*blast* blight, wither
25	*is Warwick . . . become* has Warwick reached
26	*towards London*. See IV.3.62.
28	*King Edward's friends must down*. Warwick's purpose when he captured the King in 1469 was only to remove the Woodvilles from their positions of influence; and he did indeed kill a number of the Queen's relatives before releasing the King.
	must down will necessarily be destroyed
29	*prevent* forestall

30   *trust not him that hath once broken faith* (proverbial: 'He that once deceives is ever suspected')

31   *sanctuary* (religious house, where residence guaranteed immunity from arrest)

32   *right* just title to the crown

33   *secure from* untouched by
     fraud trickery

IV.5   The scene is located in the grounds of Middleham Castle in Yorkshire. Historically Edward escaped from there in March 1470 and marched triumphantly to London, driving Warwick to go to France to seek aid from Louis XI (the visit dramatized in the second half of III.3). After Warwick's subsequent invasion, Edward was forced to leave the country and went to Holland in September 1470. In this scene Shakespeare dramatizes the events of the first escape (lines 1–19); but he makes the King's party have as their destination Holland rather than London. (stage direction) *Sir William Stanley*. Born in 1435, he was the second son of Thomas, first Baron Stanley, and the brother of the Earl of Derby. He was always a Yorkist, but it was nevertheless his intervention at the Battle of Bosworth in 1485 that enabled Richmond to defeat Richard III. He was beheaded in 1495 for his part in the Perkin Warbeck conspiracy.

1–19   *Now my Lord Hastings ... the park corner.* In Hall, Edward's escape in March 1470 was effected by Sir William Stanley and Sir Thomas Borough: 'King Edward, being thus in captivity, spake ever fair to the Archbishop and to the other keepers, but – whether he corrupted them with money or fair promises – he had liberty divers days to go on hunting; and one day on a plain there met with him Sir William Stanley, Sir Thomas of Borough, and divers other of his friends, with such a great band of men that neither his keepers would nor once

248

durst move him to return to prison again' (page 275).

3   *chiefest thicket of the park* most heavily wooded section of the hunting grounds

5   *the Bishop* (the Archbishop of York; see IV.3.54)

6   *usage* treatment

7   *but* only

8   *disport* entertain

9   *advertised* (accented on the second syllable) informed

10   *make* come

11   *Under the colour of his usual game* on the pretext of following his usual practice while hunting

14   *game* quarry

17   *close* hidden

18   *case* circumstances

19   *horse* horses

20–26   *But whither ... be hanged.* Compare Hall's account of Edward's flight to the continent in September 1470: ' ... quickened by having knowledge that some of the Earl of Warwick's power was within a half day's journey and less of his tail, [Edward] with all haste possible passed The Wash (in greater jeopardy than it beseemed a prince to be in) and came to the town of Lynn, where he found an English ship and two hulks of Holland ready (as fortune would) to make sail and take their journey; whereupon he, being in a marvellous agony and doubting the mutability of the townsmen, taking no further leisure for his sure succour and safeguard, with his brother the Duke of Gloucester, the Lord Scales, and divers other his trusty friends, entered into the ship' (page 283).

20   *Lynn* (King's Lynn, a seaport in Norfolk)

21   F has a full-stop after *Flanders*, but it is clear that Hastings does not know the plan and is merely guessing correctly.

23   *requite* repay
      forwardness zeal

25   *go along* come with us

IV.6   The scene is located in the Tower of London. Shakespeare draws together for the scene events which happened at different times historically: (1) Henry's release from the Tower; (2) the appointment of Warwick and Clarence as Protectors; (3) the re-establishment of the Lancastrian succession and the confiscating of Edward's property; (4) the sending for Margaret and her son; (5) the meeting between Henry and the Earl of Richmond; (6) the news of Edward's escape to the court of the Duke of Burgundy; (7) Richmond's flight to Brittany. The various passages from Hall are cited in the relevant notes.

(stage direction) *Somerset*. See the note to the opening stage direction of IV.1. At this time the head of the house of Beaufort was Edmund (1438–71), the fourth Duke, who is depicted by Shakespeare as the appropriate guardian for the young Earl of Richmond. Historically, it was Richmond's uncle, Jasper Earl of Pembroke, who brought him to meet Henry VI and took him to Brittany in 1471; see the note to lines 96–102.

young Henry Richmond. This was the son of Edmund Tudor, Earl of Richmond, and Margaret Beaufort, the great-grand-daughter of John of Gaunt. At this time he was thirteen years old. On Edward IV's recovery of the throne in 1471, he was taken to Brittany and there remained until he invaded England in 1485 and defeated Richard III at Bosworth. He was crowned Henry VII in October of the same year and married Elizabeth, the daughter of Edward IV, thus uniting the white and red rose factions.

1–20   *Master Lieutenant . . . cannot hurt me*. This is based upon Hall's account of Henry's release by Warwick and Clarence in 1470: 'Upon the twelfth day of October [Warwick] rode to the Tower of London, which was to him without resistance delivered, there took King Henry VI out of the ward where he before was kept, and was brought to the King's lodging and there served according to his degree. And the twenty-fifth day of the said month, the Duke of Clarence, accompanied with the Earls of Warwick, Shrewsbury, and the Lord Stanley . . . , resorted with a great company to the Tower of London, and from thence with great pomp brought King Henry VI, apparelled in a long gown of blue velvet, through the high streets of London' (page 285).

5   *enlargement* release

      due fees. It was customary for prisoners to pay the gaoler on their release for food and services provided during their imprisonment.

6   *challenge* demand as their due

10   *requite* reward

11   *For that* because

13   *Conceive* begin to feel

      moody gloomy

14   *of household harmony* which fill the house with music

18   *author* originator

      instrument means, agent

19   *spite* malice

20   *low* humbly

21–52 *And that the people . . . his ease*. In the parliament of 26 November 1470, 'the Earl of Warwick, as one to whom the commonwealth was much beholden, was made ruler and governor of the realm, with whom as fellow and companion was associated George Duke of Clarence, his son-in-law' (Hall, page 286).

22   *thwarting stars* malign fate

25   *fortunate* favoured by fortune

26   *still* always

      famed for reputed to be

28   *spying* foreseeing

29   *temper with* conform to what is determined by

31   *in place* here

251

32   *sway* power of government

33   *thy nativity* the special conjunction of stars when you were born

34   *olive branch* (conventional symbol of peace)

       laurel crown (classical symbol of military victory)

36   *free* willingly given

37   *only for* as sole

43   *latter* final

47   *repose myself* rely

49   *yoke* join

50   *supply* take

53–5   *And, Clarence, now . . . be confiscate.* At the November parliament in 1470, after Henry's reinstatement, Edward 'was declared a traitor to his country and usurper of the realm . . . and all his goods were confiscate and adjudged forfeited; and like sentence was given against all his partakers and friends' (Hall, page 286).

55   *confiscate* confiscated

56–7   *What else? . . . his part.* In the November parliament of 1470, the Lancastrian succession was re-established: 'The crowns of the realms of England and France was by the authority of the same parliament entailed to King Henry VI and the heirs males of his body lawfully begotten, and, for default of such heir male of his body begotten, then the said crowns and dignities were entailed to George Duke of Clarence . . . and further, the said Duke was by authority aforesaid enabled to be next heir to his father, Richard Duke of York' (Hall, page 286).

56   *What else?* assuredly

57   *want* lack

59–63   *Let me entreat . . . is half eclipsed.* Compare Hall: 'Queen Margaret, after that the Earl of Warwick was sailed into England, ever forecasting and doubting the chance that might happen, did never cease to pray to God to send victory to her friends and confederates; which when she knew by her husband's

letters to be obtained, she with Prince Edward her
son and her train entered their ships to take their
voyage into England' (page 286).

62   *doubtful fear* uncertain apprehension

65–76   *My lord of Somerset . . . hurt by me.* Compare Hall:
         'Jasper Earl of Pembroke took this child, being his
         nephew, out of the custody of the Lady Herbert,
         and at his return he brought the child to London to
         King Henry VI; whom when the King had a good
         space by himself secretly beholden and marked both
         his wit and his likely towardness, he said to such
         princes as were then with him: "Lo, surely this is
         he to whom both we and our adversaries, leaving
         the possession of all things, shall hereafter give room
         and place." So this holy man showed before the
         chance that should happen, that this Earl Henry,
         so ordained by God, should in time to come (as he
         did indeed) have and enjoy the kingdom' (page 287).

66   *so tender* such affectionate

69   *divining thoughts* thoughts which prophesy the future

78–88   *That Edward is escapèd . . . that may betide.* This is a
         reflection of Hall's account of the events following
         Edward's escape from Middleham Castle: 'When
         the Earl of Warwick and the Duke of Clarence had
         knowledge how the King, by treason of them that they
         put in trust, was escaped their hands, and that in one
         moment of time all their long studies and forecasts
         were brought to non-effect or conclusion, they waxed
         angry and chafed without measure; and, by and by
         calling together all their chief friends, began to consult
         again' (page 276).

78   *your brother* (the Archbishop of York)

79   *he* (your brother)

81   *conveyed* carried away secretly

82   *attended* waited for

88   *A salve for any sore that may betide* (proverbial:
         'There is a salve for every sore')
         betide occur

253

89   *like not of* am not pleased by

90   *Burgundy.* Charles the Bold (1423–77) was married to Edward IV's sister, Margaret, and was an implacable enemy of Louis XI. He did provide Edward with money and ships for his invasion of England in 1471 (Hall, pages 289–90).

94   *misgive me* give me a presentiment of

96–102   *Therefore, Lord Oxford ... about it speedily.* The decision to take Richmond to Brittany was not taken by the Earl of Pembroke until after the Lancastrian defeat at the Battle of Tewkesbury in 1471: 'The Earl in good haste ... was ... conveyed to Tenby, a haven town in Wales, where he, getting convenient ships for to transport him and his over the sea into France, with his nephew, Lord Henry, Earl of Richmond, and a few of his familiars took ship and, by Fortune's leading, landed in Brittany' (Hall, pages 302–3).

96   *prevent* forestall

100   *like* probable

       down be executed

IV.7   The scene is located outside the gates of the city of York. It is based upon Hall's account of (1) Edward's trickery in taking over the city, after his landing at Ravenspurgh; (2) the meeting with Sir Thomas Montgomery a few days later at Nottingham when he proclaimed himself king. The passages used are cited in the relevant notes.

3   *interchange* swap

4   *wanèd state* diminished rank

8   *Ravenspurgh* (a town on the Yorkshire coast at the mouth of the Humber). Compare Hall: 'He sailed into England and came on the coast of Yorkshire to a place called Ravenspurgh; and there, setting all his men on land, he consulted with his captains to know

to what place they should first for succour resort
unto; for he imagined that no way could be for him
sure, having so small a company of soldiers' (page
290).

9   *as* as though

10–19   *The gates made fast ... unto Henry.* Compare Hall:
'King Edward ... came peaceably near to York, of
whose coming when the citizens were certified,
without delay they armed themselves and came to
defend the gates, sending to him two of the chiefest
aldermen of the city, which earnestly admonished
him on their behalf to come not one foot nearer nor
temerariously to enter into so great a jeopardy, considering that they were fully determined and bent to
compel him to retract with dint of sword' (page 291).

10   *made fast* locked up

11   *stumble at the threshold* (a proverbial sign of bad
luck)

12   *foretold* forewarned

13   *abodements* forebodings

15   *repair* return

16   (stage direction) *on the walls.* The Elizabethan theatre
possessed an upper acting area which would be used
for this entry.

        brethren (aldermen)

20–39   *But, master Mayor ... follow me.* Compare Hall:
'with lowly words and gentle entreatings, requiring
most heartily the messengers that were sent to
declare to the citizens that he came neither to demand
the realm of England nor the superiority of the same,
but only the Duchy of York, his old inheritance. ...
And so with fair words and flattering speech he
dismissed the messengers, and with good speed he and
his followed so quickly after that they were almost at
the gates as soon as the ambassadors. The citizens,
hearing his good answer that he meant nor intended
nothing prejudicial to King Henry nor his royal

authority, were much mitigated and cooled and began to commune with him from their walls ... but he gently speaking to all men and especially to such as were aldermen, whom he called worshipful and by their proper names them saluted, after many fair promises to them made, exhorted and desired them that by their favourable friendship and friendly permission he might enter into his own town. ... The citizens, partly won by his fair words and partly by hope of his large promises, fell to this pact and convention, that ... they would receive him into their city' (pages 291–2).

23   *challenge* lay claim to

25–6   *when the fox hath once got in his nose, | He'll soon find means to make the body follow* (proverbial)

30   *stout* valiant

31   *fain* be glad

32   *'long of* due to

39   *deign* are willing

    (stage direction) *Montgomery*. Although Shakespeare calls him *Sir John*, according to the chronicles this was Sir Thomas Montgomery (d. 1495), who with Sir Thomas Borough joined Edward not at York but at Nottingham: '[Edward] came safely to the town of Nottingham, where came to him Sir William Parr, Sir Thomas a Borough, Sir Thomas Montgomery, and divers other of his assured friends with their aids, which caused him at the first coming to make proclamation in his own name, King Edward IV, boldly saying to him that they would serve no man but a king' (Hall, page 292).

50   (stage direction) *march* (strike up a marching beat)

51   *debate* discuss

56   *keep them back* prevent them

57   *pretend* lay claim to

58   *stand you on nice points* do you make such subtle distinctions

60   *meaning* intentions

61   *scrupulous wit* reasoning which hesitates because of scruples

63-4   *we will proclaim ... many friends.* Compare Hall: 'But when the fame was blown abroad that King Edward without any detriment was in safe time come to Nottingham, princes and noblemen on all sides began to fall to him' (page 292).

63   *out of hand* immediately

64   *bruit* news

66   *diadem* crown

68   *champion.* Montgomery refers to the position of King's Champion, who was the warrior surrogate for the monarch, issuing and answering challenges on his behalf.

69-75   *Sound trumpet ... Edward the Fourth.* In Hall, the proclamation is made at Nottingham; see the note to the stage direction at line 39. Historically Edward took an oath concerning his intentions to the citizens of York and was much criticized for his perjury.

69   *Sound trumpet* let the trumpet sound

73   *gainsays* denies

77   *serve* favour

78   *harbour* lodge

79   *his car* (Phoebus's chariot)

80   *horizon* (accented on the first syllable)

81   *We'll forward towards Warwick and his mates.* After leaving Nottingham, Edward 'In the mean season ... came to Warwick, where he found all the people departed, and from thence with all diligence advanced his power toward Coventry and in a plain by the city he pitched his field' (page 293).

    forward march on

    mates (used contemptuously) supporters

83   *froward* refractory

    evil ill

    beseems befits

86   *day* victorious outcome of this day of battle

87   *that once gotten, doubt not of large pay.* This is an echo of Hall's comment that Edward 'gathered a great host by reason of his money' (page 292).

IV.8.1–32   The scene is located in the Bishop's palace in London, where Henry was lodged after his release from the Tower (see V.1.45). There is no specific event in the chronicles on which this scene is based. It reflects Hall's account of Edward's march south-ward in 1471, during which he 'did daily increase his power (as a running river by going more and more augmenteth)' (page 293), and also Warwick's plans to wait at Coventry to be joined by the forces of Oxford, Montague, and Somerset. Historically, Edward challenged Warwick to battle at Coventry. Only when the Earl refused to venture outside the city walls did he proceed to London and seize King Henry (see lines 33–64 and the note to the stage direction at line 32).

(stage direction) F includes Somerset in this entry; but there is no evidence for his presence and he is omitted from the orders Warwick gives in lines 11–18.

1   *Belgia* (Flanders; see the note to IV.5.20–26)

2   *hasty* quick-tempered
     blunt rude, uncivilized

3   *the narrow seas* (the English Channel)

4–5 *with his troops ... to him.* See the headnote to this scene.

5   *giddy* fickle, irresponsible

7–8 *A little fire is quickly trodden out; | Which, being suffered, rivers cannot quench* (proverbial: 'Of a little spark a great fire')

8   *being suffered* allowed to go unchecked

11   *son* (son-in-law)

20   *girt in with* surrounded by

258

21   *Dian* (Diana, goddess of chastity)

22   *rest* remain

23   *stand not* do not wait

25   *Hector* (Priam's eldest son, the protector of Troy)
      my Troy's true hope. There was a widely held belief
      that London was founded by Brutus, the grandson
      of the Trojan Aeneas, and named originally 'Troy-
      novant' (the New Troy).

27   *Well-minded* virtuously disposed

29   *seal my truth* ratify my loyalty

31   *at once* together

32   *let's meet at Coventry.* In Hall, Warwick 'without
      delay marched forward toward Coventry to the in-
      tent to set on his enemies' (page 293); but he is
      frustrated by Clarence's negligence and defection
      and Montague's lack of support.

32   (stage direction) In F there is no entry direction here;
      and many modern editors assume this is a continuation
      of IV.8, printing it as such by replacing Somerset's
      name in F's opening stage direction with that of
      Exeter. However, there are convincing arguments that
      Shakespeare designed IV.8.33–64 to be a separate
      scene: (1) in F there is a stage-clearing '*Exeunt*'
      after line 32; (2) there is no more indication in IV.8
      that Exeter is present before Henry's address to
      him at line 34 than there is for Somerset; (3) Henry
      seems to be referring (lines 35–6) to the troops Warwick
      planned to raise at lines 9–18 as already having been
      mustered; (4) Edward's allusion to Warwick's
      remaining at Coventry (lines 26–7) makes no sense if
      Warwick has left the stage to set out from London
      only twenty-five lines previously; (5) the tone of
      Henry's opening lines to Exeter implies the beginning
      of a new scene, as he identifies the place and proceeds
      to discuss what is obviously news of Warwick's

and Edward's actions following the decision taken earlier in IV.8; (6) a comparison between lines 1–32 and lines 33–64 and the section in Hall on which they are based suggests dramatization in two scenes rather than one. However, although it is thus a separate scenic unit the present edition preserves the traditional numbering for convenience of reference.

The location of the scene is the Bishop's palace in London. Compare Hall's account of Edward's march from Coventry to London: 'When ... King Henry's friends saw the world thus suddenly changed, every man fled, and in haste shifted for himself, leaving King Henry alone, as an host that should be sacrificed, in the Bishop's palace of London, adjoining to Paul's Church, not knowing of whom nor what counsel to ask, as he which with trouble and adversity was clearly dulled and appalled; in which place he was by King Edward taken and again committed to prison and captivity' (page 294).

33   *palace*. See the previous note.

35   *power* forces

37   *doubt* danger

seduce the rest. Hall suggests that Warwick suspected (prior to Clarence's actual desertion of him) that 'he should be deceived by the Duke of Clarence', and that he 'grudged against his brother, the Marquess, for letting King Edward pass' (page 293).
seduce attract loyalty to himself from

38–50   *That's not my fear ... follow him*. Compare Hall's analysis of Henry's character: 'a man of no great wit, such as men commonly call an innocent man ... whose study always was more to excel other in godly living and virtuous example than in worldly regiment or temporal dominion, in so much that, in comparison to the study and delectation that he had to virtue and godliness, he little regarded, but in manner despised, all worldly power and temporal authority' (pages 285–6).

38   *meed* worth, merit
        fame a good reputation
39   *their* (the people of England's)
40   *posted off* postponed
43   *water-flowing* (flowing like water)
45   *subsidies* (property taxes, which in the fifteenth
        century were levied by the monarch intermittently
        when he needed funds)
46   *forward of* eager for
        erred turned against me, strayed from their duty as
        subjects
48   *challenge grace* lay claim to their favour
50   (stage direction) *À York! À York!* rally to York.
        F's reading, '*A Lancaster, A Lancaster.*', is an obvious
        error; the cries offstage clearly announce the arrival
        of Edward's forces as they charge Henry's guards.
52   *shame-faced* modest, retiring
55   *stops thy spring* your source of power is stopped up
58   *towards Coventry.* Historically, Edward had been to
        Coventry and confronted Warwick before the inci-
        dent dramatized in this scene took place.
        bend we let us direct
59   *peremptory* presumptuous, overbearing
60–61   *The sun shines hot; and, if we use delay, | Cold biting
        winter mars our hoped-for hay* (proverbial: 'Make
        hay while the sun shines')
60   *use delay* hesitate
61   *hoped-for hay* expected harvest
62   *betimes* quickly
        join link up with each other
63   *take* capture
        great-grown (who has become so powerful)

V.1   The scene is located before the walls of Coventry in
        Warwickshire. Historically the confrontation between
        Warwick and Edward at Coventry took place before the
        Yorkists' capture of Henry in London and before

Clarence's defection. Shakespeare rearranges the chronology of events so that the Coventry flyting immediately precedes the Battle of Barnet, which took place on 14 April 1471. For the scene Shakespeare draws on various sections of the chronicles covering the events between Edward's march to Coventry from Nottingham and the Battle of Barnet. The passages used are cited in the relevant notes.

1, 5   *post* messenger

3, 6   *By this* by this time

3   *Dunsmore* (a town between Daventry and Coventry)

6   *Daintry*. This is the Elizabethan pronunciation of Daventry.

    puissant powerful

    (stage direction) *Sir John Somerville*. He has been variously identified as Sir John and Sir Thomas (d. 1500). The Somerville family estates were in Aston Somerville, Gloucestershire, some thirty miles from Coventry.

7   *son* (son-in-law)

8   *nigh* close

9–10   *At Southam ... two hours hence*. In Hall, Warwick suspects Clarence's loyalty, 'yet he had perfect word that the Duke of Clarence came forward toward him with a great army' (page 293).

9   *Southam* (a town ten miles south-east of Coventry)

12–13   *Here Southam lies; | The drum your honour hears marcheth from Warwick*. Warwick hears Edward's drum, which is approaching from the town of Warwick in the south-west. Somerville points in the south-easterly direction in which Southam lies.

13   *Warwick*. The town is south-west of Coventry, and is the site of Warwick's castle.

14   *unlooked-for* unexpected

15   (stage direction) *March. Flourish* (the sound of marching music and a fanfare of trumpets)

16   *trumpet* trumpeter

parle (summons to a conference before fighting)

18   *unbid spite* unwelcome irritation

    sportful. The reference is to Edward's notoriously lascivious nature.

19   *Where slept our scouts* why were our lookouts so ineffective

20   *repair* approach

21–4   *Now, Warwick, wilt thou ... these outrages.* In Hall, 'it was concluded amongst the three brethren to attempt the Earl of Warwick if by any fair means he might be reconciled or by any promise allured to their part' (page 293); but in Holinshed, Edward, 'for the advancement of peace and tranquillity within the realm, offered large conditions: as a free pardon of life to the Earl and all his people' (III.307).

27   *patron* defender, protector

30   *make the jest against his will.* Richard takes Warwick's reference to Edward as a duke to be a joke and wonders how he resisted referring to his part in making Edward a king.

33   *do thee service.* Richard sarcastically adopts the language of a feudal tenant acknowledging a gift from his lord of the manor

35   *if but by* if only because it was

36   *Atlas* (the mythological giant who bore the world on his shoulders)

42   *forecast* forethought

43   *the single ten* (the highest non-picture card in the pack)

44   *fingered from the deck* slid from the pack

48   *time* opportunity

49   *when* (an exclamation of impatience)

    Strike now, or else the iron cools (proverbial: 'It is good to strike when the iron is hot')

51   *other* (other hand)

52   *bear so low a sail ... strike.* See the note to III.3.5.

57   *Wind-changing* (1) as fickle as the wind's direction;

  (2) able to change the direction of the wind

57 *change* change side

57-72 (stage directions) *Enter Oxford ... into the city.*
  The names of Warwick's supporters appear in a
  list given by Hall of the forces composing the Lancastrian army before Barnet: 'In the Earl's army were
  John Duke of Exeter, Edmund Earl of Somerset,
  John Earl of Oxford, and John Marquess of Montague'
  (page 295); but Holinshed has some of these men
  joining him at Coventry: 'There came to the Earl
  of Warwick, whilst he lay thus at Coventry, besides
  the Earl of Oxford, the Duke of Exeter, and the
  Lord Marquess Montague, by whose coming that
  side was greatly strengthened and the number much
  increased' (III.309).

57 (stage direction) *colours* flag-bearers

61 *So* if we do
  set upon our backs attack our forces from the rear

63 *bid* offer

64 *but of small defence* only weakly fortified

65 *rouse* roust out (as when hunting a grounded animal)

66 *want* need

68 *buy* pay dearly for

69 *dearest* most vital

70 *The harder matched, the greater victory* (proverbial:
  'The more danger the more honour')
  harder matched more powerful the opposing forces

71 *happy* fortunate
  (stage direction) *Somerset.* See the note to the opening
  stage direction of IV.1.

73 *Two of thy name* (Edmund (d. 1455), second Duke,
  killed at the first Battle of Saint Albans; and his
  son Henry (1436-64), third Duke, beheaded after
  the Battle of Hexham)

76 *sweeps along* proceeds proudly

77 *Of force enough* with an army sufficiently strong

78 *to* towards

right justice

79   *nature* natural feeling

81–105   *Father of Warwick . . . is brother-like.* This is based on
Richard's actions at Coventry: 'When each host was
in sight of other, Richard Duke of Gloucester,
brother to them both, as though he had been made
arbiter between them, first rode to the Duke and
with him communed very secretly; from him he
came to King Edward and with like secretness so
used him that in conclusion no unnatural war but a
fraternal amity was concluded and proclaimed; and
then, leaving all army and weapon aside, both the
brethren lovingly embraced and familiarly communed
together' (Hall, page 293).

81   *Father* (father-in-law)

     know you what this means. Q1's version of Clarence's
arrival may indicate how the scene was produced on
the Elizabethan stage: 'Sound a Parlie, and *Richard* and
Clarence whispers togither, and then Clarence takes
his red Rose out of his hat, and throwes it at *War-
wike*.' This action seems to echo Richard's role as it
is described in the chronicles; see the note to lines
81–105.

83   *ruinate* bring to ruin

84   *lime* cement

85   *trowest thou* do you believe

86   *blunt* rough, rude

87   *bend* direct

89   *Perhaps thou wilt object my holy oath.* See the note to
line 106.

     object raise an objection against me by naming

90–91   *To keep that oath were more impiety | Than Jephthah,
when he sacrificed his daughter* (proverbial: 'An un-
lawful oath is better broken than kept'). The Israelite
general Jephthah vowed that if he were granted
victory over the Ammonites he would sacrifice the
first person he saw on his return from battle. It was

his daughter, coming to welcome him home (Judges 11.34).

92   *trespass made* sin already committed

96   *stir abroad* move outside (the city walls)

97   *thy foul misleading me.* In Holinshed, Clarence is swayed by consideration of the manner in which he had been won over to Warwick's side: 'the Duke of Clarence began to weigh with himself the great inconvenience into the which as well his brother King Edward as himself and his younger brother the Duke of Gloucester were fallen through the dissension betwixt them, which had been compassed and brought to pass by the politic working of the Earl of Warwick and his complices' (III.307).

99   *blushing* (with shame)

101   *faults* offences

102   *unconstant* disloyal

106   *O passing traitor, perjured and unjust.* Compare Hall: 'When the Earl had heard patiently the Duke's message, Lord, how he detested and accursed him, crying out on him that he, contrary to his oath, promise, and fidelity, had shamefully turned his face from his confederates and allies. But to the Duke's messengers he gave none other answer but this: that he had liefer be always like himself than like a false and a perjured duke' (page 293).
    passing unsurpassed

107–8   *What, Warwick ... thine ears?* Compare Hall: 'And the next day after that [Edward] came thither, his men were set forward and marshalled in array, and he valiantly bade the Earl battle, which mistrusting that he should be deceived by the Duke of Clarence ... kept himself close within the walls' (page 293).

109   *Alas* forsooth
    cooped shut in

110   *I will away towards Barnet presently.* In Hall, Warwick hears of the capture of Henry and so follows Edward's

army south: 'he saw that all cavellations of necessity were now brought to this end, that they must be committed to the hazard and chance of one battle, wherefore he rested with his army at the town of Saint Albans, partly to refresh his soldiers and partly to take counsel what was best to do. . . . And from Saint Albans he removed to a village in the mean way between London and Saint Albans called Barnet, being ten miles distant from both the towns' (page 295).

Barnet (a town in Hertfordshire some seventy miles from Coventry)

presently immediately

V.2   The location is the battlefield at Barnet on 14 April 1471. According to the chronicles, the battle was fiercely fought until noon without either side getting the upper hand. Edward threw fresh troops he had kept in reserve into the battle, and this move turned the tide in favour of the Yorkists. There is no historical evidence for Edward and Warwick fighting hand-to-hand; but Hall describes Warwick's death and Edward's personal participation in the battle on the same page: 'But when [Warwick's] soldiers, being sore wounded, wearied with so long a conflict, did give little regard to his words, he, being a man of a mind invincible, rushed into the midst of his enemies, where as he (adventured so far from his own company, to kill and slay his adversaries, that he could not be rescued) was in the midst of his enemies stricken down and slain. . . . Some authors write that this battle was fought so near hand that King Edward was constrained to fight his own person and fought as sore as any man of his party, and that the Earl of Warwick, which was wont ever to ride on horseback from place to place, from rank to rank, comforting his men, was now advised by the Marquess his brother to relinquish his horse and try the extremity by hand strokes, which if he had been on his horseback might fortune to have escaped' (page 296).

2   *bug* bugbear
    feared frightened

3   *sit fast* make sure your position is firm

11 *cedar.* As the tallest plant of the vegetable kingdom, this tree was an Elizabethan symbol of sovereignty.

12 *the princely eagle* (Richard Duke of York)
    eagle (the bird which corresponded to the king in the Elizabethan avian hierarchy)

13 *the ramping lion* (Henry VI)
    ramping rampant, rearing angrily. The lion was considered the king of beasts and the royal coat of arms carried lions rampant.

14 *over-peered* towered over, overlooked
    Jove's spreading tree (the oak, which was the counterpart of the cedar among the deciduous trees)

15 *kept* protected

18 *search* perceive

22 *bent his brow* frowned

23-5 *Lo, now my glory . . . now forsake me.* Hall stresses how death came 'with his dart to take from Warwick all worldly and mundane affections' (page 296).

24 *parks* hunting grounds
    walks pleasure grounds

25-6 *of all my lands | Is nothing left me but my body's length.* This contrast between the earthly ambitions of the great ruler and the size of the grave which finally held his remains was a commonplace taken from Latin literature; Shakespeare later gave memorable expression to it in *Richard II*, III.3.153-4, and *1 Henry IV*, V.4.87-91.

28 *die we must* (proverbial: 'All men must die')

29-32 *Ah, Warwick . . . couldst thou fly.* In the account of

268

these events by Philippe de Commines in his *Memoirs* (translated into English by T. Danet in 1596), it is noted that if Warwick had waited for the Queen's forces he would have been victorious. Also in this account the Battle of Tewkesbury follows directly from Barnet, as it does in the play.

31–2   *The Queen from France ... news.* In the chronicles, Queen Margaret lands in England on the same day as the battle, having been delayed by bad weather: 'Queen Margaret, having knowledge that all things in England were now altered and brought into trouble and broil by reason of King Edward's late return into the realm, gathered together no small company of hardy and valiant soldiers, determined with all haste and diligence, with Prince Edward her son, to sail into England; but yet once again (such was her destiny) being letted for lack of prosperous wind and encumbered with too much rigorous tempest, a day after the fair, as the common proverb saith, landed at the port of Weymouth in Dorsetshire. When she had passed the sea and taken land, it was to her declared how that King Edward had gotten again the garland and that King Henry her husband was desolately left post alone and taken prisoner, how the Earl of Warwick and his brother were both slain and dead' (Hall, page 297).

31   *puissant power* mighty army

35   *with thy lips* (with a kiss. The soul was believed to fly upwards from the mouth at the moment of death.)

40–47   *Montague ... farewell, Warwick.* Compare Hall: 'The Marquess Montague, thinking to succour his brother, which he saw was in great jeopardy, and yet in hope to obtain the victory, was likewise overthrown and slain' (page 296).

41   *latest* final

45   *mought* might

50   *Away, away, to meet the Queen's great power.* Historic-

ally, 'after this field ended, the Duke of Somerset with John Earl of Oxford were in all post haste flying toward Scotland; but fearing the jeopardies that might chance in so long a journey, altered their purpose and turned into Wales to Jasper Earl of Pembroke; every man fled whither his mind served him' (Hall, page 297).

(stage direction) *bear away his body*. As the Elizabethan stage had no front curtain, all dead bodies had to be carried from the stage.

V.3   The location of the scene is another part of the battlefield at Barnet.

(stage direction) *in triumph*. Historically Edward left Barnet to return to London, where he was 'greatly rejoiced and comforted, after the manner of a victorious conqueror' (Hall, page 297).

2   *graced* favoured

5   *sun* (the heraldic symbol of the Yorkists; see the second note to II.1.25)

7-9   *those powers ... fight with us*. In the chronicles the Queen loses heart after Barnet on hearing of the news of Edward's victory and Henry's imprisonment. She retires to Beaulieu in Hampshire and only decides to renew the war under the influence of Somerset.

8   *Gallia* France
        arrived landed on

12   *very* mere
        beams (of the sun of York)

13   *every cloud engenders not a storm* (proverbial: 'All clouds bring not storms')
        engenders not does not produce

14   *the Queen is valued* the Queen's army is estimated to be *thirty thousand*. The chronicles give no number for the Queen's forces; Philippe de Commines in his *Memoirs* gives forty thousand.

15 *with Oxford*. In the chronicles only Somerset is named among those who joined the Queen after she had taken sanctuary at Beaulieu (Hall, page 298).

16 *time to breathe*. Historically this was exactly what the Queen and her allies had between Barnet and Tewkesbury (Hall, page 300).

breathe rest, catch her breath

18 *advertised* (accented on the second syllable) informed

19 *they do hold their course toward Tewkesbury*. Historically the Queen camped at Bath in order to augment her forces, then marched to Bristol, bypassed Gloucester (where Richard was influential), and stayed at Tewkesbury (Hall, page 300).

20 *the best* triumphed

21 *straight* at once

willingness rids way eagerness to travel makes the distance seem shorter

22-3 *as we march ... along*. This seems to have been suggested by Hall's summary of Somerset's arguments to the Queen: that the war should be resumed 'with all haste possible and extreme diligence, lest their company by tarrying might be diminished and King Edward's power increased and augmented, considering that all this time he had no army gathered together, for so much that at the last battle the very strength of his chief soldiers was weakened and appalled' (page 298).

V.4 The location is the open ground near Tewkesbury on 4 May 1471. The Queen's attitude in this scene is in marked contrast with that found in the chronicles, where she is dispirited and fearful after hearing the news of the Yorkist success at Barnet and of Henry's capture. It was only by Somerset's persuasion that she was deterred from fleeing to Wales with her son. See the notes to V.3 and to lines 1-38 below.

(stage direction) *Oxford.* The chronicles make it clear that Oxford was not at Tewkesbury. After Barnet he seized and occupied Saint Michael's Mount in Cornwall until he surrendered to Edward in 1474 and was imprisoned for twelve years; see the note to V.5.2.

1–38   *Great lords ... lament or fear.* The idea for this stirring speech of encouragement may have come from Hall's description of Margaret's actions after the lines of battle had been drawn up: 'When all these battles were thus ordered and placed, the Queen and her son, Prince Edward, rode about the field, encouraging their soldiers, promising to them, if they did show themselves valiant against their enemies, great rewards and high promotions, innumerable gain of the spoil and booty of their adversaries, and above all other fame and renown through the whole realm' (page 300). The extended use of the ship metaphor is very close in treatment to lines 1359–77 of Arthur Brooke's *The Tragical History of Romeus and Juliet* (1562), a poem that Shakespeare used as a source of his play of the same name.

1–2   *wise men ne'er sit and wail their loss,* | *But cheerly seek how to redress their harms* (proverbial: 'One must not wail a mischief but find out the remedy')

2   *cheerly* cheerfully
     redress their harms repair their damage

4   *holding-anchor* anchor (which moors)

6   *our pilot* (Henry VI)
     meet fitting

7   *fearful* frightened

8   *With tearful eyes add water to the sea* (proverbial: 'To cast water into the sea')

10   *in his moan* during his laments

11   *industry* hard labour
     saved prevented

12   *fault* crime

15   *tackles* rigging

18	*of* from
	shrouds sail-ropes
	tacklings rigging
19	*Ned* (Prince Edward, her son)
20	*charge* duty, responsibility
21	*from* leave
23	*shelves* sandbanks
	wrack shipwreck
24	*speak them fair* address them respectfully
27	*ragged* jagged
28	*bark* ship
34	*If case* should it happen that
37–8	*What cannot be avoided	'Twere childish weakness to lament or fear* (proverbial: 'What cannot be cured must be endured')
41	*magnanimity* greatness of spirit
42	*naked* unarmed
	foil defeat
	man at arms fully equipped soldier
45	*betimes* at once
47	*like spirit* similar disposition
51	*faint* faint-hearted
52	*grandfather* (Henry V)
54	*image* likeness
55	*hope* (promising young prince)
59	*his* (my)
62–3	*it is his policy	To haste thus fast.* In his portrait of Edward, this is one of the qualities that Hall stresses: 'in great affairs and weighty causes quick and diligent' (page 341).
62	*policy* cunning strategy
63	*unprovided* unprepared
65	*forwardness* eagerness
66	*pitch our battle* align our forces in battle order
70	*add more fuel to your fire* (proverbial)
74	*gainsay* forbid
77	*state* kingship
80	*makes this spoil* wreaks this destruction

V.5   The location is the battlefield at Tewkesbury. The Q1 stage direction at V.4.82 gives some idea of how the ebb and flow of the battle was conveyed on the Elizabethan stage: see the Account of the Text, page 297.

1   *period* end

2   *Away with Oxford to Hames Castle.* Oxford was not present at the battle. After Barnet he 'both manfully got and valiantly kept Saint Michael's Mount in Cornwall; [but] either for lack of aid or persuaded by his friends, gave up the Mount and yielded himself to King Edward, his life only saved, which to him was granted. But to be out of all doubtful imaginations, King Edward sent him over the sea to the Castle of Hames, where by the space of twelve years he was in strong prison miserably kept and diligently looked to' (Hall, page 304).

Hames Castle (a stronghold in Picardy)
straight immediately

3   *For Somerset, off with his guilty head.* Compare Hall: 'on the Monday next ensuing was Edmund Duke of Somerset ... beheaded in the market-place at Tewkesbury' (page 301).

For as for

6   *stoop* (1) submit; (2) bend (to the headsman's block)
fortune fate

8   *Jerusalem* (the New Jerusalem, Heaven: Revelation 21.2)

9–10   *Is proclamation made ... life.* Compare Hall: 'After the field ended, King Edward made a proclamation that whosoever could bring Prince Edward to him alive or dead should have an annuity of an hundred pounds during his life, and the Prince's life to be saved' (page 301).

9   *who* he who

11–40   *lo, where youthful ... me with perjury.* Compare Hall: 'Sir Richard Crofts, a wise and a valiant knight, nothing mistrusting the King's former promise, brought forth his prisoner, Prince Edward, being a goodly, feminine, and a well-featured young gentleman, whom when King Edward had well advised, he demanded of him how he darest so presumptuously enter into his realm with banner displayed. The Prince, being bold of stomach and of a good courage, answered saying: "To recover my father's kingdom and inheritance from his father and grandfather to him, and from him, after him to me lineally devoluted." At which words King Edward said nothing, but with his hand thrust him from him (or, as some say, struck him with his gauntlet); whom, incontinent, they that stood about, which were George Duke of Clarence, Richard Duke of Gloucester, Thomas Marquess Dorset, and William Lord Hastings, suddenly murdered and piteously manquelled' (page 301).

11   *youthful*. Edward was eighteen at this time.

13   *Can so young a thorn begin to prick* (proverbial: 'It early pricks that will be a thorn')

14   *satisfaction* atonement

18   *mouth* spokesman

19   *chair* throne

23-4 *you might still have worn the petticoat | And ne'er have stolen the breech* (proverbial: 'She wears the breeches'; compare *Part Two*, I.3.144)

23   *still* always

24   *breech* breeches

25   *Aesop* (the Greek sixth-century fabulist, who was reported to have been a hunchback)

26   *currish riddles* (comments of the kind associated with the Greek philosophers known as Cynics; but also 'doggish, mean')

      sorts not with are inappropriate to

27   *brat* (not always used contemptuously) child

31   *charm* silence

32   *Untutored* badly brought up

32   *malapert* impudent

37   *right* legal claim (to the throne)

38   *the likeness of this railer* (the image of your mother)

39   *Sprawlest thou* do you writhe in pain

42   *Marry, and shall* by the Virgin Mary, I will
    (stage direction) *offers* is about

46–50   *Clarence, excuse me . . . the Tower.* In the chronicles, the murder of Henry VI takes place after the Yorkist forces had returned to London.

48   *be sure to* you may be certain you will

51–67   *O Ned . . . . sweet young Prince.* Hall stresses that the Queen 'passed her days . . . languishing and mourning in continual sorrow, not so much for herself and her husband, whose ages were almost consumed and worn, but for the loss of Prince Edward her son' (page 301).

55   *were by to equal* had been there to compare with

56   *in respect* by comparison

62   *untimely* prematurely

63–4   *You have no children, butchers; if you had, | The thought of them would have stirred up remorse* (proverbial: 'He that has no children knows not what love is')

63   *You have no children.* This was not true: Edward had several, and Clarence one son.

64   *remorse* pity

65–7   *But if you ever . . . young Prince.* Hall comments, after recording the death of Prince Edward: 'The bitterness of which murder some of the actors after in their latter days tasted and assayed by the very rod of justice and punishment of God' (page 301).

66   *Look* I hope you can expect

67   *deathsmen* executioners
    rid destroyed

68   *perforce* by force

69   *dispatch* slay

70   *Here sheathe thy sword.* Margaret offers Edward her breast.

72   *do thee so much ease* release you from your grief (by killing you)

75   *usest to forswear* are in the habit of perjuring

78   *Hard-favoured* ugly in appearance

79   *alms-deed* act of charity

80   *puttest back* reject

81   *charge* order

       bear her hence. Compare Hall: 'Queen Margaret like a prisoner was brought to London' (page 301).

82   *come* may happen

84   *all in post* at full speed

86   *sudden* prompt in action, impulsive

87   *common sort* ordinary soldiers

90   *a son* (Edward V, born in 1470; a daughter, Elizabeth, had been born in 1465)

V.6   The location of the scene is a cell in the Tower of London. It is based upon (1) Hall's account of Henry's death following Edward's victory at Tewkesbury: 'Poor King Henry VI, a little before deprived of his realm and imperial crown, was now in the Tower of London spoiled of his life and all worldly felicity by Richard Duke of Gloucester (as the constant fame ran), which, to the intent that King Edward his brother should be clear out of all secret suspicion of sudden invasion, murdered the said King with a dagger' (page 303); and (2) Hall's character portrait of Richard: 'he was little of stature, evil-featured of limbs, crook-backed, the left shoulder much higher than the right, hard-favoured of visage, such as in estates is called a warlike visage, and among common persons a crabbed face. He was malicious, wrathful, and envious, and, as it is reported, his mother the Duchess had much ado in her travail, that she could not be delivered of him uncut, and that he came into the world the feet forward, . . . and, as the fame ran, not untoothed. . . . He was close and secret, a deep dissimuler, lowly of countenance, arrogant of heart, outwardly familiar where he inwardly hated, not letting to kiss whom he thought to kill, despiteous and cruel, not alway for evil will but ofter for ambition and to serve his purpose; friend and foe were all indifferent where his advantage grew; he spared no man's death whose life withstood his purpose. He slew in the Tower King Henry VI, saying "Now is there no heir male of King Edward III but we of the house of York".... Some wise men also ween that his drift lacked not in helping forth his own brother of Clarence to his death, which thing in all appearance he resisted, although he inwardly minded it' (pages 342–3).

1   *book* (prayer-book)

3   *'Tis sin to flatter* (Daniel 11.32)
     better (than flattery)

4   *were* would be

5   *preposterous* invert the natural order of things

6   *Sirrah* (a form of address used to a social inferior)

7   *reckless* thoughtless, careless

10   *Roscius* (the greatest Roman actor, who died in 62 B.C. and whom the Elizabethans used as the standard of great tragic acting)

11   *Suspicion always haunts the guilty mind* (proverbial: 'Who is guilty suspects everybody')
     Suspicion fear of something bad about to happen

12   *The thief doth fear each bush an officer* (proverbial)

13–14   *The bird that hath been limèd in a bush, | With trembling wings misdoubteth every bush* (proverbial: 'Birds once limed fear all bushes')

13, 17   *limed* (trapped by the use of bird-lime)

14   *misdoubteth* suspects

15   *hapless male* unfortunate father
     bird (young bird, offspring)

16   *fatal* death-dealing
     object. Henry views Richard as 'a thing of death'.

17   *my poor young ... killed.* The reference is to Richard's stabbing of Prince Edward at Tewkesbury.

18–20   *what a peevish ... was drowned.* Daedalus was a famous Athenian inventor who constructed the labyrinth to contain the Minotaur for King Minos of Crete. He escaped from his subsequent imprisonment in Crete with his son Icarus by making wings for them both. Icarus, intoxicated with flight, flew too near the sun, which melted the wax with which the feathers were fixed to the wings, and he fell to his death in the sea.

18   *peevish* childish

19   *office* function

19–20   *fowl ... fool.* These two words were pronounced sufficiently alike for there to be a quibble here.

20   *for all* despite

22   *denied* forbade

       course departure

23   *sun.* The reference is to the badge of Edward; see the second note to II.1.25.

25   *envious gulf* malicious whirlpool

27   *brook* endure

28   *history* story

38   *mistrust no parcel* do not suspect any portion

40   *water-standing* (flooded with tears)

42   *timeless* untimely

44   *owl* (a bird of ill-omen)

45   *The night-crow cried, aboding luckless time* (proverbial: 'The croaking raven bodes misfortune')

       night-crow (bird of ill-omen, probably an owl or night-jar)

       aboding predicting, foreboding

47   *rooked her* crouched

48   *pies* magpies

       dismal sinister

51   *indigested* uncompleted

64   *purple* blood-red

69	*that* what
71	*forward* (emerging feet-first from the womb)
73	*right* claim to the throne
74	*wondered* was astonished
79	*crooked* (one syllable)
	answer conform with
81	*'love', which greybeards call divine*. Compare 1 John 4.7: 'love cometh of God'.
82	*like* who resemble
84–8	*Clarence, beware ... be thy death*. For Shakespeare's full dramatic treatment of Richard's responsibility, see Act I of *Richard III*.
85	*I will sort a pitchy day for thee* (proverbial: 'It will be a black day for somebody')
	sort a pitchy day choose a black day, arrange a fatal future
86	*buzz abroad* spread about (rumours of)
87	*of* for
88	*purge* clear away, expel
91	*Counting myself but bad till I be best* because I consider myself the lowliest in the land until I achieve the crown
93	*triumph* exult
	of doom on which you face God's judgement

V.7	The location is the royal palace in London. There is no basis for the scene in the chronicles, though some details are taken from Hall; see the notes below. (stage direction) *the infant prince* (Edward, Prince of Wales (1470–83), later Edward V, murdered with his brother Richard in the Tower)
1	*Once more*. Edward reflects the seesawing of fortunes during the play.
2	*Repurchased with* regained at the cost of
4	*in tops* at the height
	pride fullness of growth

5   *Three Dukes of Somerset*. See the notes to I.1.16 and
to the opening stage direction of IV.1.

6   *For* as
undoubted fearless
champions outstanding warriors

7   *Two Cliffords*. See the notes to I.1.7 and to the stage
direction at I.1.49.
as namely

8   *two Northumberlands*. See the notes to I.1.4 and to
the stage direction at I.1.49.

9   *coursers* chargers

10   *bears*. The allusion is to Warwick's heraldic device of
the bear chained to the ragged staff, which he inherited with his title from his father-in-law. See the
notes to the opening stage direction of I.1 and also
Part Two, V.1.144.

11   *chains* (by which the bears were fastened to the
stake during a bear-baiting)

13   *suspicion* anxiety
seat throne

14   *And made our footstool of security*. This is almost
identical with a line in Marlowe's *The Massacre at
Paris*, 14.41.

17   *watched* stayed awake during

21   *blast* blight
head (1) Edward's head; (2) the ear of corn
laid (1) put to rest (in death); (2) flattened

22   *looked on* respected, highly regarded

23   *thick* strong, sturdy

25   *Work thou the way* you make a path, you devise a means
thou (himself)
that (his shoulder)

28   *duty* loyalty, obedience

30   *brother* brother-in-law

31-2   *that I love . . . fruit* (proverbial: 'Many kiss the child
for the nurse's sake')

31   *tree* (family of York)

33–4   *so Judas kissed ... harm.* The comparison with the betrayal of Christ may have been suggested by Hall's comment on Richard's 'not letting to kiss whom he thought to kill' (page 343).

34   *when as* when on the contrary

38–40   *Reignier, her father ... her ransom.* Margaret's ransoming took place in 1475, four years after the Battle of Tewkesbury. Compare Hall: 'Queen Margaret like a prisoner was brought to London, where she remained till King Reignier, her father, ransomed her with money, which sum (as the French writers affirm) he borrowed of King Louis XI; and because he was not of power nor ability to repay so great a duty, he sold to the French King and his heirs the kingdoms of Naples and both the Sicils, with the county of Provence' (page 301).

39   *the Sicils* (Naples and Sicily)

40   *it* (the sum borrowed)

41   *waft* convey by sea

42   *rests* remains

43   *triumphs* public displays of celebration

45   *sour annoy* bitter troubles

AN ACCOUNT OF THE TEXT

THE Third Part of *Henry VI* exists in two versions. The first of these was published by Thomas Millington in octavo format in 1595 ('Q1') under the title *The true Tragedie of Richard Duke of York*, which was reprinted by the same publisher in 1600 ('Q2') and in 1619 by Thomas Pavier, who combined it with a version of *Henry VI, Part Two* and called them together *The Whole Contention betweene the two Famous Houses, Lancaster and Yorke* ('Q3'). The second version appears in the first Folio edition of the collected plays of 1623 ('F'), where it is the eighth play in the Histories section and is called *The third Part of Henry the Sixt, with the death of the Duke of Yorke*. It is obvious that there is a close relationship between these two texts; but its exact nature is still a matter of scholarly debate.

F is clearly the superior text and is about one third longer than Q. Behind the work of the two main compositors of the Folio volume, who (with the help of a third man) did the typesetting for this play, there appears to be Shakespeare's own manuscript. The evidence for authorial copy is abundant. Many stage directions are descriptive and literary rather than theatrical (for example, those at III.1.12, III.3.0, and IV.3.27) and some stage directions for exit implicit in the text are omitted (for example, at I.1.184, 186, and 188). Some minor roles are assigned by name to known actors in the company by the author: Sincklo and Humphrey (Jeffes) are cast as the two Keepers in III.1, and Gabriel (Spencer) is indicated as taking the part of the Messenger to York at I.2.47. There are also indications that the roles assigned to some characters were changed during the course of composition. The most remarkable example of this is Falconbridge, who is referred to at I.1.239 as having control of the Dover Straits, but whose part seems to have been assumed by Montague, who inappropriately speaks as if he were Falconbridge at I.1.209. Montague's relationship to Warwick is also not clearly grasped in the early scenes, where he is treated as York's brother (see the Commentary to I.1.14). Some inaccuracy in the use of the chronicles (for example, in the marriages arranged for Warwick's daughters with Clarence and Prince Edward at III.3.240–50 and IV.1.118) is also likely to be of authorial origin.

Q is a much inferior text and looks as though it is a deliberately shortened version of the original play. The line of narrative is the same as in F, and many of the speeches are very close to their counterparts in F; but at many points material seems to have been transposed or appears to be a poor paraphrase of what is found in F. Some minor characters are dropped, such as the three Watchmen in IV.3 and the Lieutenant of the Tower in V.6. Lines are included which are recollections of other plays, and the whole text is poetically inferior. Q's stage directions often read like descriptions of what took place in a particular production rather than instructions of what should be performed. Some of these (for example, at I.1.0. and 49 and V.1.81) strike one as stage business not demanded by but permitted by the F text.

Various theories have been elaborated to account for the features of these two texts and to explain the relationship between them and its origin:

1. Some scholars argue that Q is an original play which Shakespeare rewrote as *Henry VI, Part Three*. Passages where F and Q agree are viewed as having been taken over verbatim by Shakespeare from his source-play; passages in F which are superior to Q are seen as indicating rewriting; and those in F which have no parallel in Q are taken to be Shakespeare's additions.

2. A more generally accepted theory claims that Q is a memorially reconstructed acting version of the play F prints. The fact that some of the roles in Q are more full and accurate

than others suggests that the actors who originally played the parts of Warwick and Lord Clifford may have helped in creating from memory the shortened and faulty version of the text that Millington published.

3. The pattern of agreement and non-agreement in variants between F and Q has been explained as being of printing-house origin. Instead of working directly from Shakespeare's manuscript, the F compositors are seen to have set type from a copy of Q 3 (and possibly Q2 in part) which had been corrected and added to by reference to such a manuscript, following the amended printed text whenever they could and consulting the handwritten copy only when it provided substantial additional material.

4. Many scholars believe that features of F and Q, whatever their relationship, can be explained only by the play's being of multiple authorship. Using mainly stylistic and some external evidence, they argue that the play was originally the work of Robert Greene, Thomas Nashe, George Peele, and Shakespeare working with them and/or revising the original play to make it fit into a three-part sequence.

The purely textual features of Q and F versions are often analysed in connexion with various pieces of external historical evidence, which are themselves susceptible to very different interpretations. For example, the first reference we have to Shakespeare as a dramatist occurs in Robert Greene's pamphlet *Groatsworth of Wit* (1592), where the dying writer appears to be warning his fellow dramatists against Shakespeare, whom he characterizes as 'an upstart crow, beautified with our feathers, that with his *Tiger's heart wrapped in a player's hide* supposes he is as well able to bombast out a blank verse as the best of you; and, being an absolute *Johannes fac totum*, is in his own conceit the only Shake-scene in a country'.

Clearly this allusion connects Shakespeare with the authorship of the *Henry VI* plays; but scholars differ as to the exact nature of the charge Greene is making. Obviously he is angered by Shakespeare's theatrical success; but is he implying that Shakespeare plagiarized his and other men's work?

Or is he irate at the spectacle of a mere actor competing with university-trained playwrights? Or is he being scornful of Shakespeare's literary imitation of his contemporaries? And what exactly is the point of the misquotation of the line at I.4.137? With widely different interpretations of Greene's tirade possible, it can easily be seen that it may be used to support a variety of theories about the origins and relationship of the Q and F versions.

According to the title-page of Q1 the play was '*sundrie times acted by the Right Honourable the Earle of Pembrooke his seruants*', a theatrical company which was forced to tour the provinces owing to the closure of the London theatres occasioned by the plague in parts of 1592 and 1593. Apparently these players went bankrupt as a result of this experience and were forced to sell up their effects. Some of their plays ultimately found their way into the repertoire of the Lord Chamberlain's Men, a company of which Shakespeare was to become the chief playwright and a leading shareholder. Like the Greene allusion, this tantalizingly incomplete theatrical history – involving as it does Shakespeare, Greene, Peele, Nashe, and Marlowe as playwrights, a company being disbanded, and plays changing hands – can be used in support of very different textual theories about *3 Henry VI*.

Thus at the moment there is no theory concerning the genesis and early history of the play which has won general acceptance; nor is there agreement about its date of composition (between 1588 and 1592), any estimate of which must obviously take into account much of the same evidence.

As F is the better version of the play it is this that the present edition follows. Only where F presents genuine difficulties has Q been used to make emendations. In the Commentary and in collations lists 1 and 3, Q's readings are recorded when they seem to throw light on possible meaning or stage practice, even where no emendation has been made in F. List 4 quotes the more substantial passages in Q which are noticeably different from those in F or constitute an addition to what is found there.

COLLATIONS

The following lists are selective. The quartos are abbreviated as 'Q1' (1595), 'Q2' (1600), 'Q3' (1619), and the editions of the Folio as 'F1' (1623), 'F2' (1632), 'F3' (1663–4), 'F4' (1685). In lists 1–3 quotations from the early editions are unmodernized, except that 'long s' (ʃ) is replaced by 's'.

I

Emendations

Below are listed the more important departures from the text of F1, with the readings of this edition printed to the left of the square bracket. Those readings adopted from or based on Q1 are identified, as are readings taken from the reprints of F. Most of the other emendations were first made by eighteenth- and nineteenth-century editors. Corrections of obvious misprints and demonstrable mislineation, the variant spelling of proper names, and punctuation changes where the sense is not significantly affected are not recorded. The speech prefixes of F have been regularized, including those for characters whose change of rank in the course of the play is often reflected in their F designations: thus Edward always appears as 'EDWARD' despite the indication 'King' at some points in F; George Duke of Clarence always appears as 'GEORGE' despite F's change to 'Clarence'; Richard Duke of Gloucester always appears as 'RICHARD', both before and after his elevation to the dukedom; and Lady Elizabeth Grey is always indicated by 'LADY GREY', both before and after she is Queen.

THE CHARACTERS IN THE PLAY] *not in* F

I.1.   69 EXETER] (Q1); *Westm.*

      105 Thy] (Q1); My

      259 with] (Q1); *not in* F

      261 from] (Q1); to

I.2.   49 MESSENGER] (Q1); *Gabriel.*

I.4.   111 She-wolf ... wolves of France,] Shee-Wolfe of France, | But ... Wolues of France,

I.4.   120 Were ... shameless.] Were ... thee, | Wert ... shamelesse.

      152–3 That ... cannibals | Would ... blood;] That ... his, | The ... toucht, | Would ... blood:

II.1.   33 'Tis ... of.] 'Tis ... strange, | The ... of.

      41 Nay ... it,] Nay ... Daughters: | By ... it,

      157 makes] (F2); make

      181 amain] (Q1); *not in* F

II.2. 89–92 Since when ... in] (F2); *assigned to George in* F1

      101 What ... crown?] What ... *Henry*, | Wilt ... Crowne?

      116 sun set] (Q1); Sunset

      133 RICHARD] (Q1); *War.*

      172 deniest] (Q1); denied'st

II.3.   44 Brother ... Warwick,] Brother, | Giue ... Warwicke,

      48 Away ... farewell.] Away, away: | Once ... farwell.

      49 all together] altogether

II.5.   119 Even] Men

II.6.   6 commixture] (Q1); Commixtures

      8 The common ... flies;] (Q1); *not in* F

      44 See who it is] *assigned to Edward in* Q1; *assigned to Richard in* F

      68 If ... words.] If ... think'st, | Vex ... Words.

      76 They ... wont.] They ... *Clifford*, | Sweare ... wont.

III.1.   1 (and throughout the scene) FIRST KEEPER] (Q1 *Keeper.*); *Sink.* (i.e. 'Sinklo')

      5 (and throughout the scene) SECOND KEEPER] (Q1 *Keeper.*); *Hum.* (i.e. 'Humfrey')

      12 SECOND KEEPER] *Sink.*

      17 wast] (F3); was

      24 thee, sour adversity] the sower Aduersaries

      55 that] (Q1); *not in* F

III.2.   3 lands] (Q1); Land

123 honourably] (Q1); honourable

III.3. 16–18 And . . . neck | To . . . mind | Still . . . mischance.]
And . . . side. | Yeeld . . . yoake, | But . . .
triumph, | Ouer . . . mischance.

124 eternal] (Q1); externall

156 peace,] (F2); *not in* F1

169–70 Nay . . . best] *prose in* F

228 I'll] (Q1); I

253 Shalt] (F2); Shall

IV.1. 20–23 Not I; | No . . . severed | Whom . . . pity | To . . .
together.] Not I: no: | God . . . seuer'd, | Whom
. . . together: | I, and . . . them, | That . . . to-
gether.

29–31 Then . . . Lewis | Becomes . . . him | About . . .
Bona.] Then . . . opinion: | That . . . Enemie, |
For . . . Marriage | Of . . . *Bona*.

89–90 Go . . . brief, | Tell . . . them.] Goe . . . thee: |
Therefore . . . words, | As neere . . . them.

93 thy] (Q1); the

124–5 Not . . . matter. | I . . . crown.] Not I: | My . . .
matter: | I stay . . . Crowne.

IV.2. 15 towns] Towne

IV.5. 4 stands] stand

8 Comes] Come

20–21 lord. | . . . Flanders?] Lord, | . . . Flanders.

21 ship] shipt

IV.6. 55 be] *not in* F

68–9 Come . . . powers | Suggest . . . thoughts,]
Come . . . Hope: | If: . . truth | To . . . thoughts,

IV.7. 45–7 Thanks . . . forget | Our title . . . claim | Our . . .
rest.] Thankes . . . *Mountgomerie:* | But . . .
Crowne, | And . . . Dukedome, | Till . . . rest.

IV.8. 17–18 well-beloved | In Oxfordshire, shalt] well
belou'd, | In Oxfordshire shalt

V.1. 78 an] (F2); in

V.2. 48 Sweet . . . yourselves;] Sweet . . . Soule: |
Flye . . . selues,

V.4.	27	ragged] raged
V.5.	50	The] (Q1); *not in* F
V.6.	46	tempests] (Q1); Tempest
V.7.	5	renowned] (Q1); Renowne
	25	shall] shalt
	30	LADY GREY] (Q1 *Queen.*); *Cla.*
		Thanks] (Q1); Thanke

2

Rejected emendations

The following list records a selection of emendations and conjunctures which have not been adopted in this edition, but which have been made with some plausibility by other editors. Many of these emendations are readings adopted from Q1. To the left of the square brackets are the readings of the present text; to the right of them are F's readings where they differ from this edition, then readings adopted from Q1, and other suggested emendations. When more than one emendation is listed, they are separated by semi-colons. All emendations made to achieve metrical regularity have been ignored in this list; and most of the substantial passages from Q introduced by some editors at various points in the play, in accordance with their theories of the relationship between F and Q, are quoted in list 4 below.

I.1.	19	hope] hap
	120	KING] NORTHUMBERLAND (Q1)
I.4.	137	tiger's] (F Tygres); tigress'
II.1.	112–13	friends, | Marched] friends, | And very well appointed, as I thought, | Marched (Q1)
	130	lazy] idle (Q1)
	189	failest] faints (Q1); fallest
II.5.	38	days, months] days, weeks, months
	119	Even] (F Men); Son; Meet
II.6.	24	out] our (Q1)
III.2.	23	blow] clap (Q1)

	132	place] plant (Q1)
III.3.	11	seat] state
	128	quit] quite (Q1)
	133	tempted] tempered
IV.1.	13	our] your
IV.2.	12	welcome] come
IV.8		(*Numbered as a continuous scene rather than divided after line 32*)
V.2.	44	cannon] clamour (Q1)

3

Stage directions

The stage directions of this edition are based on those in F. The more important changes and additions to the F directions are listed below. The normalization of characters' names, minor adjustments in the order in which characters are listed, and the provision of exits and entrances clearly demanded by the action but omitted in F are not recorded. All asides and most indications of characters addressed are editorial, as are corrections of 'Exit' to 'Exeunt'. The readings of this edition appear to the left of the square brackets; to the right of the brackets are stage directions from Q1 wherever they have been adopted as or form the basis for those of the present edition, and the F readings. Quarto stage directions which have not been adopted in the present text, but which clarify the action or provide evidence of possible Elizabethan staging, are quoted and discussed in the Commentary.

I.1.	0	*with white roses in their hats*] (Q1); *not in* F
	16	*He throws down the Duke of Somerset's head*] *not in* F
	49	*soldiers*] *the rest*
		with red roses in their hats] (Q1); *not in* F
184, 186, 188		*Exit*] (Q1); *not in* F
	206	*Exeunt York and his sons*] (Q1); *not in* F
207, 208,		
	209	*Exit*] (Q1); *not in* F

I.1.   210 *and the Prince of Wales*] (Q1); *not in* F

       263 *Exeunt Queen and Prince*] (Q1); *not in* F

       273 *Flourish*] (*at the head of* I.2 *in* F)

I.2.   47 *a Messenger*] (Q1); *Gabriel.*

I.3.   0 *Alarum*] (*at the end of* I.2 *in* F)

       2 *and soldiers*] *not in* F

       9 *dragged off by soldiers*] *not in* F

       34 *He lifts his sword*] *not in* F

       47 *He stabs Rutland*] *not in* F

       48 *He dies*] *not in* F

I.4.   50 *He draws his sword*] *not in* F

       60 *They fight and York is taken*] Fight and take him. (Q1); *not in* F

       95 *She puts a paper crown on York's head*] *not in* F

       175 *He stabs York*] *not in* F

       176 *She stabs York*] *not in* F

       178 *He dies*] *not in* F

II.1.   42 *Enter a Messenger, blowing a horn*] *Enter one blowing*

       94 *of Montague*] (Q1); *Mountacute*

II.5.   54 *Alarum. Enter at one door a Son that hath killed his father, with the dead body in his arms*] Enter a souldier with a dead man in his armes. (Q1); *Alarum. Enter a Sonne that hath kill'd his Father, at one doore: and a Father that hath kill'd his Sonne at another doore.*

       78 *Enter at another door a Father that hath killed his son, with the dead body in his arms*] Enter an other souldier, with a dead man. (Q1); *Enter Father, bearing of his Sonne.*

       113 *Exit with the body of his father*] Exit with his father. (Q1); *not in* F

       122 *with the body of his son*] with his sonne. (Q1); *not in* F

II.6.   30 *He faints*] *not in* F

       41 *Clifford groans and then dies*] (Q1); *Clifford grones*

III.1.   o *Enter two Keepers, with cross-bows in their hands*]
                Enter two keepers with bow and arrowes.
                (Q1); *Enter Sinklo, and Humfrey, with Crosse-
                bowes in their hands.*

                12 *Enter King Henry, disguised, with a prayer-book*]
                Enter king *Henrie* disguisde. (Q1); *Enter the
                King with a Prayer booke.*

III.2.   35 *Richard and George go out of earshot*] *not in* F

III.3.   161 *Post blowing a horn within*] (*follows line 160 in* F)

IV.1.   6 *attended ... as queen ... and other courtiers*]
                not in F

IV.3.   60 *They lead him out forcibly*] (*follows line 58 in* F)

IV.6.   o *of the Tower*] *not in* F

IV.7.   34 *below*] *not in* F

                39 *Sir John*] *not in* F

IV.8.   o *and Oxford*] Oxford, *and Somerset.*

                32 *Enter King Henry and Exeter*] *not in* F

                50 *'Â York! Â York!'*] A Lancaster, A Lancaster.

                51 *Richard*] *not in* F
                   their] his

                57 *Exeunt some soldiers*] Exit

V.1.   6 *Sir John*] *not in* F

                10 *A drum is heard*] *not in* F

        59, 67,
                72 *He leads his forces into the city*] *not in* F

                81 *He takes his red rose out of his hat and throws it at
                Warwick*] (Q1); *not in* F

                113 *Edward and his company*] *not in* F

V.2.   49 *He dies*] (Q1); *not in* F

V.5.   o *Flourish. Enter Edward, Richard, George, and
                their army, with the Queen, Oxford, and Somer-
                set, prisoners*] Flourish. Enter Edward, Richard,
                Queene, Clarence, Oxford, Somerset.

                6 *Exeunt Oxford and Somerset, guarded*] Exit Ox-
                ford. (*after line 5*) Exit Sum. (Q1); *Exeunt.*

        11, 82 *guarded*] *not in* F

V.6.   o *Enter King Henry the Sixth and Richard below,*

		with the Lieutenant of the Tower on the walls] *Enter Henry the sixt, and Richard, with the Lieutenant on the Walles.*

V.6.   6 *Exit Lieutenant*] not in F

          93 *with the body*] not in F

V.7.   o *Flourish. Enter Edward and Lady Grey, as king and queen, George, Richard, Hastings, a nurse carrying the infant prince, and attendants*] Enter king *Edward, Queene Elizabeth*, and a Nurse with the young prince, and *Clarence*, and *Hastings*, and others. (Q1); *Flourish. Enter King, Queene, Clarence, Richard, Hastings, Nurse, and Attendants.*

4

Variant and additional passages in Q1

In general Q1 offers an inferior and truncated version of the text in F; but at certain points there occur passages in Q1 which either are noticeably different in content and expression from their counterparts in F or constitute genuine additions to what is found in F. Below are quoted, in modernized form, the more substantial of such passages, each printed below a reference to the appropriate point in the text of this edition.

I.4.1–6 The army ... bechancèd them:

    Ah, York, post to thy castle, save thy life!
    The goal is lost. Thou house of Lancaster,
    Thrice happy chance is it for thee and thine
    That heaven abridged my days and calls me hence.
    But God knows what chance hath betide my sons;

II.3.7–13 For this world ... pursuit:

    That we may die unless we gain the day.
    What fatal star malignant frowns from heaven
    Upon the harmless line of York's true house?
       Enter George

GEORGE

Come, brother, come; let's to the field again,
For yet there's hope enough to win the day.
Then let us back to cheer our fainting troops,
Lest they retire now we have left the field.

WARWICK

How now, my lords? What hap, what hope of good?

II.3.15–22 Thy brother's blood ... ghost:

Thy noble father in the thickest throngs
Cried still for Warwick, his thrice valiant son,
Until with thousand swords he was beset
And many wounds made in his agèd breast;
And, as he tottering sate upon his steed,
He waft his hand to me and cried aloud
'Richard, commend me to my valiant son!'
And still he cried 'Warwick, revenge my death!'
And with those words he tumbled off his horse;
And so the noble Salisbury gave up the ghost.

III.3.1–43 Fair Queen ... sorrow:

LEWIS

Welcome, Queen Margaret, to the court of France.
It fits not Lewis to sit while thou dost stand.
Sit by my side, and here I vow to thee
Thou shalt have aid to repossess thy right
And beat proud Edward from his usurped seat,
And place King Henry in his former rule.

QUEEN

I humbly thank your royal majesty
And pray the God of heaven to bless thy state,
Great King of France, that thus regards our wrongs.

IV.4 Q1 reverses the order of scenes 4 and 5 and has the
following exchange as scene 4:

Enter the Queen and the Lord Rivers

RIVERS

    Tell me, good madam, why is your grace
    So passionate of late?

QUEEN

    Why, brother Rivers, hear you not the news
    Of that success King Edward had of late?

RIVERS

    What! Loss of some pitched battle against Warwick?
    Tush, fear not, fair Queen, but cast those cares aside.
    King Edward's noble mind his honours doth display;
    And Warwick may lose, though then he got the day.

QUEEN

    If that were all, my griefs were at an end;
    But greater troubles will, I fear, befall.

RIVERS

    What, is he taken prisoner by the foe
    To the danger of his royal person then?

QUEEN

    Ay, there's my grief; King Edward is surprised
    And led away, as prisoner unto York.

RIVERS

    The news is passing strange, I must confess;
    Yet comfort yourself, for Edward hath more friends.
    Then Lancaster at this time must perceive
    That some will set him in his throne again.

QUEEN

    God grant they may; but, gentle brother, come
    And let me lean upon thine arm awhile,
    Until I come unto the sanctuary –
    There to preserve the fruit within my womb,
    King Edward's seed, true heir to England's crown.   *Exit*

After V.1.77:

GEORGE

    Clarence! Clarence for Lancaster!

EDWARD

    Et tu, Brute? Wilt thou stab Caesar too?

A parley, sirrah, to George of Clarence!

> *Sound a parley, and Richard and Clarence whispers together; and then Clarence takes his red rose out of his hat and throws it at Warwick*

V.4.1–49 Great lords ... his help:

QUEEN

Welcome to England, my loving friends of France,
And welcome, Somerset and Oxford too.
Once more have we spread our sails abroad;
And though our tackling be almost consumed,
And Warwick as our main mast overthrown,
Yet, warlike lords, raise you that sturdy post
That bears the sails to bring us unto rest;
And Ned and I, as willing pilots should,
For once with careful minds guide on the stern
To bear us through that dangerous gulf,
That heretofore hath swallowed up our friends.

PRINCE

And if there be, as God forbid there should,
Amongst us timorous or fearful man;
Let him depart before the battles join,
Lest he in time of need entice another
And so withdraw the soldiers' hearts from us.
I will not stand aloof and bid you fight,
But with my sword press in the thickest throngs,
And single Edward from his strongest guard,
And hand to hand enforce him for to yield,
Or leave my body as witness of my thoughts.

V.4.82 *Alarum, retreat, excursions. Exeunt*:

> *Alarms to the battle. York flies; then the chambers be discharged. Then enter the King, Clarence and Gloucester, and the rest, and make a great shout, and cry 'For York! For York!' And then the Queen is taken and the Prince and Oxford and Somerset. And then sound and enter all again*

GENEALOGICAL TABLES

TABLE 1: *The House of Lancaster*

Edward III m. Phillippa of Hainault
1312–*1327*–1377

Children of Edward III:

- Edward, the Black Prince, 1330–76
  - Richard II, 1367–*1377–1399*–1400
- William of Hatfield, d. infancy
- Lionel Duke of Clarence, 1338–68
- John of Gaunt m. Blanche of Lancaster, 1340–99; m. Catherine Swynford
  - Henry IV (Bolingbroke), 1367–*1399–1413*
    - Henry V m. Katherine of Valois, 1387–*1413–1422*
      - Henry VI m. Margaret of Anjou, 1421–*1422–1461–1471*; 1430–82
        - Edward, Prince of Wales, 1453–71
    - Thomas Duke of Clarence, 1388?–1421
    - John Duke of Bedford, 1389–1435
    - Humphrey Duke of Gloucester, 1391–1447
  - John, 1st Earl of Somerset, 1373?–1410
    - John, 1st Duke of Somerset, 1403–44
      - Margaret m. Edmund Tudor, Earl of Richmond
        - Henry VII (Richmond), 1457–*1485–1509*
    - Edmund, 2nd Duke of Somerset, c. 1406–1455
      - Henry, 3rd Duke of Somerset, 1436–64
      - Edmund, 4th Duke of Somerset, 1438–71
    - Henry, Bishop of Winchester and Cardinal, d. 1447
- Edmund Langley, Duke of York, 1341–1402
- Thomas of Woodstock, 1355–97
  - Thomas Duke of Exeter, d. 1427
- William of Windsor, d. infancy
- Joan m. Ralph Nevil, 1st Earl of Westmorland
  - Cicely m. Richard Duke of York, 1411–60
  - Thomas Montacute, Earl of Salisbury m. Alice, 1388–1428
    - Richard, 1st Earl of Salisbury m. Alice, 1400–1460
      - Richard de Beauchamp, Earl of Warwick, 1382?–1439
        - Anne m. Richard Earl of Warwick (Kingmaker), 1428–71
          - Isabella m. George Duke of Clarence, 1449–78
          - Anne m. Edward Prince of Wales, 1453–71

NOTE: Names of persons appearing in the play are in heavy type. Italicized dates are those of reigns; other dates are those of births and deaths.

TABLE 2: *The House of York and the line of the Mortimers*

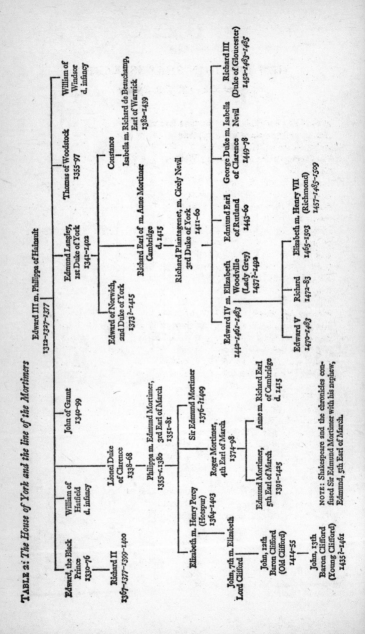

NOTE: Shakespeare and the chronicles confused Sir Edmund Mortimer with his nephew, Edmund, 5th Earl of March.

NEW PENGUIN SHAKESPEARE

General Editor: T. J. B. Spencer

All's Well That Ends Well Barbara Everett
Antony and Cleopatra Emrys Jones
As You Like it H. J. Oliver
The Comedy of Errors Stanley Wells
Coriolanus G. R. Hibbard
Hamlet T. J. B. Spencer
Henry IV, Part 1 P. H. Davison
Henry IV, Part 2 P. H. Davison
Henry V A. R. Humphreys
Henry VI, Part 1 Norman Sanders
Henry VI, Part 2 Norman Sanders
Henry VIII A. R. Humphreys
Julius Caesar Norman Sanders
King John R. L. Smallwood
King Lear G. K. Hunter
Macbeth G. K. Hunter
Measure for Measure J. M. Nosworthy
The Merchant of Venice W. Moelwyn Merchant
The Merry Wives of Windsor G. R. Hibbard
A Midsummer Night's Dream Stanley Wells
Much Ado About Nothing R. A. Foakes
Othello Kenneth Muir
Pericles Philip Edwards
The Rape of Lucrece J. W. Lever
Richard II Stanley Wells
Richard III E. A. J. Honigmann
Romeo and Juliet T. J. B. Spencer
The Taming of the Shrew G. R. Hibbard
The Tempest Anne Righter (Anne Barton)
Timon of Athens G. R. Hibbard
Twelfth Night M. M. Mahood
The Two Gentlemen of Verona Norman Sanders
The Two Noble Kinsmen N. W. Bawcutt
The Winter's Tale Ernest Schanzer

'It should be acknowledged now that the present RSC is a national treasure' – *The Times*

Since its formation in 1960 the Royal Shakespeare Company has become one of the best-known theatre Companies in the world. Its central concern is Shakespeare and in its four theatres – the Royal Shakespeare Theatre and The Other Place in Stratford, the Aldwych and the Warehouse in London – the Company performs more Shakespeare each year than any other theatre company. It is perhaps only fitting, therefore, that the company performing Shakespeare more frequently than anyone else should get together with this country's largest publisher of his plays.

Find out more about the RSC and its activities by joining the Company's mailing list. Not only will you receive booking information from all four theatres but also priority booking, an RSC quarterly newspaper, special ticket offers and special offers on RSC publications. It is also possible to buy the Company's famous silk screened posters by mail order – there are posters in stock, for example, for almost all Shakespeare's plays as well as for the new plays and classics staged at the Aldwych.

If you would like to receive details and an application form for the RSC's mailing list please write, enclosing a stamped addressed envelope, to: Mailing List Organizer, Royal Shakespeare Theatre, Stratford-upon-Avon, Warwickshire CV37 6BB. Please indicate if you would also like details of the RSC posters available.